Prince of Luster

Candace Sams

author of *Starlaw* and *Fusion*

CRIMSON ROMANCE

F+W Media, Inc.

Published by
Crimson Romance
an imprint of F+W Media, Inc.
10151 Carver Road, Suite 200
Blue Ash, OH 45242. U.S.A.
www.crimsonromance.com

ISBN 10: 1-4405-8191-6
ISBN 13: 978-1-4405-8191-5
eISBN 10: 1-4405-8192-4
eISBN 13: 978-1-4405-8192-2

Cover art © 123RF/Angela Harburn and 123RF/Alessandro Guerriero

To Lee and to everyone who looks to the stars in wonder.
Good reading to you!

Chapter 1

In the distant future, on another world

Having leisurely serviced his two lovely guests some hours ago, Marcos Starlaw had opted for fresh air in the palace gardens rather than the stuffy ballroom where a party was currently taking place. He'd left his fetching lasses behind only because they'd wanted to shower in private. There was no doubt in his mind they'd meant to compare notes on his lovemaking prowess. No doubt they'd found the liaison with him delightful. But if they hadn't, there were plenty of other lovelies to take their places.

In any event the women had re-joined him after they'd finished their ablutions, and all three were now back at it. One sweet thing was on his lap kissing him deeply; the other leaned over his shoulder watching and caressing his manhood through his uniform leggings. He was on the verge of suggesting they go back to his quarters, when someone loudly cleared their throat. The noise had the desired effect. The tryst was broken.

Marcos turned his head to find his older brother, Darius, standing on a walkway, watching him and his girlfriends. A deep scowl marred his sibling's features. And in an old, recognizable posture, Darius had his hands on his hips. He wasn't going away until some matter or other was addressed.

Sighing deeply, Marcos gently brought the girl on his lap to her feet. Then he stood to face whatever anger his sibling might unleash. "What is it, Darius?"

"Your guests must excuse us. Our parents have requested our presence in their council chamber."

"Right now?" Marcos asked.

"Yes. *Now.*"

Marcos sighed heavily and turned to his two, waiting beauties. "Sorry, my darlings. Duty calls. Have the guards summon you a shuttle back to the city. I apologize for not seeing you both safely home. I'm afraid this is most chivalrous option I can devise under the circumstances."

The girls whined but pulled their dresses back in place and walked away.

Marcos sauntered toward his older brother. "This had better be good!"

"When you're called to the council chamber, you know it is."

"Lead the way, oh gallant prince and future king of all Luster," Marcos jovially remarked as he lifted his chin, raised one brow, and made an elaborate show of dusting off his black, law enforcer's uniform tunic.

"Marcos … get serious, or Father might just have you confined to your quarters."

"Please. He hasn't grounded me since I was sixteen."

"If he'd seen what you were doing with those two women, within sight of the ballroom and guests who're still quite sober, he might have done worse. We have important visitors at the ball tonight. You've barely made an appearance. How do you think that looks?"

"*Protocol,*" Marcos derisively responded. "Father and Mother love it so … until they get in their chambers at night and the lights go off." He laughed bawdily. "Creator's blood … when they're upstairs they don't care if the entire castle hears them. I swear, Darius, it's like listening to wild cats mating in the forest. Their precious decorum doesn't mean much then."

"For the love of—have you no shame?"

Marcos made no other comment, but silently joined his brother. They slowly walked toward the second floor of the castle and the council chambers located there. But right before they opened the massive, bejeweled, metal doors that led to the inner sanctum, where all royal decision-making took place, he couldn't contain one last barb. "I really don't know how your beautiful daughter came into this world. You're such a prude."

"I am *not* a prude."

"Yes, you are."

"I am not." Darius blinked and shook his head. "We sound infantile. For the last time, will you get serious? You're well over thirty and the commander of a galaxy-class enforcer vessel. Act like you deserve the commission."

"Of course, Commander Starlaw. Anything you say, Commander Starlaw. Kiss your butt, Commander Starlaw? Should I get on one knee to do it, or will you bend over to make the target more accessible?"

"Just open the damned doors and go in!"

"Oh, no," Marcos insisted. "You go first; age before intelligence."

Darius growled out an obscenity, pulled the doors open, and entered the domed room.

Marcos, as second-born prince, followed. Their father stood behind the high throne-like chair at the end of a marble table. Mother sat to their father's right. Their elderly but ever-faithful advisor stood—like a wizened old wizard in all the obligatory robes—to his father's left.

"Father, I see you're in full uniform tonight. You're looking especially ... *kingly*," Marcos quipped as he ignored his sire's frown. Then he walked forward, took his mother's hand, and kissed it. The extra little smooch wasn't for decorum, but because he loved her with all his heart and wasn't afraid at his age to show it. "How is the most beautiful woman in the kingdom tonight?" he asked as he gazed into his mother's blue eyes and winked.

As always, she visibly tried to suppress a smile.

Although he was clueless to matters leading up to this meeting, the situation probably demanded more formality, and he was behaving like he didn't care. In truth, he didn't. As far as he was concerned, Dar and Maelle Starlaw were his parents *first*. They were his king and queen *last*.

The king shook his head. "Marcos, if you weren't such a good commanding officer I'd never put up with your nonsense. The guards tell me you were cavorting with women all day. I suppose that's why you couldn't make it to the ball when we were presented?"

Marcos made his way around the table, grabbed his father in fierce hug, and planted a resounding smack on his sire's cheek. "You're an old fake. You'd be upstairs with Mother if all this pomp and circumstance weren't necessary." He paused as his sire, like his mother, tried not to grin. "I know you have to behave like a royal hemorrhoid," Marcos continued, "but I love you anyhow."

Darius sighed heavily, rolled his eyes, and shook his head.

"Take that forbidding look off your face, brother. You love me, too. After all, I'm adorable whether you want to admit it or not. So we may as well admit it." After diverting his sibling with that piece of wisdom, Marcos plopped into a chair, put his booted feet on the council table, and clasped his hands behind his head. "So ... what's up, Pop?"

Dar cleared his throat. "Please try to pay attention. Our advisor has news to share."

Marcos turned to the older man with the long white hair and even longer white beard. "And how are you this evening, Hannibal?" He winked and leaned toward the elderly man. "I hear you've been romancing those dancers from the Andromeda Bar again, you old demon. Things must be hanging very well these days, eh?"

Hannibal responded by placing the fingers of one hand to his lips. "Why, Prince Marcos ... I would never ... at my age?"

"Can we get down to business?" the king sternly asked.

Marcos waited for Darius to take a seat.

Nothing in these dull meetings was ever resolved until everyone had a butt in a chair and leaned expectantly forward. Sadly, the night had started out so well. He could have been in a big, warm bed with two beautiful women pleasuring him. Instead, he was in conference.

When Hannibal struggled to gather his star-embossed robes about his old figure and fought to pull out a very heavy chair, Marcos surreptitiously slid it back by using one booted foot. For that small favor and show of respect, he finally got Darius to smile.

"All right, Father. We're here," Marcos announced. "We're all seated and waiting with bated breath. As I told Darius when he found me in the garden, I hope this is very important. If not, I've just left two young beauties to find amusement elsewhere."

Dar shook his head, briefly closed his eyes, then opened them again. "Despite the interruption in your love life, there are rather pressing matters, Marcos." He glanced at Hannibal and nodded for the elderly advisor to begin.

Hannibal cleared his throat. "We have news that pirates may be operating in or near the Delta Seven planetary system. They may have access to *fire plasma*."

Marcos sat up straight, immediately dropped his playful façade, and faced his father. There were few things he took more seriously than weapons of mass destruction. "Possessing the formula alone warrants a death penalty. I saw what that substance did during the wars."

"That's exactly why we have to find out what's happening on Delta Seven," the king replied. "The governor of that planet is Adaman Forrell. He insists there's nothing wrong, but the latest news from other sources says that plasma is being stockpiled under his watch. Enforcers in that area don't confirm it. But your mother, as ambassador to several colonies in that outlying sector, suspects marauding ships *are* present, and that they might be threatening the population into keeping quiet. Add it up. Pirates plus plasma … there's nothing passive in that state of affairs."

Marcos glanced at Darius before speaking. His sire hadn't just sent for him and his brother without some plan on how to handle the situation. "What do you intend to do, Father?"

"I'll need someone to get to that planet without being associated with the Constellation League or its enforcers. Someone who can covertly report back, find any cache of banned weapons, and identify leaders of any pirate faction … assuming one does exist. As of now, all this is just suspicion. There aren't many people on Delta Seven. It's small and there are only two communication sources. One belongs to the governor. The other is public but isn't transmitting for some odd reason."

Marcos slowly smiled. "I'm your man."

"The blazes you are!" Darius asserted.

Marcos slowly stood. "I'm the only enforcer in this room without family. I go," he firmly insisted.

"What are *we* if not your family?" the king angrily asked. "And what makes you two young bucks think I wouldn't go myself?"

Marcos's gaze turned to his sire's solid and imposing presence. From a distance, his father could easily be mistaken for himself or Darius. The long black hair was the same. His father had the green eyes of the Starlaw clan and the massive build of all the men of their lineage. He was still exceedingly virile and athletic. But his safety came first.

"Father, you're the king of Luster. It's possible that citizens of an outlying planet, even though it's a planet with which we hold diplomatic ties, may never recognize you. Especially if you're out of royal trappings. They don't hold to tradition in such places, so your image may not have been widely circulated. But all that considered, we can't risk it. First, if anything goes wrong, you'll be blamed. Second, if there're pirates present who *do* recognize you, you'll be targeted. Third, we'd only intervene for the sake of diplomatic alliances agreed on by some ancestor. Our own people might not understand your absence. Finally, as for that remark about not having family, you know what I meant. I have no wife or children. I'm the only one who should do this. My experience with similar matters trumps everyone's."

General hubbub erupted, but Marcos raised his hands for silence. "Father, I know how to disguise myself. Having just mentioned experience …I've been in covert ops for years. Darius, on the other hand, has only dealt with criminals in a uniformed capacity. He has duties here. He can't make any plausible excuse to leave his occupation as head of ground enforcers. He'd be more likely recognized than I would be…" He took a deep breath and continued. Everyone was staring at him, which meant no argument against his statement was logical. "Now, it's my guess you want someone you can explicitly trust. You called me here; I've negated every other candidate in the room. I'm the only choice left." He stared at Darius and silently challenged his brother to say otherwise. But no sound came from his sibling. Only a look of fear crossed Darius's features. His older brother was concerned for his safety, and Marcos knew it.

The king glanced at his wife before speaking. "Because the planet is our ally, we can't just land and demand a search. That would make us an aggressor to an allied world whose governor isn't responding completely to our simple ambassadorial queries and hails. All other planets with whom we share similar treaties would lodge every complaint imaginable. We simply cannot land on any allied world without making sure we've been diplomatically cleared and everyone in charge is agreeable. That's why we've got the damned treaties in place. And we can't arm you as we might on any insertion mission into some backward society. While Delta Seven isn't state-of-the-art in many aspects, we must assume its citizens have all our latest technology. Any equipment you might take with you could be detected."

"Then I won't use any," Marcos relayed.

Darius leaned forward and voiced his concern. "Marcos … you'd be out of contact. You'd have to approach the planet in an unmarked shuttle. In the event you needed help, any authority on the ground has our capabilities to detect and intercept transmissions. If there's something wrong in their constabulary ranks or if Forrell is in collusion with some kind of enemy illegally producing fire plasma … you could be in real trouble. The last thing they'd want on the ground is a League enforcer. Just as Father says, Governor Forrell isn't cooperating with our requests for information. At this time, he can be considered a suspect. Again … we cannot land without risking diplomatic censure from a great many sources."

"How else are we to find out about plasma being stockpiled, much less distributed to pirates? We all know I've infiltrated criminal factions much closer to home; factions that should have recognized me as a member of the royal household were it not for my use of disguises. I know what I'm doing, and you know it too. There is no other choice. That's why I'm here. Is it not?"

Darius quickly turned to his father. "I should be with him. I, too, can change my appearance."

Marcos adamantly shook his head. "I've already expressed myself where Darius is concerned. He needs to be home, looking after his duty and his family. And I work best alone." He took a deep breath and turned to his father. "If pirates have plasma, how long do you think it'll be before they use it to attack every colony in that sector? I just have to verify our suspicions, then rendezvous with an enforcer ship in deep space. If nothing's wrong, we'll know soon enough. The whole thing shouldn't take more than a week. No diplomat on the Delta Seven mining colony will ever know an enforcer spy from Luster was present."

The king slowly nodded. "But if you *do* find evidence of criminal activity, and Forrell is involved, then there will be sufficient cause to mount an enforcer rescue of innocents. Even our allies should agree on that matter. We can deal with fears over how we learned of such treachery later. I daresay those colonists in the area would thank us for the help if they *are* threatened. First we must establish what, by the name of Chronos, is going on! When the governor of the very colony we suspect starts hedging and won't communicate the way anyone else would, to ordinary hails and requests for reports, there's reason to worry."

"Marcos … I don't like this," Darius complained. "You've never gone undercover on an allied world. If you're caught, alliances between Luster and Delta Seven could be deemed null and void. You could be put to death as a spy—"

"As was *always* the case during the war years, Darius." He clapped his older brother on the shoulder. "I won't get caught. That I won't have enforcer technology doesn't mean I can't communicate. There are other ways. I'm not without resources, hence my having returned safely each and every time."

The king gazed into Marcos's eyes. "There's another problem."

"Which is?" Marcos asked.

"Because some of our politicians here demanded permission from Delta Seven to land—and with much greater zeal than necessary—our motives are suspected by officials on the surface of that colony. We've been informed that we won't be allowed to set foot there for at least five months," the king said. "While this in no way alters *your* mission, it makes sending help even more difficult should circumstances grow exigent." Dar leaned forward. "Connect Forrell and his minions to any criminal actions, especially in regards to fire plasma, and all this is a moot point. I'll have enforcer ships there in short order, no matter what anyone thinks or says."

"Diplomacy or the lack thereof! It boggles the mind," Marcos said as he ran one hand through his hair and considered all he'd heard. He gazed into his mother's eyes, Hannibal's, and finally Darius's. "I'll be all right as long as I can maintain my alias. I'll be just another gem merchant, trying to make a decent living by buying whatever the mines of Delta Seven yield. If there's anyone there who wants to keep my mouth shut, they'll present themselves in short order. I'm almost certain other merchants have been threatened with having their ships and crews seized or destroyed if they didn't cooperate. This is assuming there's no logical explanation for all this foolishness. However, if this *is* all some terrible misunderstanding, someone will owe me a month's liberty in the Starlaw mountain stronghold, with all the women and wine I desire."

Darius snorted. "I should have known you'd come up with some kind of extra payment for your efforts."

"Sorry, brother. But I count myself a hedonist to the extreme. When I get back, I want the castle in the north ready for my use."

"Just make sure you come back," Darius sternly responded.

Chapter 2

Two weeks later, Marcos boarded an outbound transport. He'd decided that outfitting an old freighter and trying to pass it off as being from another world would be unnecessary. In fact, a succession of transfers from one shuttle to many others would make his trip virtually impossible to trace. This would leave little possibility of his parents being held responsible for any breach of diplomacy, assuming he was caught. He took on the alias Marcos Orlandis, using his real first name in the rare instance anyone would ever recognize him and call out his name. In that highly unlikely event, the hope was that he could shut them up before they said anything more. His cover story was set.

By the time three months passed, he'd sport a beard, his hair would be much longer, and the clothing he wore wouldn't pinpoint his origin as being from one place or another. He'd look very much like any moderately successful gem merchant, looking for the ultimate deal in medium-grade, rare stones that would set him up for life. Not even his own family would recognize him as their brother or son. If he bore the green eyes of his sire, thousands in many sectors of space claimed that feature. Only acting like someone of regal heritage would undo his cover. Drawing attention to himself wasn't an option. He meant to let the role consume him. He *would* be a nondescript merchant.

. . .

As he finally neared Delta Seven—after the predicted three months of utterly boring travel through innocuous sectors of space—his appearance in the mirror reflected that he'd achieved the desired result. He in no way resembled a prince of Luster.

When the last of many long shuttle transfers landed on the outskirts of the central town known as Prosperity, he'd versed himself in every aspect of Delta Seven's habits and customs. He turned as the last permitted transport off the planet for weeks left him behind, and made his way to the nearest tavern.

Walking through the small town revealed first clues that something was indeed wrong. For a mining colony, Delta Seven should have had its share of wealthy merchants and business owners. Their lives and property wouldn't match the elegance of those residing on Luster, but the storefronts indicated anything *but* business as usual. Instead, they'd been scorched and were in terrible disrepair. Serious confrontations had recently occurred. Probably since the last enforcer patrols had visited. And now that someone had seen fit to end larger and objective law enforcer landings for months, whoever had committed the damage couldn't be held responsible.

He walked into the only tavern, sat on a stool at the bar, and put his pack close to his feet. There was nothing in his belongings but clothing, travel papers necessary for interplanetary business, and those tools someone in the gem merchant profession would use. There were a few personal items, but nothing to indicate who he was or where he was from. His money was sewn into the lining of the long, brown cloak he wore. Pushing the hood off his head, Marcos placed his order with the barkeep.

"Orion whiskey. No ice."

The barman nodded.

Marcos noted how the man's eyes darted around the room, as if he was looking for someone or worried for some reason. After filling his order, the barkeep leaned across the counter and spoke in a soft voice.

"If I were you, friend, I'd take yourself to some other part of the planet and wait for the next shuttle out. Strangers aren't welcome here these days."

Marcos casually sipped some of his drink before responding. "Why is that?"

"Local problems. We have unruly criminals lurking. They'd steal for nothing but the pleasure of it."

The barman quickly moved away as a number of people entered the small establishment. Marcos had his back to them so as not to look as if he was protecting himself. But he'd seen a look in his host's eyes that boded no good.

Pretending he hadn't a care in the world, he sat still, with his gaze on his glass of whiskey. Someone soon tapped him on the shoulder. He slowly turned and saw two local constables, laser weapons strapped to their right sides. Both men were wearing helmets. The gear was typical police issue. The lasers were new and very like what the best-equipped enforcers on Luster wore. "Can I help you, gentlemen?" he casually asked.

The bigger of the two enforcer officers spoke. "We understand, from the shuttle pilot, that you disembarked at the outer-city landing pad. Do you have travel documents and identification?"

"Of course. I can't very well do business without them." Marcos reached for the pack at his feet, but the smaller of the two constables grabbed it up and proceeded to search the interior.

When the man found the folder containing the faked ID, he handed it to his comrade.

Marcos watched as the first constable looked over the documents and compared the video-imprinted photo to his likeness. "As you can see, everything's in order," Marcos insisted.

"It would seem so. These papers say you're here to buy gems from local miners. Anything in particular?"

Strange question from a constable. "No, no particular type of stone. Anything will do as long as the quality is decent. And what I can afford."

"And how long do you intend to stay?"

Marcos cautiously regarded the two men before replying. "No longer than it takes to obtain enough to sell. I'm a freelance trader. Just trying to make a living without having to give up my share of any gem sales to a large broker."

The constable handed the paperwork back. "I'd make your trip a short one."

"I noticed the store fronts. There seems to have been a number of fires lately. Is there some trouble I should be wary of?"

"Dissidents. They don't like Governor Forrell's policies, and they've taken to attacking some of the business owners who do. Some of them are just thieves, really. If I were you, I'd get your business done and leave as soon as possible."

Marcos nodded. "I'll certainly take that into consideration. And I thank you most kindly for the warning. All I want it some sellable gems, and I'll be gone."

"The next shuttle isn't due for a few weeks. Where will you be staying?"

It was on the tip of Marcos's tongue to tell them it was none of their damned business, but he was sure there was a specific reason the question was being asked. "At the Celestia Inn. I'm told a man can get a cheap room there and meals for a little extra."

"There's a curfew … I'm sorry, what's your name again?"

Marcos knew he was being tested. "Marcos Orlandis … from the Allusion star sector."

"Haven't ever been there."

"Not much to see," Marcos commented. "Just a lot of planet clusters with a couple of business outposts. I could probably do better elsewhere, but managing the transport fees to one of the bigger planetary trade systems is out of the question right now."

The constable looked him over, and then gazed into Marcos's eyes for a moment. "You don't look much like any of the other gem merchants who've come through this sector lately. Anybody doing business here is usually on his last credit. Your clothing looks fairly new."

Marcos shrugged. "One has to look as successful as he can if he wants to be taken seriously by gem salesmen. They'll take advantage of a buyer if they think he's desperate. Or looks as though he is."

The constable laughed. "That's probably true in any profession." He nodded curtly. "Just be sure to get to your room before the sun sets and stay there. The curfew is lifted at dawn."

"Guess I'll be doing all my business during the daylight hours." He thanked the two men, then watched them walk away. From his conversation with the one law enforcer, he knew two things.

First, the man doing the talking was certainly lying about dissidents attacking the merchant buildings he'd just seen. The storefronts he'd walked past had been badly burned, and by advanced weaponry not associated with any rebels who'd likely be scrounging what arms they could. Even the stone of the sturdiest structures had been severely scorched. He'd seen such damage before, by Warlords on numerous planets where their murderous cults had tried to rule or take over by force. Driving specially equipped shuttles through the streets and firing advanced munitions on storefronts had been a way to issue warning. Such tactics were meant to instill fear into the hearts of anyone who opposed that faction. Warlords and their minions had been at the core of recent war that'd killed billions. Small groups of them still tried to set up strongholds on planets just like Delta Seven.

Second, that enforcer had likely been to the Allusion planetary system. But so had Marcos. The description he'd given of the Allusion planets and their businesses was quite accurate.

It seemed that some of the rumors surrounding this planet were true. As to pirates or Warlords being the culprits, that remained to be seen. But if either of those groups had fire plasma—and had ever openly demonstrated its destructiveness—no one on this or any other sparsely populated mining colony would dare take a stand. Doing so would be suicide. Survivors of such attacks were worse than dead. They were always horribly mutilated and suffered until their open wounds closed. And that happened very slowly.

Fire plasma was normally dispersed broadly and tended to kill or maim innocent civilians not considered at war with anyone. It was a means to terrorize, nothing more. That was why all law-abiding, sentient planets and colonies banned the substance.

Marcos considered everything he'd seen and heard so far. There wasn't enough evidence to use against any one or any group. He had to dig to get to the heart of the issue.

In order to look as though he was the merchant he claimed to be, he said nothing more except to order a meal to go with his drink. He moved to another part of the bar so he could surreptitiously keep his eyes on the door.

The sun would set in less than an hour; he didn't want to cast any doubts as to his identity by violating the curfew. He was sure he'd be watched as he left the tavern. Maybe later in the night, when he wasn't being spied on, he'd drop the façade of the lowly gem merchant and become what he was—a master of stealth and cunning.

But something told him to go carefully and trust no one. He'd only been off the shuttle a very short time before the local constables had approached him. Apparently, anyone coming into or leaving the colony was being accounted for. That lent even more credence to the stories and rumors that'd reached the house of Starlaw. Marcos understood the secrecy his father employed in not contacting other allied planets to aid in this mission.

As ruler of the planet heading up the entire League, Dar Starlaw felt utterly responsible for any arising law enforcement problems. To keep hordes of criminal gangs and scores of petty tyrants who'd like to get their hands on a weapon of mass destruction equally clueless, his sire had opted to keep the mission quiet, to take care of matters himself and without involving any allied planets or their glory-grabbing, fame-hungry dignitaries. The last thing Dar wanted or needed was to have fire plasma, and the chemical recipe to make it, spread throughout an entire sector of space. Unsure of how allied diplomats might want to leak or even openly boast about their world's part in such a dangerous mission, Marcos understood why his father had opted to leave them clueless. If those same self-serving fools did as they had on so many occasions and opened their mouths about the mission too soon or alluded to it inappropriately, their tactical ignorance could result in a lot of innocent deaths. Criminals would use any information as an excuse to raid. This was the way Marcos's father had always operated, even if being so closed-mouthed wasn't always in accordance to treaties.

Marcos applauded his father's efforts and loved him even more for his boldness and carelessness of heroic titles that went with mission success. His sire didn't and never had needed to make a showing of himself to rule effectively. Instead, the king of Luster enforced with as little presence as possible. In that regard, Marcos was determined to keep his real purpose as secret as he could, honoring his father's attempts to deal with any likely problem before it blew up and became an intergalactic issue.

By chance or portent, Marcos suddenly remembered his family's final warnings as he'd left home. Even when operating as a spy during the wars, he'd been assured there was someone close to back him up. If he slipped up now and his worst fears were accurate, this lowly planet might become his tomb. As long as he played his part and kept his head down, he'd get the information he came for and could steal whatever transport needed to get off the surface. At least some transportation that'd get him into deep space and the backup waiting there.

Marcos swallowed the last of his drink, picked up his belongings, and headed toward the inn. He prayed to the Creator that his extensive research about the planet and its businesses was correct. If he slipped up and revealed himself, he might be lucky if anyone even found his bones. Pirates were known to do hideous things to captured enforcers. Worse things to any allied planet's royalty. It was the allies, after all, who'd finally vanquished the Warlords in the last battles. Thus ending years and years of conflict.

As he suspected, his short walk to the inn was shadowed. The men following him weren't particularly good at what they were doing, or they just didn't care that he knew. If that were the case, he'd have to carefully weigh every single move he made and every contact's credibility.

He wasn't a coward, but the odds were against him. For a moment, he wished for a companion, if only to help watch for trouble. But that meant an extra person's life would be at risk. There was no reason to put some other soul in danger when he didn't intend to be on the surface longer than necessary.

After registering at the inn and seeing that the innkeeper behaved in much the same nervous manner as the tavern employee, Marcos quickly retreated to the second-floor room he'd been assigned. It was dark and small. The conveniences and furnishings were made of old-fashioned wood and fabrics, and they looked as though they'd seen better days. The walls were stained, and the mirror over the leaning dresser was cracked. The primitive nature of his surroundings made him wish for the clean, technologically advanced houses of his home world. Everything on Luster was made of pure-white marble that shimmered in the sunlight. And that same marble glowed under the moon's radiance. Forests and hills were green, lush, and bountiful. This place in which he found himself was full of grays, browns, and the dingiest colors. It was like walking into the reverse of all he knew. It was like being at war again. But even after years of battle as an enforcer officer, the small cabin of any Lusterian vessel was still cleaner and friendlier than this ugly little hamlet. That drove home the need for swift but careful action. The sooner he got his information, the quicker he could see Luster again.

After what seemed like an appropriate amount of time to unpack, Marcos switched off the old-fashioned wall lights and waited. He watched the empty street outside the dirty window without standing too close. After several hours passed, the light from Delta Seven's crescent moon revealed that no one lurked about. But then a sudden movement caught his eye.

A small figure crept out of the shadows. It moved stealthily through the darkness like a feral feline. He watched and waited to see what new intrigue was afoot. As the moonlight outlined those who'd followed him to the inn, it now delineated the movements of this new player in the stealth game.

• • •

Nova Drayton moved as swiftly as she dared, but stopped in the shadows to make sure her way was clear. Guards were usually posted at regular intervals along the streets and thoroughfares. But the decimated shops on this lane were no longer considered worth the time. Their owners had learned their lesson or were dead. Still, she was exceedingly careful. The fact that this section of town wasn't so guarded made it easy for a thief like her to steal small morsels of food from each abandoned establishment.

She'd long since dispelled conscience where stealing was concerned. And she'd given up trying to guess who might help her and who wouldn't. The constables were paid by Forrell. He owned them, and the pirates owned the governor. As a result of their constant torture of the town folk—liberally applied to obtain news of dissidents—neighbor turned on neighbor. The past two years had amounted to a study in survival. And no one could be trusted. But after a year of learning by doing, she'd become a very good thief. She knew where all the best food and goods were stored, long forgotten or given up by their owners. She took too little to be of notice to the looting pirates. But it was enough to grow her pantry. As the weather turned colder, and it would very soon, she'd need warmer clothing as well. What clothes she had from the previous year were threadbare. And she'd find a few things for little Una, too. A few blankets and some canned meats would do nicely.

The small puppy was her only family now. She was thankful she'd found the wandering animal before the cruel pirates did. It didn't take much imagination to understand what they'd do to a helpless creature, just for sport. She'd already seen what they'd done to every human or other sentient being in the marketplace and surrounding homesteads. All the horror was inflicted to make sure the citizens knew the pirates were in control. Her burned, scarred flesh was another of many reminders. As the weeks grew closer to wintertime, if she had enough food and clothing stored, she wouldn't have to come into town at all. She could stay in her little cave with Una, live out the coldest months in warmth, and pray that help would come.

But what form would such help take? What did the Constellation League care about some small planet's plight?

Before some of her friends were killed in the market that fateful day the pirates made an example of them, she'd heard a message had been smuggled out. But no one had come. The Constellation League enforcers to whom the message was supposedly sent cared as little for their poor planet's problems as did the ruler of Luster. As head of the entire League enforcer cadre, it was Dar Starlaw's responsibility to see that all remained safe. And the man hadn't done his job. And for that, she hated him. But she still hoped someone would help—anyone who might even take her small collection of coins for a ticket on a shuttle, to any place in the known universe. As far as she was concerned, any hole would be better than Delta Seven and the small town of Prosperity. Everything here she'd once loved was dead. All but her little Una.

• • •

Marcos watched as the diminutive figure crept about. Whoever the person was, he was covered from head to toe in a dark cloak and hood. It was the typical mantle of outer-world colonists, but a fashion that even those ornately dressed on Luster sometimes wore. The mode of dress was not unlike the brown cloak Marcos had brought with him. But the garment type was the only similarity shared by him and this nightly creeper. Even from his vantage point on the second floor, he could tell his frame dwarfed the party he watched. Whoever it was, he was good. Very good. The operative moved swiftly and gracefully. Marcos well believed the party might be a master thief. Perhaps it was someone working for the pirates, perhaps not. But if the thief's alliances were with criminals, why creep about in such a decimated area and after an established curfew?

He watched as the small figure stopped in front of one of the merchant shops, looked up and down the darkened streets, and lifted a stone slab on the walkway by the front entrance. His attention was captured by the effortless way the culprit slid beneath the stone and pulled it back into position from underneath.

There were probably tunnels dug beneath the buildings as there were on many mining planets. Old-fashioned steam tunnels often concealed pipes that fed directly into the buildings and provided heat and/or water conduits. Someone with a working knowledge of such channels could easily access them, and find their way into any building. Marcos remembered finding refugees hiding in such places during the war years. They had often sheltered there as a last sanctuary from the fighting, and in violation of local law. Gaining access to them was forbidden in most places because of their use in looting.

Intrigued by the act being played out before him, he watched for the return of the little thief. About a half hour later, the thin stone was pushed aside, and a bag was tossed onto the walkway. The thief easily emerged, pushed the stone back in place, and quickly stopped to throw a handful of street dust back over the area. Presumably, this was done so no one could tell the walkway had been disturbed. He slowly smiled and nodded.

Very good indeed.

Movement from down the street caught his attention. Constables were on patrol. Even from a distance, he recognized their uniform badges and side arms in the moonlight.

He glanced at the small figure struggling to tie up a sack. Apparently, the little thief hadn't expected them. It could be they were only present because of *him.*

Marcos watched the cloaked figure move away, but it wouldn't be soon enough for the constables not to notice.

Why did he care? A thief was a thief, and he'd incarcerated enough in his time to understand any *other* constable's enforcement of very similar laws. Still, something with the situation wasn't right. If a person wanted to steal, why do it from a burned-out mercantile likely not to hold anything of real value? Nothing but food, water, or perhaps some medicine.

Glancing between the two approaching constables and the small form, logic warred with compassion. The latter won.

He moved closer to his open window, put his hands on the edge, and slammed it hard. The sound echoed to the street below, and the thief looked up. Marcos saw the cloaked figure's attention move not only up to where he stood, but quickly down the street where the constables now moved faster. The sound had alerted them as well. His act was all he could think of doing on the spur of the moment, without risking his mission.

As if by magic, the thief backed quickly into the shadows and became one with the dark columns and window ledges of the buildings. Marcos saw the constables trot up to the front of the inn. They quickly glanced around and finally pulled search beams from their uniform belts. In doing so, they made themselves obvious to anyone who cared to look out the window. They no longer cared if anybody knew they were present. He held his breath as their lights were directed to the areas on either side of the street.

One of the constables drew his laser and aimed it straight at the wall where Marcos had last seen the small figure. But there was nothing there.

Marcos let out a sigh of relief and watched as the guards searched a few minutes longer, then finally made their way back the way they'd come. It suddenly dawned on him that the thief had to be a woman or a young girl. In the moonlight, the bandit's shoulders were narrower than a man's. But it was really his experience with the female anatomy that gave rise to his conviction.

The grace with which the gloved hands had grabbed at the sack, and the slight swaying motion of the body as she moved, left him in little doubt. And he was that much happier for his decision to slam the window. He didn't want to think about what might happen to the little thief if corrupt constables caught her. He was sure the men who'd confronted him earlier weren't the kind of enforcers to honor a female prisoner's rights. They were surly-looking sorts better suited to criminal activity themselves. The way they'd questioned him right after finding out he'd arrived was, in and of itself, suspicious.

He smiled, turned away from the window, and decided to get some sleep.

•••

Nova huddled near the small fire in her cave and held Una close. "I don't know why someone would help me," she whispered to the white, round ball of fuzz in her arms. "Whoever it was could just have easily called out to the constables and picked up a nice reward. And what were the local enforcers doing there in the first place? They're never walking the street in front of the inn these days. It makes no sense."

Una sighed in contentment and stuck her cold black nose against her mistress's cheek.

"I'll have to be much more careful. But I bet if I go to the marketplace tomorrow, I'll find out if there's anyone new in the area. Someone who obviously doesn't know about the bounty on thieves's heads. What do you think?"

Una yawned, gazed adoringly up, and cuddled closer.

"That's what I'll do, then. I'll go to the marketplace tomorrow."

No one would recognize her or care about her presence if they did. She was one of hundreds of victims who all looked the same now. That was one of two sad advantages to have come from the fire plasma. Not many people were recognizable if they survived exposure. And she'd feign her usual slow limp so no one would ever think her capable of thievery. The one *other* good thing the burning substance had done was render her so hideous that even the pirates who lurked near the market wouldn't touch her. There were now too many willing and *unscarred* prostitutes present.

As beautiful as the prostitutes were, they were no more than slaves. They'd been originally brought in to service Forrell's butchers, but were now unable to leave Delta Seven except by permission. And that would never come. She knew it even if the whores didn't. In fact, no one who came was ever allowed to leave unless there was a suspicion their presence would be missed elsewhere. And until each visitor's purpose could be determined the governor kept travelers isolated. These days, the only new people to arrive were those down on their luck seeking a few low-grade gems, or those looking to barter for supplies. The real booty that might have drawn fortune and given every citizen on Delta Seven a chance at prosperity was in the hands of the pirates and Forrell. No one would ever know what they'd done. No one cared. Least of all the king of Luster and his elite enforcers from the Constellation League. Unlike the lesser trained, underpaid, and easily bribed local enforcers, they were supposed to have been Delta Seven's next line of protection in the event anything ever went wrong. Where were they now?

She wondered, as she had for the thousandth time, whether the king himself wasn't in on the lucrative secret Forrell and his henchmen hid on the little, backwater mining colony.

She also wondered if she'd ever see her real face under all the scar tissue. If she'd ever get to a planet where a medical incubation unit wouldn't be ransomed for only those who could pay the exorbitant prices the pirates and Adaman Forrell demanded.

"I hate this place!" she bitterly spat out. "And we'll leave it one day, Una. You'll see. But we can't depend upon anyone but ourselves. Even that person I saw in the window could be an enemy. We can't trust anyone."

• • •

After eating a hasty breakfast, Marcos decided to head to the center of town and visit the merchant district.

Attempts at friendly conversation with the inn's staff had been met with dour nods or curt answers. People who were living under normal circumstances didn't behave in such a way. Not if they expected repeat business or a good recommendation. In fact, the innkeeper and his staff acted as though they didn't care if he was present or not. That and the lack of citizenry on the street the afternoon before added to his growing sense of trepidation.

Remembering the careful research he'd done on where gem sales were held, Marcos donned the brown cape and cloak that seemed part of a merchant's garb everywhere, and made his way to the center of the market. There were more people out there, but they hurried and avoided making eye contact. He presumed they were busy getting their business and errands done before the night's curfew. But he couldn't help smiling when he remembered one little denizen that had obviously found a way to defeat that ban and the brawny looking constables who might have captured her.

Turning a corner and heading west, he found the larger, gray stone building that should house the gem sellers. His research consisted of out-of-date records, but what knowledge he had from Lusterian records of this small planet still held true. At least so far.

Again, he was struck by the difference between the browns and grays of this dismal planet and the colors, smells, and beauty of Luster. As he approached the building he sought, men and women stood in small groups and haggled over goods and raw, uncut gems. He walked into a foyer where an officious looking little man was busy weighing stones and recording their specifics.

"I'd like to put my name on the buyer's list. Are you the man to speak to?"

The official looked up and stared a moment before speaking. "You're the one who came on the shuttle yesterday."

"I see good news travels fast," Marcos quipped. When the man stared longer than was considered polite, Marcos continued. "I'm Marcos Orlandis. I'd like to barter with some gem dealers if that's acceptable."

"Y-yes, of course. I'll let you into the dealer's room, but you'll have to step through our security gate. Procedure, you understand."

"Of course." Marcos waited for the man to lock up the stones he had been weighing before servicing him. The security gates were no problem. He'd already been through several, and that was the unfortunate reason he couldn't hide even an older weapon on his body or his small pack of clothing. Advancements in technology, even in this part of the galaxy, were such that he couldn't conceal even the smallest compression grenade or laser firearm. He'd had to go through a security checkpoint to get on the last shuttle to Delta Seven, and still another one when he got off it. Such stringent tests were to make sure no weapon got smuggled for or by anyone intending to do harm. Or anyone seeking to stop harm already *caused*.

While the intense searching wouldn't have caused notice in traveling to a major planet, he wondered what there was on this depressing little hole in the cosmos that encouraged chances of arrest. If thievery was the reason for the advanced security, then what was being protected? From what he'd seen, there simply wasn't anything on Delta Seven other than ordinary necessities. The storefronts barely displayed any valuable merchandise. Other than gems, there seemed to be nothing to commend this planet to anyone. Even the stones he'd seen were of low grade.

He followed the thin, little man to the security gate, walked through, and waited for the arched doors on the other side to open. As usual, the security system couldn't detect the micro transmitter embedded in his right breast. The transmitter would do him little good unless an enforcer vessel was in very close orbit around the planet, but Darius and Father had insisted that he have it implanted.

He walked into the gem seller's area and found only one salesperson huddled over a table. To that man's right, however, Marcos recognized the tall, balding pate of Delta Seven's governor. All the images of the man were superior to what was presented in real life. Adaman Forrell looked like an individual who wasn't happy. His face was pinched, and sweat poured from his brow despite the cool air of an early Delta Seven autumn. The man's color was both pale and red; he seemed to have difficulty breathing.

For some reason, Marcos knew his presence had been expected. Having the governor at a common market sale was so obviously wrong that his instincts went into overdrive. He slowly walked forward, trying to maintain control over his situation.

Adaman Forrell held out his hand. "Welcome, Marcos Orlandis. We've been expecting you."

Warily, Marcos took the extended hand the governor held out and shook it. His persona would not know this man. "And you are?" he nonchalantly asked.

"Pardon my lack of manners. I'm Governor Forrell. I'm in charge of administering affairs on our humble little planet. Please, do take a seat." He motioned to a chair in front of the gem seller's table.

"I'm honored, sir. I didn't expect to meet with the esteemed governor of the planet. How is it you know my name?" Marcos glanced at the gem salesman and noted how the man kept his eyes on the stones he displayed.

"Ah, we have so few visitors here. Unfortunately, our merchandise isn't the best to be had. When any gem merchants arrive, news travels quickly. Gossip on small colonies is the fastest form of communication in the entire universe, you know." Adaman smiled and poured wine from a nearby decanter.

Marcos took a glass when it was offered. But he'd only drink when he was sure the governor did. "I'm a lowly merchant, sir. I'm sure you must have more important duties than to oversee my poor dealings."

"Actually, this is the highlight of the month for me, Mr. Orlandis. While I do get news from the rest of the planets in this sector, it's often old. I was wondering if I might watch your transaction and query about recent news. Why, it's such an occasion when anyone visits here."

The ingratiating tone of voice and false smile did nothing to calm Marcos's anxiety. Likely, the governor had been waiting for him to make an appearance all morning. "I'm at your disposal, sir. Ask what you will while I survey this good merchant's offerings. While I'm a man of very moderate means, I'd like to get the best stones I can. Gems from outlying planets are impossibly expensive. For someone of my lowly income, that is."

Adaman bowed his head politely. "Of course, Mr. Orlandis, I totally understand your situation. We on Delta Seven are the last to gain attention of businessmen of any kind. We want to make the best possible impression so that you leave here satisfied and can relay our fair dealings to others who seek our reasonable prices. If only we could afford to offer the casual visitor more to see and do. But without business, that isn't possible."

"A vicious circle to be sure. One can't offer more unless there's more income."

"You have a perfect understanding of our predicament," Forrell said. "Now … please survey our best merchant's stones, and forgive me if I pick your brain for news while you do so."

Marcos pulled out a gem viewer from his pocket, leaned forward, and looked over the merchant's jewels. The seller still remained silent, obviously preferring to let the governor do all the talking.

"I see you have one of the newer electronic gem magnifiers. Our merchant will give you a very reasonable price even with the small but acceptable flaws you'll undoubtedly find. We here on Delta Seven pride ourselves on our honesty. Let no man say otherwise," Forrell congenially insisted.

Marcos looked over the stones. After having researched the subject extensively, the gems he viewed were not even of fair quality. Even the semi-precious stones weren't what he knew to be acceptable. But his research led him to know the worth of what he saw. He looked them over again and made his best offer. "I can give you five hundred credits for the lot. No more." Again the merchant kept silent.

Adaman put out his hands in a supplicating gesture. "Please, Mr. Orlandis. Do look again. Surely you can offer seven?"

"That's all I can afford, Governor Forrell. And that's certainly all these stones are worth. They're costume quality, but nothing better."

"Surely the rubies are a bit better than average?"

Marcos slowly shook his head and stared Forrell in the eyes. He wasn't dealing with the merchant at all, and this entire little scenario was more than it appeared to be.

"You do drive a hard bargain," Forrell acknowledged. "But if that's the best offer, I'm sure we can have your stones wrapped and conclude the deal. Still, I am anxious to hear what news you may have. I was hoping you'd linger over the merchandise a bit longer so we might talk."

"If you'll allow me the honor of buying us a drink at the local tavern, sir, I'll answer any questions I can."

"Splendid!" Forrell clasped his hands together and turned to the merchant. "Have Mr. Orlandis's stones packaged and delivered to his room at the inn immediately. And make sure he gets the same jewels he's viewed. We don't want him leaving here with any impression of us but an honest one. I insist that he doesn't pay for them until the purchase is complete and he's satisfied."

The merchant bowed his head slightly, gathered the stones up into a small pouch, and quickly left.

Marcos watched the man go and got the impression he was glad to be out of the room and away from Forrell. The salesman moved a little too quickly, his eyes had a wary, anxious look, and his hands had shaken as he'd gathered the gems.

"Now. Let's retire to the tavern and have our drink. Of course, our meal will be my way of thanking you for a successful business deal. If you'll give me a moment to change into something less officious than these robes of office, I'll join you in the foyer outside."

Marcos waited until Forrell strode from the room. Afterward, he slowly turned and walked toward the arched doors and noted again how gray all the building stone was. Every structure reminded him of an old castle dungeon. His mood turned as dour as all the colors of the town. Sitting with the suspicious governor and sharing a meal wasn't his idea of a good time. But it was one way to get closer to the planet's primary official and find out what might be going on. Marcos knew his business dealings should have been made with the merchant of his choice, and he should have had the opportunity of viewing different stones. Not with the one gem salesman and limited variety Forrell seemed to have chosen. But it would make perfect sense if Forrell wanted to keep track of what Marcos was told, what information he might be exposed to.

Marcos knew he was being watched constantly. Not because there were any outward signs of surveillance equipment, but just because the hair on the back of his neck was standing straight up. Someone was suspicious about him. His transaction had been too easy. Forrell was being too solicitous of a minor merchant's needs, and there was a considerable lack of trust and freedom to move about the streets or the planet's surface. Even though Delta Seven was a humanoid colony, it wouldn't have been uncommon to see other races. But to see no other races among the population at *all* was strange. And there should be other merchants like *him*.

In the short time he'd been on the planet's surface, he'd come to believe there was something illegal and exceedingly dangerous going on. His worst fears had been realized. There'd been no mistake. Failure to maintain contact with allies, such as Luster, had been purposely done. And not because of some perceived diplomatic slight.

With a few well-placed questions, he hoped to find out more without making the governor suspicious. He had to get further into the main marketplace and find anyone who might be willing to talk openly. That would be the most dangerous part of his entire mission and must be accomplished quickly.

"I'm so sorry I took longer than expected, but there was some minor business I needed to address. I hope you didn't mind the wait."

Marcos turned as Adaman Forrell entered the room from a side entrance. The man could hardly be missed. He was wearing a caftan-type robe that was a bright melon orange. It contrasted so absurdly with his pallid complexion that Marcos felt the need to avert his gaze lest he say something tactless. "No trouble at all, sir." He bowed slightly. "Shall we retire to the inn and enjoy a cold drink?"

"You've taken the words right from my mouth, Mr. Orlandis. Let's not tarry."

After making their way to the tavern and placing their orders, Marcos took his time and held off asking any leading questions until the governor was half inebriated. But plenty of questions had been asked of him.

"So, you've no family and make your home where you please. Ah, a wanderer's life is so uncomplicated. I envy you, my friend."

Marcos leaned forward and refilled the governor's goblet with ale. "I hope to settle down some time. But the urge to make my fortune drives me. I hold back a little profit from each sale in the bigger markets. Perhaps, by doing so, I can save enough to eventually purchase some particularly exquisite stones. Even just a few. Then, I can one day count myself among those gem merchants whose offerings are noteworthy."

Forrell waved his hand toward the ceiling. "Wishing on stars as do all merchants. That's the eternal dream. To have better goods, bigger sales, and excessive profits while working fewer hours."

Marcos lifted his goblet in a toast. "Here's to merchants everywhere."

"Well said." Forrell lifted his goblet to his lips and glanced over the top at the four large men at the other end of the bar. "Uh, I suppose you'll want to leave our little planet right away?"

Marcos carefully studied Forrell's face as he sipped his own drink. He didn't think the other men in the bar were there because of their thirst. They'd only come in a few minutes after he and the governor had found a seat and ordered their meal. "I'd heard shuttles were few and far between. I suppose I'll have to wait a few weeks for the next one to be available?"

"Oh, there'll you'll be in luck, my friend. We have a shuttle coming tomorrow evening. It's bringing supplies. With a word from me, we can have you on your way as soon as possible."

"Luck is with me, then. But since the shuttle won't be arriving until tomorrow, I'd like to see something of your major market area."

Forrell put his drink down and carefully cleared his throat. "I'm sorry, Mr. Orlandis, I'm afraid our larger section of town is off limits to outer-worlders such as yourself. It's guarded and our constables wouldn't let you near it."

"And why is that?" Marcos noted the way Forrell swiped at his sweating brow and how his hands shook.

"I'm afraid we have a problem with a few dissidents. They don't like me or my policies and have found a way to take their anger out on my local supporters. Why, they've attacked decent merchants, stolen goods from miners, and have caused the population untold chaos, and quite recently too. I'd hate it if something were to happen to you. A stranger might make a target. Ransoming you might be one means of instilling the fear they seek. The marketplace simply isn't safe right now. As I've said, our constables are patrolling the area, but it's difficult to find these thieves and malcontents. Some of our honest and noble citizens are coming forward and helping root them out, one by one. But until we have them arrested, it wouldn't be prudent for you to put yourself in harm's way. And I can assure you, there's nothing in the major marketplace for a merchant such as yourself. We have only a few vendors selling wares and food the locals need, but nothing noteworthy."

Marcos asked the obvious question. "Why not call League enforcers to handle the lot of them?"

Forrell shook his head. "It isn't necessary. By the time Constellation League personnel could arrive, months will have passed. Our own local constabulary will have these criminals under arrest by then. At that time, a jury of their peers will try them. Justice will be served." He shrugged and sighed heavily. "For now, I'm afraid the major areas are simply off limits. As I've said, we'll rectify the entire situation shortly."

"Yes. I can see that if something were to happen to me, it could be newsworthy enough as to be a deterrent to other visitors."

Adaman nodded in agreement. "Precisely."

Marcos pretended to acquiesce. "Perhaps I'll see the main part of your city on another visit, when your situation has been tactically contained by your local constables."

"Of course. Never fear, my good fellow. We'll settle the problem before long. And there are some merchants near the inn you can certainly visit. I'm sure they'd be happy to have your business. Some sell clothing, trinkets, and local crafts. That area is quite safe, and you're welcome to shop there. Until curfew, that is."

There were a dozen more questions he'd liked to have asked. But as he was being watched and covertly questioned as it was, Marcos kept the rest of his queries to himself.

The morning passed without incident, and he left the governor drinking at the tavern. He retreated to his room, telling Forrell that he needed to check on the delivery of his stones and make payment to the merchant's delivery person. In actuality, he now had another idea in mind.

As he was sure he was being watched, he waited until the late afternoon, finalized his gem transaction, then pretended to do some shopping in those streets near the inn, where his presence wouldn't be questioned.

As he ducked in and out of one shop or another and tried to blend in with the locals, the constables following him were finding it increasingly difficult to delineate his form from any other. There were many lofty, muscular men in the vicinity. Many were miners and worked very hard for a living, as exemplified by their hands, forearms, and strong upper bodies. They were of a similar build to him, so his task was easy.

To make himself even harder to discern, he hunched forward by inches, making himself seem shorter.

At some intersections he turned right, left at others. Then he deliberately backtracked and pretended to go back into a store to look at something he was considering buying. The merchants took no notice of his antics.

When he was sure no one followed, he slipped out the side entrance of one shop, through an alley, and among the back of a row of stores. He was finally lost to his pursuers. He had only an hour or two of light left; curfew loomed. He made his way straight to the major part of the small colony, by way of back streets and lonely alleys. He assumed the men following would be too embarrassed or too afraid to admit they'd lost their quarry. Something told him the latter of those two excuses would be the reason he really got away.

People on the planet were frightened. It was in the air, in every person strolling by, in every child with a downturned face. It was even prevalent among the business folk with whom he'd talked. If they hadn't come right out and said it, their faces certainly had showed it. They'd constantly glanced toward the streets where the constables lurked. And they'd been willing to take anything he'd offered for their goods, sometimes at an extreme loss. To those who rarely sold goods, some money was better than none. Especially if one had a family to feed.

Marcos still carried the money he'd hidden away in his cloak, along with the gems he'd purchased. With those, he hoped to bribe someone in the main part of the city into telling him the truth. Surely someone would talk and keep their mouth shut. If he could convince one good witness that help was on the way, then he could leave with testimony of what was actually happening. But he had to have someone step forward. So far, he'd seen nothing that didn't corroborate Forrell's statement that "dissidents" were causing disaster, but his intuition and instincts were not enough.

Before this night was over, he'd have his answers. He'd be on the shuttle tomorrow and return in months with a fleet of Constellation League star ships behind him.

He smiled. Cunning evasion of this small colony's law enforcement was easily accomplished.

As he approached the major part of the small city and tried to blend in with the cloaked and hooded citizens, his smile melted. Appreciation of his stealth reverted to intense and immeasurable horror. As he saw the faces of those in the market, he understood why so many wore hoods of one kind or another. It wasn't just the fashion. The garments were worn to cover raw, open wounds or old, terrifying scars.

Fire plasma.

Now he knew why he'd been kept from this part of the city. Here, hooded garments were necessary to protect open, burned flesh from the sunlight. Children, the elderly, and people his age were all scarred.

From his cursory inspection, one out of every three of the citizens had been exposed to the plasma. He pulled the hood of his own cloak closer to his face. He strolled among them, barely able to contain anger. This was how a population was kept silent. But why? Why would anyone do this to another soul?

Suddenly, a woman cried out.

He instinctively turned toward the sound, as everyone else did. It was then that he witnessed the reason no non-humanoid races were present.

What he'd seen thus far had made his blood run cold; it froze in his veins now.

Chapter 3

Limaxians.

He stared in horror at the brown-clad, slug-like creatures. Each was almost seven feet in height. A crowd formed around them. No one wanted to get too close.

Limaxians oozed about the galaxy after leaving the primordial soup of their own planet. Their home world of Maximus was unfit for any other life form save their own. Even in the recent wars between the allies and various races calling themselves Warlords, the Limaxians took neither side, preferring to live off the carnage war always brought. While he'd only seen them when they were chased from some battlefield, where it was said they ate the flesh of dead allies and enemies alike, Marcos knew them to be unconscionable killers.

He watched as the eyes protruded from the grayish, flat face of the biggest of the three. Its fang-like teeth jutted out from gums that secreted some kind of foul-smelling ooze. Whatever the substance was, it was also present over the rest of their bodies. This one was particularly large, muscular, and had its two-fingered appendage that served for a hand around a merchant's throat. Marcos watched as the big *slug*, as they were called, laughed and taunted the frightened man in front of the humans.

The Limaxian appearing to be the leader tossed the man to the ground and placed his booted foot over the merchant's throat. "What do I have here?" the slug loudly announced. "This pathetic creature isn't even intelligent enough to know that he should never cheat higher life forms ... such as us."

Marcos would have given his right arm for a good laser weapon or even a large club. Anger rose as the slug continued to browbeat the frightened man on the ground. Marcos slowly made his way through the crowd and toward the cloaked, foul-smelling alien. Clearly, the slug doing the talking was the leader. It was now apparent why there were no other alien beings on Delta Seven. Slugs would kill or run them off if they could. They only allowed humans to live and exist in their proximity because they considered them a subordinate species, worthy of subjugating or eating if the notion struck them. Because of their size, strength, and propensity to wander in packs, it was easy for the slugs to do as they pleased. Especially against an unarmed, untrained civilian population.

Marcos only saw them as filth that needed to crawl back under the slimy rocks of their home world and leave the rest of the galaxy alone. They were incapable of any cognitive thought above brutality. But the crowds still needed to find food, supplies, what commiseration they could amongst one another. Hence their grouping together now. They'd likely stopped to watch out of fear of what would happen if they left. Limaxians liked to put on a show of force. Anyone not wanting to watch their gruesome displays, anyone even appearing to leave, might be thought of as a dissenter.

• • •

From her position to the east of the crowd, Nova watched the massive slug pick the elderly merchant up off the ground. A scream rang out as a young woman ran forward and threw herself at the feet of the slimy being that also led the local pirates, and went by the name of Prometheus Worthy. Whether that really was his name didn't matter. Everyone knew he was associated with the governor. They'd all been at the slug leader's mercy at one time or another. She suspected this particular foe had been the one who'd ordered her father dragged out of their cottage in the middle of the night. Nova's mother had done much as the young woman was doing now and pled for her family member's life. But the begging had only gotten both her parents killed.

The girl at the slug leader's feet knelt and held her hands up in a supplicating gesture. "Please, let my grandfather go. I beg of you," she cried.

Nova physically cringed. Slugs disliked humans enough. But they hated the ones who showed weakness. She only saw death for the old merchant and his granddaughter.

"Prometheus hears your cry, little one. And I will save his life if you agree to service me in my chambers tonight."

Nova bit her lower lip and winced in revulsion.

The girl looked up at the slug leader called Prometheus and slowly stood. She raised her face up and spit in his.

Angered beyond measure, Prometheus threw the elderly man aside, grabbed the girl and raised her over his head. He brought one knee up. "See how easily your kind dies? How brittle your bodies are and how easily demolished?"

Before the slug could bring the girl's body down and break her back over its knobby knee, a big man in a cloak stepped forward. Nova held her breath, as she was sure everyone around her did. The big merchant stood boldly and bravely, tempting fate with his baritone voice.

"Why don't you put her down and fight someone who can defend himself, you greasy son of a bitch!"

Nova froze and waited to see what would happen next.

Prometheus growled out a curse, dropped the girl to the ground, and turned toward the sound of the huge merchant's voice. He motioned his two other comrades forward.

"Who are you? Who, among the lot of cowards, has the audacity to speak to Prometheus Worthy in such a way?"

"I spoke. I'm the one you want, you gutless mass of garbage. Fight a man if you will."

Nova finally found the courage to move back when the rest of the crowd did. She could only see the speaker from a distance and couldn't get a good look at his face. He still had his hood pulled up, but his voice rang out with the commanding courage of an avenging angel. To her eyes, he stood tall, broad of shoulder and marvelously gallant. She watched him saunter forward as if he'd take on the world. It gave the young girl Prometheus almost killed time to get to her feet. She and her grandfather fled the slug leader's wrath by disappearing into the growing crowd.

"You foolish, wonderful man," Nova muttered under her breath. "No one will help you."

The miners, merchants, and the rest of the crowd would stand by and watch him die. Just as they'd stood by and watched while her father, mother, and other several other brave miners had met their fates.

Indeed, her parents had been among the first and the last citizens to defend their small colony. After that initial example of power and control, the slugs owned them all. She sighed and felt deep pity for this stranger among them. Surely he was new to this world, or he wouldn't have been so valiant. It was an unfortunate fact that the defender's death would not only be excruciating, it would be degrading. Prometheus would see to that. He'd make the brave man an example.

"Come forward, human. Let me see you."

The bold man in their midst did as the slug asked, and finally pushed his hood back. He stood before Prometheus, lifted his chin, and glared into the ugly alien's black eyes.

Nova gasped at the audacity shown. But she felt her heart leap at the show of courage few had seen for a very long time.

"Ah, the new gem merchant," the slug said.

The bold man slowly smiled, then spoke loudly. "While you seem to know me, I'm afraid I haven't had the pleasure."

"Our acquaintance will be short-lived. Before another hour passes, your body will hang in the town square. Then, my comrades and I will quarter you and dine on your flesh tonight," Prometheus promised.

"I don't think so."

Prometheus lurched forward. "And why is that, merchant?"

"Because you'll have to kill me first. And I don't intend to die today. And certainly not at the hands of an oversized snail."

The slugs behind Prometheus growled in anger.

Nova instinctively winced, but she couldn't leave. The man standing up to the slug leader deserved to be heard. He deserved to have his final hour witnessed and remembered.

Prometheus glanced over his shoulder at his companions. "Finally, a human that's worthy of a warrior's death." He turned his head back toward the tall human before him and studied the man carefully. "I think there's a better way to deal with you. Something that will make a lasting impression." He motioned to one of his compatriots. "Codge … come forward. It would amuse me to watch this puny human fight before we kill him."

"I hear and obey my leader."

The slug known as Codge walked in front of Prometheus, hissed loudly at the rebel in their midst, and drew out a long sword from a sheath at his side.

Prometheus drew one of his own swords, from among several he carried, and tossed it to the human.

As on all worlds these days, swords of all kinds were ancient weapons Limaxians carried, along with more modern side arms. Their presence struck fear in the hearts of any adversaries. It was one thing to see someone cut down with a tekion phaser. That was quick, painless, and virtually bloodless. But it was quite another to see someone beheaded. There were few sights more hideous or fearful to a crowd that an enemy wished to keep subservient. And everyone who'd witnessed such an event never forgot it. Nova had seen it too often and knew firsthand.

"Let's see what you're made of, gem merchant. Let's see if you can fight a Limaxian brawler with the same courage you boast. Fight well, and I'll kill you quickly. Fight poorly, and you'll die shrieking in agony."

The brave man took a fighting stance, took off his cape, and tossed it aside.

Nova still couldn't see the stranger's face clearly. The retreating crowd was so dense that their retreat forced her to reverse with them. But the one feature she made out were the striking green eyes of the lone human facing Codge. They were as bright as new blades of grass or buds on a tree. And even from that distance, she could see the firm set of his strong jaw, and the long black hair that flowed straight down his broad back and shoulders.

She prayed that this courageous stranger would live. That he would somehow survive what was to come. "Please, don't let him die," she whispered.

The brave man lifted his sword, glared at Codge, and readied himself.

Prometheus sat on a nearby metal cargo box and raised his hand. "Take him, Codge."

Codge growled, immediately faced the human before him, and brought his sword up.

The weapon the human fighter had been given was meant for a man twice his weight. But there was room on the hilt for two hands. He balanced himself but maintained a light stance, probably so he could move quickly.

Nova put one hand to her mouth as she watched the fight unfold.

Codge lunged at his quarry and swung high. The man she immediately dubbed *Green Eyes* instead of just *the brave man* ducked and moved to the slug's left.

Codge faced Green Eyes again and thrust forward with his entire weight.

Nova saw Green Eyes parry the sword aside and strike low. The tip of his blade nicked Codge's stomach. A gray blotch appeared on the fighting slug's brown shirtfront just above his enormous buckle. There was an overwhelming stench of rotting meat, and Nova knew the human had scored a minor victory.

Codge looked down at his small wound and emitted a howl of anger. Just as she was sure Green Eyes intended, the alien lunged at him blindly several times. The human dodged or parried the blows away from his body.

Nova heard a murmur from the crowd, and someone shouted out a cry on behalf of the human defender. Other people rallied and called out encouraging words.

Finally!

This was what the people needed. Someone who could take them from the depths of despair, motivate them out of their hopeless state, and join them together again. Instead of acting selfishly, they began to speak with one voice and heart. More cries came, and she saw the human fighter continue his taunting game with the oversized, slimy savage.

As Codge repeatedly attempted to regain a position of power, Green Eyes removed each effort with one expert blow after another. Soon, Nova saw the huge slug begin to tire. He became clumsy, and his ill-timed strikes were further misdirected because of his uncontrolled anger.

"I thought you said you could fight," Green Eyes taunted. "I've scraped things from the bottom of my boot with more class than you."

Enraged by the insult, Codge bellowed and lunged uncontrollably.

Green Eyes knelt on one knee, letting the slug's blade miss him by inches. And before the creature could recover and deliver one more strike, Green Eyes turned his blade sideways and cut deeply into the mucous-coated body. Gray blood gushed forth.

Green Eyes stood, backed away, and kept his sword up. But the fight was over. Codge was down on both knees, his sword lay on the ground, and his appendage-like hands gripped his ugly wound.

Prometheus slowly stood. He walked toward his fallen comrade and looked down. "Codge ... get up and finish him."

"I-I can't, my leader. My wound prevents it."

Prometheus snarled, withdrew another sword from a sheath on his back, and swung it once.

Everyone watched as the slug leader's minion lost his head. It rolled in the dust of the street. Women near Nova screamed in horror; she wasn't one of them. Green Eyes had surely sealed his fate in the most horrifying way. Prometheus would never kill him quickly now, not when the embarrassment of such a defeat had been witnessed. And not when the leader of the slugs had to slaughter one of his *own* cutthroats to reassert his position.

Prometheus circled the body of his comrade while glaring at the crowd. He slowly turned his attention back to the human who'd succeeded in rallying the people. He pointed the tip of his sword at Green Eyes. "You'll pray for death, human. You'll know the meaning of agony before this day is done." He looked at the other slug present and issued a severe order. "Cell disrupter—on stun."

Nova and the crowd quickly backed away once more. She stared at the helpless green-eyed warrior and sent a prayer for him to the Creator Goddess. Their hero turned to face the slug to which Prometheus had spoken.

Green Eyes bravely charged the second slug, but not before that gray hulk pulled a side arm and fired. Nova flinched and physically lurched when the hero's entire body convulsed. He'd received the full brunt of the electrocuting stunner. In an instant he lay quite still. There'd be worse done to him this night. Tears filled her eyes.

The courageous, green-eyed combatant would indeed wish himself dead, and very soon. She and everyone around her knew what would happen. They'd all seen it before. In this instance, however, the horror would be inflicted on someone who'd stood up for someone *else*. Just as her parents had.

Prometheus turned on the crowd with his cellular disrupter drawn. "No one leaves. No one."

Nova watched as the slug leader and his assistant dragged the limp human fighter by the arms to two granite support columns located in front of one of the stores Like all the others on that block, the columns had been charred by similar activities as what would soon take place. The unconscious man was pulled into a standing position. His wrists were then strapped to the columns.

"Wait until he regains his wits. I want him awake," the slug leader commanded.

Nova put her hands to her face when Prometheus grabbed the front of the green-eyed stranger's shirt and pulled it off with one swift move. She still couldn't see the human's face because his head lolled forward. But his upper body was perfection. The muscle of his pectoral area, his biceps, and abdomen looked as though they'd been sculpted from metal. His tanned skin glowed in the light of the Delta Seven sun. And though the leader of the pirate slugs told the humans not to leave, they all still backed away. By now, there was quite a distance between the victim and the witnesses, as always. From her perspective, the helpless fighter appeared even smaller, though he still towered over men and women standing at the edge of the circle behind him.

Even if the brave man opened his eyes now she doubted she'd see their striking shade of green. That's how far she and the crowd with her had moved away. She didn't dare fight her way forward.

There was nothing she could do now for the only brave soul among them.

"Bring me the diffuser," Prometheus ordered his aide. "I want it set for a direct, non-spray stream. It will create the most impact against his bare flesh."

The slug aide bowed and lumbered away to do as his leader bid.

Prometheus then put his hand on the back of the unconscious man's head, grabbed a section of black hair, and pulled it so that his intended victim's face was upward. "Wake up, human excrement. Wake up, I tell you!"

He slapped his captive, and Nova repeatedly shuddered when everyone else did. The fighter came awake and shook his head free from the big slug's grasp. He struggled against the bonds holding him, but the ropes had been tied tight enough that bright red blood was now visible from his wrist wounds.

"You're a coward," the fighter cried out. "Your entire race is. That's why the known universe will having nothing to do with your kind. Why don't you untie me and fight like a warrior? Or are you afraid I'll do to you what I did to Codge? Maybe if you lose, that other slug will take your head off, is that it? Is this the way you deal with defeat?" he ranted as he pulled at his bindings.

Nova swallowed hard and shook her head. The man was only making things harder on himself. He had no idea what was about to happen. But his loud questions—meant to encourage the crowd—infuriated Prometheus into action. She watched as the behemoth struck Green Eyes over and over. But the human stranger never cried out during the blows. With each strike to the face or body, she saw him lift his head and glare proudly at his torturer. She wished with all her heart she could see his countenance clearer, before he died. But she'd forever remember the baritone timbre of his voice. It rang out—clear, strong, and proud. He repeatedly defied the beast hitting him.

Finally, when Prometheus could withstand the taunts from his victim no longer, and his beating wouldn't shut his captive's mouth, the slug leader pulled out a dagger and dragged the edge of it across that beautiful torso. Blood gushed forth, and Nova's eyes filled with tears again. She swiped at them with the sleeve of her robe and wanted to leave before watching any more. But she couldn't. If she tried, and even managed, to get away from any pursuing slug minions, ten would be tortured in her place, just as an example to the rest.

"Someone stop him, please," she whispered. But no one came forward. The crowd moaned in protest and many covered their faces. Mothers held children to them and tried to protect the youngest of them from seeing the hideous scene.

He lunged at the tied human before him and continued to strike him harder.

"Sir, the diffuser," the slug aide said as he ran forward and tried to push the long, rod-like device into his leader's hands.

Prometheus carelessly shoved his underling aside as he grabbed his final means of torture. He also grabbed up the diffuser's attached canister, and put the butt end of the dispenser rod against his shoulder.

Before now, Nova had never stopped to wonder how or why the entire device looked so much like some ancient flamethrower. It was meant to do much the same thing with the chemicals stored in the containment canister.

She wished once again to be far away, not witnessing this horrifying event. She, like most of the women in the large crowd, cried out as Prometheus turned on the diffuser. The awful, telltale sound of a turbine starting always preceded the blast of fire plasma that followed. But *she'd* been running when she and the other dissenters had been hit. Only her head and back had been struck. The green-eyed stranger would take the full force of the plasma, right to his torso. He'd likely burn to death right before their very eyes. And though she'd been ordered to stay, just as everyone else, she could have looked away. Instead, pity for the man who was about to be burned stayed her fear. He deserved to be remembered. Up until he took his last breath.

As Prometheus wielded the long rod and the canister dispensing chemicals through it, she kept her eyes riveted on the courageous soul still tied and helpless in front of them all.

The stream of volcanic-like plasma shot out the end of the Prometheus's barrel. It struck the tied figure directly in the upper torso and lit him on fire. And this time he *did* scream.

His agonizing cries were heard throughout the marketplace. And after the plasma hit his body and clung to it in red-hot globs, the stuff quickly went gray as it cooled. That was the worst part of what it did. The gooey substance would stay there resisting removal and searing flesh from bone. Surely he would die soon, but not before he felt every drop of the chemical seep through his skin. He had the sense to put his head down when he saw the blast coming. That meant he'd either heard of fire plasma or his act was simply one of instinct; Nova couldn't tell which. But the small movement likely protected his eyes from any residual spattering. In the end, it wouldn't matter if he got any into his eyes or throat. He'd die from the horrific burns, and more slowly because he *hadn't* ingested the stuff.

She saw him writhe and pull at his ropes as he cried out in pain. Parts of the plasma went over his shoulders and were probably flung across his back. Some of the glowing and cooling gobs of chemical were even spattered down his arms and on his hands. It then caught his hair on fire. The long, once-lovely sheen of thick black locks began to smoke.

While it would have been better for him to take the plasma head-on, and stand totally still so he'd breathe it in and end his life quickly, how could anyone do so? She hadn't been able to. The pain was too great; the instinct to shake if off was primal.

Some of the chemical landed on the rope binding him. He fell from his tied position and began rolling in the dust of the street, trying to be free of the substance burning his flesh. It now slid downward and began to burn away clothing. He clawed at the globules but it did no good. Nova remembered the pain, and felt hot tears fall down her cheeks. No one should have to die like this. No one.

Prometheus turned to the crowd.

Nova kept her gaze lowered and pulled her hood more closely to her head. This was the part where they were all warned *again*. She'd seen and heard the speech so often.

"Let no one come near him. Anyone who does so will suffer the same fate."

The slug leader slowly ambled away. But as he got near his aide, he loudly muttered, "Let him lie here so the people can see him. When curfew comes, take his body to the hole and dump it along with Codge's."

The aide bowed. "Yes, my leader."

Nova wept harder now. The figure writhed helplessly, and everyone was inflicted with his screams, but there was nothing anyone could do. His brown pants and tall boots were melting right into his skin. He was so far away, but she felt closer to him at that moment than she'd ever felt to another living soul. Not just because she'd been exposed to the plasma herself, but because this brave man had been so abused and no one helped. That included *her*.

Once the crowd was finally allowed to leave, they did so in great masses. No one wanted to see more than they had.

She stealthily crept back to her little, hidden cave, sobbing with each step.

There was no hope left. The next transport crews, whether they were offloading supplies or picking up gems, would be severely restricted to the airfield outside of town. The population who'd witnessed the carnage wouldn't be allowed to speak to anyone working aboard those shuttles. Prometheus wouldn't allow witnesses to testify as to his brutality.

She knew what everyone else did, even if no one spoke it. They were, more than ever before, truly alone.

•••

Marcos could no longer move. His pleas for help went unheard, and the plasma kept burning. He groveled in the dirt and scooped handfuls of dust over his flesh, in an attempt to stem the fire.

"P-please let me die," he begged. "Please, please, please … "

No one came near, and night finally fell. His breathing became shallow, and he struggled to clear his lungs. Even as he pled for release from life, autonomic responses kept him breathing. He cursed the ability the human body had for compensating when all physical hope was gone.

He heard someone approach. Heavy footsteps fell on the earth around him.

"Put him in the back of the hauler with Codge," one voice growled out. "We'll take them to the pit as Prometheus ordered. The incinerators are due to burn off bodies tomorrow."

"Hurry, then," a second voice advised. "There's a whore waiting for me at the tavern, and I have a taste for human women."

Marcos lay quite still as two slug minions conversed, and as they heaved his body into their hovercraft sled. He bit his lip against crying out, even as he was thrown in, and some of his burned flesh came loose. In the dim light he could see it falling from his forearm, like water fell from his body in a shower.

"Did you hear something?"

"If he's still alive, the incinerators will take care of him tomorrow. I'll lay odds he won't survive the night at any rate. No one has ever been burned that badly and survived."

Thankfully, Marcos felt himself losing consciousness. Blackness finally engulfed him just as his body was dumped among the other dead of Delta Seven.

• • •

In the cave that now served as her home, Nova wept harder. She held her pet in her arms and rocked the small animal back and forth.

"They didn't have to do that to him, Una. They could have just killed him outright. There was no reason to hurt him so badly. I've never seen anyone get that much plasma."

The puppy whined, licked its mistress's face, and put one tiny paw on her chest.

"If only I could have done something," she sobbed. "I'm no better than all the others I've blamed for not standing up."

As Nova sat there, she imagined those beautiful green eyes as the man had stared courageously at his attackers. Perhaps someone would look for him. But if he were a lone gem merchant as rumors claimed, then he would be incinerated without anyone even saying words over him. There were many at the pit that'd died because of exposure to fire plasma or some illness. At least some of them had family who would ask the Goddess for acceptance into the next life.

Nova gently put Una aside and stared at the entrance to her cave.

"I can at least do that much. No one goes to the pits long after dark, not even the slugs."

She grabbed her cloak and made her way to the marketplace. Stealth was her companion as it always was. Unfortunately, to get to the death pits where the bodies were thrown on Prometheus's orders, she had to go back to the scene of the horror first. The pits were only a short distance on the other side. But the journey vividly reminded her of the shrieks and moans she'd so recently heard.

As she crept through the shadows and listened, she sensed she was alone on the street. The day's events found the slugs drinking in the tavern and loudly boasting of their prowess in killing a tied man. She actually heard them laugh about it.

With grim intent, she kept to the shadows and made her way to where the stranger had been tied.

In the light of the full moon, the stranger's cloak and shirt still lay on the ground. Nova grabbed the garments and held them to her chest. For some reason, no one had picked them up. Likely, everyone had ignored them in order to get away as soon as they'd been allowed, just like she had.

Guilty pain settled in her heart. She looked across the marketplace once more and stared at one of the columns. It was still smoking. There was even a black, oval burn mark where the stranger had fallen to the ground. It led to a trail of ash and charred bits of other clothing where he'd dragged himself and rolled in the dirt. "No one should have to die like that," she whispered again, then hurried away toward the pits.

When she arrived, there were only a few bodies, but some of them had been there for a week or more awaiting incineration. The smell was indescribably abominable. But she clenched her jaw and searched through the rocks and rubble. Then she found him.

He lay on a pile of loose stones, his hands reaching for the sky in a clenched posture. She'd seen that before, when the last stages of death overtook the victims. They'd tried to breathe, then had gasped their last as they'd clawed and writhed for air.

She knelt beside the horrible, scorched figure and placed his cloak and shirt over him. They were his property after all. And putting them in the pit with the man meant no one would steal them.

She clasped her hands together, looked toward the night sky, and quietly prayed.

"Creator Goddess, please let this brave stranger come into another life. Please lead him to an existence where he'll be rewarded for his deeds this day. Have pity on him, I beg you."

One reaching hand slowly turned toward her and stretched outward.

Nova almost froze in horror.

"H-help me … *please*," he croaked.

She swallowed hard, took a deep breath, and glanced toward the heavens before pulling the cloak and shirt off his face. She finally got a good look into the open green eyes of the stranger. In that poignant moment, the moonlight illuminated his face, as if to punctuate the last remnants of a battling god.

"You can't be alive," she whispered. "No one could have survived that much plasma."

"P-please …" he begged as he stretched his hand toward her again.

She put out one shaking hand on the side of his head. He weakly cried out. By some miracle, his beautiful eyes had been spared, though the rest of his body seemed burned beyond recognition.

In the moon's light, those striking eyes begged for some tender mercy in the universe; mercy not shown on Delta Seven in a very long time.

She couldn't leave him. In that moment, Nova knew she'd been brought there by the Goddess's hand.

"I-I'll take you someplace safe," she quietly told him. "But you're too large for me to carry." She thought for a moment. If she'd been brought there for a reason, then there was a solution to the problem of getting him to safety. He might not last long thereafter, but he'd be with someone who'd help him into the next life.

It suddenly occurred to her that the slugs had parked their hovercraft outside the tavern. Attached to one was a hauler—likely the very one that'd carried her victim to this pit.

She remembered how to operate a hovercraft, though those she was used to were different from the small conveyances slugs brought from their cargo ships.

Still, it was worth trying. She could take one, have the stranger to her cave in just a few minutes, and get it back before the Limaxians ever knew what happened. They'd likely be so drunk that they'd never know the transport had been moved.

"I'll be back," she said as she whispered down to the surviving hero of the day. "Do you hear me? I'm coming back. Don't give up. Just keep breathing. Okay?"

He barely nodded, but he'd understood.

With new purpose and courage to go with it, Nova re-covered the stranger's torso with his cloak and shirt. She gently touched his cheek one time before making her way back up the rocky hillside, over the dead, and through the garbage.

She ran faster than she'd ever run in her life.

Please let him be alive when I see him again.

Chapter 4

Marcos lay in pain so deep that he began to imagine someone had come. That was the cruelest part. To lie there believing another soul said they'd help, only to really be alone, was worse than anything he'd ever experienced.

He begged again to die.

Every move he made pulled more loose skin from his body and drove him into a new round of torment. The rocks beneath him felt like glass wedging its way into his body. Every breath he took was worse than the last. He looked into the night sky and thought of home, his siblings and their families. And he thought of Darius's two-year-old daughter, Cory, and all the other nieces and nephews in the castle nursery he wouldn't hold again. The children he wouldn't ever conceive with some woman drifted into and out of his tortured mind.

The worst part was knowing his family would never have a shred of his body left to bury.

Marcos began to cry, using the last of his body's fluid in the process. The damage done to his torn, bleeding, and burnt form was nothing compared to what was being done to his spirit. It was as though someone had ripped who he was, and all he'd been, away. He reached up to the sky as best as he could and bitterly pled for his family to know where he was and to have them find some small remnant of his remains: a finger bone or a lock of what was left of his hair. Anything they could bury with the dignity that was now denied him.

The whole thing was his fault.

He'd wanted to save that elderly merchant, had gone off mission and paid the price. Anger over seeing an innocent tormented— and disgust over witnessing how a young girl was forced to beg for a man's life—had driven him to open his mouth when he should have kept it closed. But no one else had stepped forward.

Too late, he'd learned why.

The entire colony had been so terrorized that no one would dare speak. He now knew what the scorch marks on the buildings meant. For every one of them, some soul had probably died; someone who might have stood for what was right, just as he'd tried to do.

Look where it'd gotten him.

He was lying among the refuse of Delta Seven with the dead and the garbage of a doomed world piled around his burned shell of a body. The pain was so great he could well wish himself dead a thousand times, but his stupidity in landing there would never be undone.

At times his mind drifted to why he'd done it. Then he'd decide again that he'd had no choice. What did it matter? That girl, the elderly man, and scores of others would probably die anyway.

Perhaps the slugs, who had to be working with consent of the governor, would kill everyone before they moved on to plunder some other world. Then what would his brave act mean? He uttered one croaking plea to the heavens.

"Please …want to … see my family again … the pain … want to die … c-can't be d-dishonored … n-not like this."

. . .

Nova stopped at the top of a small rise, only a few feet from where Green Eyes slumped. She heard his plea, and her heart broke.

For two years, she'd seen the result of public torture. Friends no longer knew friends. Longtime business adversaries no longer quarreled because there was nothing left to fight over. The Limaxian pirates and the traitor Adaman Forrell had taken everything for themselves. In that one small way, they were all united. Indeed, the citizens had two things in common: their hatred of the governor, and the loss of hope.

The first time the fire plasma was used, that display had taken all fight from every heart. The second and successive times were meant to make scurrying cowards of every man, woman, and child.

Nova renewed her vows of hatred for an empire where an allied king—one who was supposed to have periodically checked on planets within the alliance—sat on a rich throne, ordering his League of Enforcers to ignore small, unimportant colonies like Delta Seven. While her world wasn't ruled by King Starlaw, as head of The Constellation League of Enforcers it was the man's duty to make sure that all law enforcement alliances were honored. So where was he? Surely he had to know something on her planet was very wrong. Even normal messages weren't getting out, at least not without Forrell's approval or censorship. And this had been the case as far as anyone had known.

She moved forward and knelt beside the weeping, green-eyed warrior.

"Don't die, Green Eyes. You're not dishonored. You stood against a malevolent beast when no one else would; even as I did nothing. But I'll help you now. I promise I'll always be here and I'll help you."

"Y-you came back."

"I wouldn't break my promise. I'll stay with you." She gently wrapped her gloved fingers around his wrist. "This is going to hurt worse than anything you can imagine. But you have to try and get into the hovercraft. We don't have much time. I'll take you someplace safe, but we have to move quickly. Understand?"

He nodded.

She took a deep breath and prayed he wouldn't cry out too loudly. When her fingers tightened around his wrist, pain sent him into spasmodic convulsions. She immediately released her grip and tried to overcome the revulsion of his burned flesh. The smell of it was unholy. But she could do him no good if they couldn't move.

"What's your name?" she quietly asked. She repeated herself several times while trying to keep him from injuring himself further. His body flailed against the rocks in a twisted, ghastly way. She almost had to sit on him before his thrashing subsided. Eventually, he breathed deeply and tried to answer her repeated request.

"My n-name is M-Marcos," he muttered.

"All right, Marcos. I'm called Nova Drayton. So we both know each other."

He simply gasped.

"We'll try again. Can you push yourself up without my help? Even just a bit?"

"N-No."

She leaned very close to him and knew the words she'd say would be cruel. But they might be what motivated him to move. "I can't carry you; you're too big. If you don't get up, then you'll be incinerated here tomorrow. There'll be nothing of you left, and anyone who ever cared about you will never know what happened. No one will admit you were ever here. It will be as though you simply disappeared."

He breathed harder. The man seemed panicked by the idea that such a thing could happen. Whatever made him do so, whether it was her words or thoughts of his own making, he finally rolled onto his side and pushed himself into a sitting position.

Nova put her hands to her face when his screams of agony echoed off the rock quarry pit around them.

"Goddess … forgive me for what I'm about to do, but I have to get you out of here."

Without telling him, Nova pulled her cloak tighter around her body to protect herself against residual plasma on his. She lifted one of his charred arms around her shoulders and pushed herself straight up with all her strength.

"Stand with me. *Now!*" she commanded.

Clumsily, Marcos did as she ordered and moved where she led. He stifled more screams as they progressed. She didn't know where the strength came from—hers or his. She simply moved forward, pushed his massive form into the hauler on the back of the hovercraft, then leapt into the driver's seat. The open design of the silver, flat transport allowed the air to flow around her and the injured man as they moved. She heard him tearing at the metal of the hauler bed with his hands. The air on his burned skin had to be agonizing. But he didn't cry out again.

She couldn't imagine the willpower it took for him to remain as silent as he did. Suppressing that kind of pain would likely cost him later. Given everything he'd been through that day, and all she'd seen of him, he was either the bravest man she'd ever known or the most foolish.

Whatever he was or wasn't, he was now her responsibility. And she wouldn't let him be caught again.

She drove straight to the outskirts of town as fast as the transport could move. There, in a small dense forest were hillsides where the miners used to work. The caves there were devoid of any sizable stones. Miners now worked on the other side of the small colony, under the strict supervision of Prometheus, his slug minions, and Adaman Forrell.

She knew every bush, rock, cave, and cranny. It was here, in a place where her father had told her it would be safe, that she now made her home. Slugs never came here, and she knew she and her green-eyed victim would be safe. He might not live the night, though some instinct told her he *could.*

The transport maneuvered effortlessly, right in front of the small opening to her cave. For someone of her size, it was easy to walk right in. But for man Marcos's height, he'd half to duck and then get on his knees before entering the small, inner chamber where he could finally stand. Standing right now wasn't the issue. Just getting him out of the transport and into a position where he could move at all *was*.

Nova hopped out of the driver's seat and loped to the hauler. Marcos lay there on his side, staring blankly and curled into a fetal position. But he was still breathing. Again, her heart melted when she saw him lying there so helplessly. His current position was in direct contrast to the bold man who'd stood up to Prometheus.

She put her face close to his and stared into his eyes. "We're someplace safe. I've been here for almost two years, and the Limaxians have never found me. Neither have Forrell's guards or the constables. They're all in collusion. But none of them thinks this place is worth the dirt piled here. You'll be safe. I have things that can help heal you if you want to survive. Do you want to live, Marcos? Do you?"

Even in the muted moonlight, even as he lay so still and quiet, he turned his gaze toward her. The expression in his bright green eyes said *yes*.

"All right, then. You're going to have to hurt some more. I have to move you inside this cave." She pointed behind her. "But once there, you'll be safe. Will you try and help me one more time?"

Slowly, Marcos pushed himself up from the floating platform. She saw the massive agony his movements caused. His eyes rolled back in his head several times, and painted an eerie picture in the moonlight surrounding them.

The pain almost sent him into unconsciousness again, but she kept talking to him. Still, he never cried out.

She witnessed strength that must have been delivered by the Goddess herself. He pushed himself into a sitting, then a standing position, and actually walked. It was one slow step at a time but he moved.

"Gods of old … I-I know what this is costing you, Marcos. But once you're inside the cave, you can cry out all you want. It's deep within the hillsides and no one will hear. I know. I screamed for days after the plasma hit *me*." She didn't add that she hadn't been as badly burned as he was.

He kept stumbling forward, and almost fell at one point.

When she reached out to help, he held up one hand in denial. The flesh from that arm dangled like skin from a roasted foul.

"D-don't touch me … may still have plasma … b-burn you."

Once more that day, Nova openly wept. Even now his concern was for someone else. "I'll use my cloak. It's eel skin, dried from creatures caught in the lakes. It'll resist the plasma for the little while it takes to get you inside the cave."

Marcos stiffly turned his head toward her, but still waved off her assistance.

She watched as, one small step at a time, he kept moving forward. He fought again to maintain his balance, and she saw his eyes roll back into his head again. His breathing came in rasping gasps.

Finally, when he actually got to the cave entrance, he fell to his knees. She watched him dig his way forward by clawing at the red dirt. Unable to hold back the sobs of sympathy any longer, she pushed the hood of her cloak back. His cloak and shirt, placed on his shoulders to keep more dirt from blowing into open wounds, now lay in the hauler. She grabbed them up as they were now the only clothing he had without any plasma attached. What was left of any other clothing was now burned into his skin. It'd be difficult to tell cloth from flesh.

Rather than put her hands on him again, she simply let him crawl forward at his own crude pace. And when he was finally through the entrance and lay on the ground in the chamber beyond, she knelt beside him.

"I have to return the transport I stole. I'll be back soon."

He lay on his side and simply stared at the cave wall. In the belief pain had taken him to a place where he couldn't hear her now, she hurried outside again.

It took but a few minutes to return the hovercraft and its attached hauler. The tavern lights were out now but she was careful to put everything back exactly where she'd found it.

Luck was with her. Almost as if her actions had been ordained and approved by the Creator Goddess herself, she heard loud snoring coming from the open iron doors of the tavern. The slugs had passed out where they'd partied. Apparently, the tavern owner had retreated to his dwelling for the night, unwilling to waken the drunken Limaxians and endure their wrath.

She crept carefully back to her cave and arrived just as the sun was coming up. Fear of finding her rescued green-eyed hero dead made her approach his still figure slowly. Light from her perpetual stone kept the chamber illuminated enough to move about. The stone had been one mined by her father when he was still alive. He'd given it to her when he first suspected there'd be trouble with Adaman Forrell. While it couldn't provide much heat, it kept the darkness at bay.

It was a time long ago when her father had made this cave into a retreat for Nova, her mother, and himself. Sadly, her parents had never been able to use it. Because of her sire's foresight, she now had a place to survive the cold winters and hot summers in reasonable comfort.

She took a deep breath, and gathered her supply of wood for the small fire. The smoke would be drawn toward the rear and dissipate while going up a very narrow tunnel to the surface. In this way, she'd avoided detection while keeping warm.

When she had a good-sized blaze, she gathered her supply of stolen medicinals and finally turned to Marcos. He was as she'd left him. His eyes stared sightlessly at the side of the cave. He still breathed, but he hadn't been alone after all.

A small white ball of fluff was curled up near Marcos's bare chest. Una wasn't close enough to cause him harm or to be burned by residual plasma. The pup instinctively knew not to get too near. But Marcos should certainly be able to hear the whirring sound the animal made. That sound was usually reserved for when Una was being stroked or held.

Marcos blinked once. One of his fingers flicked near the puppy's nose. Something in her new patient registered the fuzzy presence.

Nova put her small basket of medicines down by Marcos's head. She stared at him and Una for a moment before speaking softly. "My dog senses you're hurt, and she's trying to help. But you know that, don't you?"

Marcos blinked again.

Nova patted the puppy's head, picked her up, and cuddled her close. "Good girl, Una. Good girl."

Marcos's eyes stayed on the puppy.

"You want her near? Is it helping you that she's near you?"

He blinked once more.

"All right. She can stay close."

When Nova put the puppy down, it immediately waddled back to Marcos and cuddled up where it had been.

Marcos's left hand moved closer to the pup's nose. As before, he was able to move one finger in acceptance of the animal's presence.

• • •

Marcos stared at the small animal. It was fuzzy and totally white except for its black eyes, black nose, and two purple antennae, which were about three inches tall. All other body parts were indiscernible.

For some reason, staring at the small beast made the pain more bearable. Hearing it breathe was comforting. Having it blow softly on his hand wasn't painful. When the girl had left him, it'd found him and lay down quite near, as if it didn't want him to be alone. As it stayed so still beside him, the pain diminished a little.

The woman spoke softly and moved closer. He recognized his surroundings as a cave and remembered her mentioning its existence.

Everything was brighter now. Flickering shadows on the red walls told him a fire had been started. A face loomed over him.

He was finally able to see her without her hood. Her cheeks, chin, and neck were scarred, likely from a previous plasma burn. Her forehead and nose had somehow escaped the dripping chemical. Her hair was gone, so he could only guess about the original color. Her eyes, however, were unbelievable. They were a shocking shade of purple, so bright they rivaled the loveliest amethysts he'd ever seen.

"P-pretty eyes," he rasped.

She smiled. "The worst of the burning is over, or you wouldn't even notice."

That one smile brought more light to his spirit than the fire brought to the cave. Her smile was the most enchantingly wonderful thing he'd ever witnessed. Her full lips parted over straight white teeth, and he actually found himself wanting to lift a hand to touch her scarred cheek.

He swallowed hard, turned on his back, and moaned as pain overwhelmed him again.

"Marcos, I have to get the remainder of your clothing cut away. If I don't, it'll cause infections later. Then I'm going to bathe you with cold water. It'll hurt. *Badly*. But the residual plasma can't be removed unless I do it."

He swallowed hard, blinked to let her know he understood, and quit trying to speak. The effort was too much.

"The pain will go on for a long time, but your skin will eventually heal over with scars. Some parts of your will body will be very sensitive. Other parts won't have any feeling at all. But the cleaning has to be done tonight," she told him. "Do you understand?"

He nodded slightly and moved his eyes in her direction.

"I'm going to move the puppy away so I can get to your body. I don't want Una exposed to any plasma. I think she helped you. The sound she makes is very reassuring. I'll put her back when I'm done. Okay?"

He breathed deeply and blinked his response once more.

"Now … as I get your clothing off, I'll apply the water."

She still spoke softly. It was calming to hear her voice but he feared her touch, no matter how gently applied.

"I'm going to start now. You can cry out if you need to."

Marcos clenched his jaw, but nothing eased the terrible, torturous hours ahead. He screamed and writhed until darkness surrounded him.

• • •

"Chronos's balls!" Prometheus yelled as he threw his tankard against the wall.

Adaman Forrell stared at the big slug and slowly shook his head. If it weren't for the wealth the bastard had helped him accumulate—which he considered his due for serving in a thankless public office—he'd poison all the odorous vermin just so he wouldn't have to hear their bellowing complaints. "What's wrong, Prometheus?" he slowly asked as he reeled in any rage of his own.

"I knew there was something about that merchant that wasn't right. Without specialized experience, no human could have stood against one of my brawlers. He handled a sword as if he was born to it. Not one in a thousand could give such a showing. But then, *Dar Starlaw*'s son would be taught to handle any number of weapons from an early age."

Adaman's hands began to shake. He fell into the nearest chair and wiped a sudden wash of sweat from his forehead. If what Prometheus said was true, they were in horrific trouble. "Dar Starlaw's *son*? I-If you believed that's who that man was, then you should have just walked away, Prometheus!"

"I didn't know who he was at the time. Besides … what choice had I? He challenged my authority in front of the population. He'd seen too much."

"Y-you could be wrong, you know. Many men learned to fight during the wars. That he bested your brawler doesn't necessarily mean he's of royal lineage."

"The man's fighting ability was too well honed," Prometheus attested. "It took time to glean his image from others who might bear such talent, but there he is." Prometheus swiveled his computer around and brought up a holographic image of the entire royal family. "See the planetary badge on his chest? He wears the insignia that designates him as a member of the royal family. He *is* a prince of Luster … second-born son of the king. His much longer hair, beard, and trappings made it more difficult to trace. But I knew him to be of noble birth. I knew it!"

Adaman wrung his hands and took slow, deep breaths to still the hammering of his heart. The slug leader's quickness to anger was going to bring down the full wrath of the Constellation League. In fact, it usually had been Prometheus's bloodlust that'd caused every problem he'd ever had during his career as governor. Letting the swaggering gem merchant go would have been a better tactic, but discretion had never been Prometheus's style. Now their backs might very well be against a wall.

"W-what are we going to do? He was obviously sent here as a spy. What are we going to do, Prometheus?" Adaman agitatedly repeated.

"Quit babbling and let me think."

"Where did you have his body taken?" Adaman asked as he stood and began to pace. Along with enduring the stench of the slug leader and his ill-kempt minions—each and every day—he now faced a very bleak future due to the idiot Limaxian's actions.

"He's in the pit with all the other dead. Right next to Codge, I should imagine."

Adaman stopped pacing and squarely faced Prometheus. He'd resort to the same tactic he'd always employed when any merchant or traveler landed on Delta Seven and had gone missing due to one of the stupid slugs's distrust. "We'll simply never admit to his having been here. When the enforcer ships arrive, I won't allow them to land. They can't unless I say so; that's the treaty I signed with them. I've already told them there's a five-month moratorium on enforcer vessels. So if they ask … I-I'll say I don't know anything about him."

"And if they should land anyway?"

Adaman momentarily put his fingers to his lips in thought. "In that event, you can have your brawlers deal with the population … hide those who're scarred from the plasma, keep them indoors on threat of death. That ploy worked before when I allowed enforcer vessels to freely land and their crews to roam about. As usual, let everyone know what will happen if they talk."

Prometheus nodded.

"If that merchant really is who you think he is, and the king learns what you did to his son and that I permitted your presence here, we'll be taken to Luster and put to death. Do you know what they do to anyone who kills an enforcer? Never mind a man of royal lineage." Adaman vehemently shook his head. "We should have left this hellhole when that first vein of rare jewels was discovered. Since they were of such exceptional quality, we had enough to build our fortunes many times over."

"You agreed to this, Forrell. Indeed, you have received five times the share you'd have been allotted if the stones had been equitably apportioned to the miners. But more gems are needed for *my* purposes. And I will not stop until I have all I require." Prometheus growled loudly before continuing. "Starlaw or not, that man's remains must be taken elsewhere. We'll have to burn his body separately and quite thoroughly to make sure there's nothing left. The bodies of any other dissidents will also be thoroughly destroyed, but it is most important that nothing be found of the so-called merchant. The king's med-techs must not be able to locate so much as an eyelash."

"Yes, yes … quite so," Adaman quickly murmured. "I'll have my constables retrieve his body immediately."

"Have your men take his carcass to the barren side of the planet, Forrell. The man's body can be fully incinerated there. And when your constables return, I and my brawlers will be waiting for them."

Adaman tilted his head. A dropping sensation in his stomach, coupled with Prometheus's feral-looking snarl, wasn't a good sign. "What do you mean to do to them?"

"Your constables can't be trusted. They'll have to be killed to keep this secret. No one must know that Marcos Orlandis was actually Marcos Starlaw."

Adaman swallowed hard and put one shaking hand around his throat. Things were going too far. There had to be a way to stop it. "B-but they're my people. My personal guard. They won't talk. I'll swear to it."

"I'll take no chances. It took me hours of searching to find this one vid-pic taken several years ago. If your constables begin to wonder why the gem merchant's body is being treated differently from all the rest, they might be able to ferret out the same information I did, through their own resources. They do, after all, monitor the other communication center on your orders."

"But why not just send your brawlers out to retrieve the body to begin with? That way, none of my constables has to die."

"You're a fool, Forrell. Have you learned nothing?" Prometheus turned his back on the image of the king's son and faced the governor.

Forrell swallowed hard, knowing he had no choice. As Prometheus said, he was in too deep to turn back now.

"I'll be with my brawlers when your constables return," Prometheus told him. "We'll kill your men before they can speak to any of the colonists. We'll spread the rumor that we caught the constables stealing from the mines. My brawlers don't like them anyway and will believe that story. No one will ever know the real reason why the constables died. That means everyone who knew about the body being moved elsewhere will be gone. There'll be no one left alive to even say where the prince's remains were taken. No one will know anything about any of this … no one but you and me."

The slug leader moved closer, and Adaman couldn't stop shaking.

"If anyone learns a Starlaw was tortured and murdered, it will have to come from you, Forrell. And I'll know where to find you. Won't I?"

Adaman backed up. "I-I would never tell," he whispered.

"I know. This little plan will make sure of it."

Prometheus pulled out a dagger and placed it against Adaman's neck.

"Just remember," the slug warned, "you survive at my pleasure. I only need you to make contact with merchants, suppliers, and Constellation League enforcers. They'll expect you to be in office. But cross me, and you'll end up like the second-born prince of Luster. Your remains will be incinerated in some little hole, and no one will even miss you. I'll make sure of it."

"I won't cross you. I swear it!" Adaman promised as he slowly backed away from the curved blade of the big slug's dagger.

• • •

Every thread of Marcos's clothing had been cut away. Nova made quite sure of that before hauling several containers of water into the cave from a nearby pond. She boiled the water to kill any bacteria, then spread a clean blanket next to her patient's body. She methodically cleansed his back, shoulders, buttocks, and thighs. And when she was sure every bit of the plasma was gone from that side of him, she rolled him onto the clean blanket and began to gently wipe down the front of his body.

As her mother had been a healer, so was she. She'd been present when many miners, merchants, tradesmen, and their children had been brought to their home because of illness or after an accident. At first, healing incubation units had been available. But when they broke down and no one had the technical expertise to fix them, it had fallen to her mother and *her* to treat all the sick and injured. They did so using olden ways of the Wiccans who were their ancestors, and who'd passed down those arts from one generation to the next.

At the time, it seemed criminal that the governor wouldn't order more medical equipment to replace what was damaged. But no amount of pleading from her father or the other miners did any good. The new incubation units never came. It was at that time the colonists of Delta Seven began to learn just what their governor was up to.

Slugs began to arrive soon after her father's last confrontation with Adaman Forrell. Forrell finally made his announcement that no medical equipment would be coming at all, and the slugs would be taking control of the population. The head constable, a political rival for the governor's position, had been murdered in his sleep along with all his family. That was when Nova's world fell apart.

The slugs came in the night and took her father, mother, and other dissenters away. She saw them burned in the square like so many others. Soon after, her home burned down while she was in the marketplace trying to rally dissenters. Some came to her aid. And when several young men of the miner's co-op demanded answers from Forrell's constables, they were killed. One of them had been her lover and might have been her husband one day.

Afterward, a crowd rioted because of the murders of their friends and family members. Nova was among them. But the slugs appeared and released streams of fire plasma on them all. That was when she was burned, while trying to escape.

When she looked down at Marcos's severely torched body, her physical pain seemed like nothing. It'd be days or weeks before he'd be able to walk or even stand. And that was if she could keep infection from setting in.

But her mother's ways, as passed down from all those ancestors, were useful. And she'd been taught them well. Not having an incubation unit had forced her to learn the ancient path and find curatives in things that existed only in nature. And that might be Marcos's only hope, the only reason he'd survive.

Of the men she'd treated so long ago, she'd never seen one so well-endowed. There were small burns over his genital area, but she believed they'd heal. The plasma had thickened early and quit running down his body. And when he'd fallen into the dusty street and thrown dirt on himself, that'd also stopped much of the glob-like substance from sliding downward. The chemical hadn't had time to sear his sex organs very badly.

There were many who ended up in the pit when their genitals were seared. She believed they might have taken their own lives even when the rest of their bodies hadn't been nearly so torched as Marcos's. Some of the men, especially, couldn't handle what had happened to their bodies in that respect. Perhaps it was the pain. Maybe it was the complete emasculation.

She only knew there were many dead who'd received fewer, less severe burns than her patient's.

She kept her mind on her task and carefully cleansed away every tiny bit of the plasma. Even the small bit on his genitals. Thankfully, Marcos didn't awaken as she this. That kind of pain might have been too much.

There'd be times when a cool cloth dipped in herbed water might help him through the night and still the aches as scars formed. But at least he would be in no further danger from burning.

It was late into the afternoon when she finished. Marcos's beautiful black hair was gone, but the lack of it would keep infection down until scars formed. She covered him with clean, dry sheets of lightweight material and checked her supplies.

She spoke quietly to the little dog lying right next to Marcos's right ear. "I'll have to provide for all three of us now, Una. But that's all right. I don't mind."

To keep an eye on him and listen for any sounds of breathing distress, Nova put more wood on the small fire, and made up a comfortable pallet nearby. Amazingly, sleep overtook her very soon. If she had her usual nightmares, she never recalled. Hours later, a horrifying shriek awakened her.

Marcos lay on his back and tried to claw away at the now-absent, lava-like ooze. In his sleep, he was reliving the entire event.

She threw herself on his body so he wouldn't re-open wounds that were already trying to heal. "Marcos, wake up! It's over," she cried.

He suddenly sat up and struck out.

She was knocked backward, against the cave wall, where she felt a sharp blow to the back of her head. Her vision suddenly tunneled, and she fell into blackness.

Chapter 5

"Perhaps someone took his body to another part of the pit," Adaman said as he wiped profuse sweat from his face and neck with a scarf.

The days now were scorching. At least Adaman felt they were, even as fall quickened. But perhaps it was just the constant company of the nasty slug leader that made him feel so clammy. The ugly slug just wouldn't leave him alone. And now, there were more problems. Prometheus stood inside Adaman's official residence staring at the barren landscape through an open window. There was one question on both their minds. Prometheus spoke of it first.

"For what purpose would someone move a corpse?"

Adaman spoke cautiously. "Y-you're people have been known to … well, I don't mean to be indelicate but … "

Prometheus slowly turned and stared. "My brawlers do occasionally eat the flesh of lower life forms, but not any that have been exposed to plasma. That would be suicide."

Adaman lowered his gaze subserviently. "I-I was only trying to suggest a p-possible reason as to why the body wasn't where it was s-supposed to be."

Prometheus paced in front of the large picture window as he spoke further. "It could be that the prince still lives."

"No … that's not possible," Adaman affirmed. "Some of my constables were in the marketplace when you blasted the man. They tell me no one could have survived such direct contact with plasma." He aggressively shook his head. "It's more likely that he fell among the rocks in the pit, and his body is wedged there someplace. The area has been blackened from so many exposures to incineration that your brawlers and my constables simply missed the body. The remains were probably destroyed along with the others when you ordered your ships to blast that area."

"I'll take no chances. Enforcers will come looking for him. We have to make sure there's no trace of a Starlaw on this planet, or we'll all face execution."

Adaman plopped down on an overstuffed sofa and stared up at Prometheus. "I had no hand in it at all and will say so as many times as it takes to convince them. Though they may not want to believe me, the enforcers will remember their frequent uncivil contact with Limaxian fighters. They'll know this was all your doing, Prometheus. You should have ignored him and let him go. He hadn't seen anything but scarred citizens. There was no proof you or I had a hand in that until you revealed yourself in the main marketplace and blasted him. I still say he's dead. He simply couldn't have lived through what you did to him."

Prometheus growled. "Take care, Forrell. No matter how you try to worm your way out of this, the king will hold you as responsible for his son's torture and death as me. And you know it. That is why you were so shocked by the news that a Starlaw might be the man I killed. That you weren't actually in the marketplace won't matter. You've cooperated with me the entire time my brawlers and I have been present on this worthless dung heap. You wanted wealth and power; I gave it to you." He snorted, then sneered. "I'll remind you again of what will happen if you cross me."

Adaman swallowed hard, clasped his hands together, then wrung them. If he didn't stop Prometheus, things would quickly go from bad to worse. "Listen to me … if you go through all the households looking for a man who is likely dead, people will know something is wrong. Rumors will start as to who you're looking for and why. We could have another rebellion on our hands, and your brawlers might have to work the mines themselves instead of depending on the forced labor of our remaining miners."

Prometheus quickly turned away. "I *will* find out what happened to the enforcer. If it were possible for him to survive, he'd be seeking medical help. Someone with knowledge of healing would be necessary."

Adaman thought for a long moment, and then a bit of trivia came to mind he'd not thought of before. "There was once a Wiccan healer helping the people. The family name was Drayton. The mother took up helping the sick and injured after I refused to buy incubation units. Her husband was Bellos Drayton. But you had them killed, didn't you?"

"I remember humans with that name causing us trouble. If they *were* dissenters, then I had my brawlers seek them out."

Adaman shrugged. "Bellos Drayton's wife was the only healer we had. She was the only person with any kind of extensive medical knowledge at all. If she's dead, there's no one to whom an injured person can go. That's why so many die and end up in the pits."

"Were there no neighbors who might have worked with his woman? Someone she may have trained in the Wiccan ways?"

"No," Adaman told him. "I can't remember anyone helping her." He sighed and shook his head in denial. "There simply isn't anyone an injured stranger could rely on. I tell you the king's son is dead. The only incubation units for the sector are those aboard your own vessels. The man has to be rotting somewhere. None of the remaining colonists would go to his aid, risking their life in the process. My constables say you had this man tied to a post, and that you didn't miss. He's in whatever afterlife he believed in." Adaman insisted.

Prometheus snarled and clenched his hands into fists. "Still … my brawlers and your constables couldn't find his body even as they located Codge's. The enforcer and my dead minion were taken to the pit together. I don't care what you say, Forrell, something isn't right. I know a Starlaw is out there." Prometheus turned toward the window again. "I will find him. I won't rest until I see his cadaver."

•••

Marcos's vision finally cleared, and he fought remnants of the nightmare. His body was covered with open wounds, but he was no longer in the marketplace or the rock pit where he'd been dumped. Then his fogged brain pieced together the events. He'd been rescued by some kind soul.

He gazed around as flickering tongues of flame leapt from a small fire. The cave in which he found himself was formed from pure red clay. The whimper of a small animal drew his attention. There was a furry mammal of some kind scooting around a small form at the base of one wall.

Then he remembered *her*.

"Creator's blood!"

He stretched one hand toward the woman and almost touched her left arm. "Please be all right. I had a nightmare and thought you were one of the slugs." He'd lashed out and remembered her attempts to hold him down. "Please say you can hear me, little one … N-Nova. Y-your name is Nova. I remember!"

To his utter relief, Nova finally came to her senses, pushed herself halfway up, and shook her head. She put one hand to the back of her neck and scooped up Una with the other.

Marcos sighed in relief. "Please forgive me, I beg you. I-I've never struck a woman in my life."

She shook her head once more and moved toward him. "Don't move. You mustn't get this red earth into your wounds, or they could get infected. Just lie still." She sat next to him, gently pulled the clean sheet back up to his shoulders, and carefully pushed him back down on his pallet.

"I'm so sorry," Marcos repeated. "Are you all right?"

She tilted her head and stared for a moment. "I was just a bit stunned. You're the one who's hurt. Don't worry about me. I know you didn't mean it."

Marcos coughed hard as the chemical in his lungs blocked his airway.

Nova helped him turn onto his stomach just as fluid drained from his mouth and onto the cave floor. "Here, use this."

He turned his head toward the soft cloth she held, and tried to stem his gut-wrenching coughs, but couldn't. He violently vomited residue of the plasma chemical he'd breathed in. Every nerve in his body felt as if it was open and torn. His lungs felt as though they'd never draw air again. But after some minutes, he finally gasped inward, and the coughing diminished.

All the while, Nova kept holding fresh cloths for him to vomit into. The residue from his throat smelled horrible and looked toxic. She must have thought it was since she threw the cloths into the fire so they'd burn. As she did so, each vomit-filled bit of fabric flared when the flames touched them. When the worst of his retching was over, she helped him lie in a propped-up position that made it easier to breathe.

He began to shiver violently. She put a blanket over his shoulders. He yelped and tried to shake it off, but she put the covering back.

"You're going into shock from the cold water I had to put on your body. It was the only way to get the remaining plasma off and stop the burning. I know you don't like the blanket, but you have to stay warm," she softly explained.

He eventually lay on his left side and gazed up at her. For the time being, he could do nothing more than shiver. Another wave of coughing began and his lungs felt as if they'd burn away. But his little savior stayed with him, right by his side.

He focused on the dulcet sound of her voice.

Occasionally, she'd rearrange the blanket around his scorched body and offer him another dry cloth to hold against his face.

Through hours of pain, torment, and anguish, he clung to the sound of her repeated words of comfort. The Creator must have sent her to him. Who else would have come to his aid and cared for him so diligently if not a messenger from the Divine One?

When he finally lay before her in an exhausted heap, she stretched out beside him and spoke quietly.

"You'll get through this. I did, and so will you. I promise." She smiled at him. "Just rest now. I won't leave you alone."

Because he was in so much agony, she was the rock to which he clung. Nothing existed but her.

Marcos finally closed his eyes and slept. The nightmare didn't return. But only because of her. Even when his dreams threatened to turn dark again, her calm presence anchored him. And he felt hope. There was a chance he could survive. If she cared enough to risk her life helping him then he *must* try.

• • •

Hours or maybe days later, he opened his eyes and felt a cool cloth being applied to the open wounds of his body. He was on his stomach and tried to rise, but she gently pushed him down. The pain was still severe, but not nearly as bad as it had been.

"I've made some vegetable broth, so you should try to eat. You coughed a little in your sleep, but I think the worst of that crap is out of your lungs. Do you feel like talking?"

He carefully turned his head toward her. "I-I feel better," he croaked.

"You look a great deal better. Your voice will come back eventually. Just don't try to say too much if your throat hurts."

"Sit ... up?" he requested.

"All right. If you feel like it. It's a good idea to move your hands, feet, and joints if you can. The scars leave them stiffened if you don't. That's why so many who've been exposed to the plasma limp or walk in a stooped posture."

Marcos carefully pushed himself into a sitting position. The light blanket on his body fell to his thighs and exposed a great deal of his torso to the cool cave air. His skin stung, and he winced, but he quickly decided that any day above ground was a good one. All thoughts of death were gone. He'd gotten this far with her help. He could go the distance.

"You said you're called Marcos. Unfortunately, that's all I know about you. Well ... I know you're supposed to be a merchant. That's what Prometheus called you."

"P-Prometheus?"

"That's the slug leader who attacked you."

"D-Doesn't ... s-sound like a Limaxian name."

"It isn't," Nova confirmed. "I think he went by the name of Garstid when he first arrived. Being the leader of the slugs, he thinks he's above humans. Using a human-sounding name is a way of making fun of us. It's just another way to show us who's master."

Marcos sat still as she picked up her cloth, dipped it into a bowl of water, and began to reapply it to his body. It hurt badly, but he closed his eyes for a moment and willed himself to accept her help. "I didn't h-hurt you?"

Nova shook her head. "It's all right, Marcos. Don't worry about knocking me against the wall. You were having a horrible nightmare. I don't hold it against you."

The cold of the cave, combined with the cool cloth, made him shiver worse. "How long?"

"How long have you been sleeping?" she asked as she readjusted the blanket over the lower half of his body. "Almost two days."

He stared at the scars over her bald head for a moment and realized he must look much the same, likely worse. The skin of her hands and forearms looked soft and normal. It seemed that just the upper part of her body had been scorched by the plasma, as the telltale scars ran across her cheeks and neck. The long caftan she wore gave him no clue as to how badly she might have originally been burned.

After turning to fill a cup with hot vegetable broth from the fire pit, she hesitated. "I know. I'm not all that attractive, but I'm alive."

Marcos lowered his gaze, ashamed at having been caught staring.

She lifted the cup to his lips and let him sip some of the hot broth.

The soup actually tasted good. It made his throat feel better when he swallowed.

"Good. You're doing much better than I would have expected. But then, I don't know how you survived at all. You've been burned quite badly." She paused. "I was running away when it happened to me. Just my head, back, shoulders, and a few spots on the front of my body were exposed."

"W-what did you do?"

"Nothing. Just like you," she angrily responded. "Slugs went into the marketplace and fired at everyone just to make an example of us. Many of the miners and merchants here tried to fight back when the slugs first landed. But we had no real weapons. My father and mother, the head constable, and many of the miners and merchants from work co-ops were killed. Anyone I ever cared about is dead. I survive only because I hide in this cave. My father thought we might have to have a safe place to stay secluded, so he prepared this cave for us. Only he and my mother never got here."

"I'm sorry, Nova."

"You've nothing to be sorry about. It was the slugs and the governor who killed everyone. But you … what you did the other day was one of the few brave things I've seen on this planet. I saved you because I think you must be a very good person. You wouldn't have risked your life for complete strangers otherwise. And a good man doesn't deserve to … well … nobody deserves what … " Her voice trailed away.

"Listen to me," he croaked. "Enforcers will come—"

"No they bloody well won't!" she shot back. "They're as bad as the slug pirates, Adaman Forrell, and the traitorous constables he's paying to keep us in line. They can all rot. Especially the king of Luster and his Constellation League enforcers. My greatest hope is that the slug warships hiding behind the moons beyond our planet will ambush the enforcers whenever they care to show up again. And that the two sides kill each other off. Maybe then Delta Seven can have some peace, and the people here can stop dying."

Marcos stared at her, speechless for the moment. How could he judge a woman who'd been through what was likely years of subjugation and pain?

"I'm sorry, Marcos. You're a victim here just like everyone else. It's the enforcers, Forrell, and the slugs I hate. I didn't mean to take my anger out on you." She gently stroked one of his cheeks and smiled at him.

"I've never heard anyone say they hated the king or enforcers before," he quietly responded.

"You'll come to hate them, too, when you have to live like an animal. Just waiting for the next time Prometheus decides to hunt out some slaves for the mines."

"I don't understand. Please … tell me what's going on here."

She took a deep breath and refilled his cup with some more hot broth. "My father and some of the other miners discovered a vein of the richest gems you can ever imagine. When the first lot went up for sale, an outer-world merchant purchased the entire shipment for an exorbitant price. We thought that finding gems of such value would be the end of hard times. And it might have been had the slugs not seized the merchant's ship in space, found the gems, and tortured him into telling where he got them."

"What happened to the merchant?"

"It's said that Prometheus killed him. I believe he'd do it to keep the gems' source a secret. He and his minions arrived here and took over not long after that. He has Adaman Forrell's complete cooperation. All the governor has to do is answer vid-calls from deep space and placate enforcers when they arrive to take on fuel or ask a few questions. He just tells them everything is all right. They believe him, don't do an inspection, leave, and don't return for months. I heard the citizens's communication center was broken into and someone tried to get a message out, but we've always believed Forrell monitors everything and garbles transmissions even as they're being sent. If they're not sent by him, that is. It's likely he's had the real person responsible for sending messages killed. I don't know."

He breathed easier and actually posed a question without sounding like some kind of reptile was lodged in his gullet. "A-and you say the slugs use the c-citizens as slave labor? To mine the gems?"

She nodded. "Slugs are lazy. They won't work for anything. That's why they resort to stealing and pirating. And putting so many of us in the mines is why there are so few of us left. When anyone gets injured, there's not any medical help. If the miners die, they're tossed into that pit where you were dumped. New people are dragged out of their homes and sent to the mines to work, and most are never heard from again."

"Why is there no medical help? Incubation units could heal your wounds."

"Forrell wouldn't order new units or repair the old ones when they broke down. You see ... if you know you can be cured of the burns, you won't be so frightened of the slugs and what they can do using the plasma. And as long as they can keep us all afraid of being burned, we won't fight back."

"Eventually, more people will be needed to mine," Marcos reasoned. "What happens when no one is left but the sick, injured, or those who are too old or young to work?"

"They'll kidnap people from nearby colonies on other worlds." She shrugged. "Occasionally, ships arrive with supplies, or merchants like you show up. Some are allowed to leave so that suspicion is averted. But they all leave with the story that this planet isn't worth visiting, and that the gems mined here are inferior. That rumor has spread, so we don't get visitors except on rare occasions. Those merchants allowed to leave are only shown what Forrell wants them to see. But any outer-worlders who ask too many questions, or make Adaman or Prometheus uncomfortable, get thrown in the mines, or they're even killed. If they have crews aboard their ships, those crews get killed or enslaved as well. I'm sure any record of their being here is eradicated. No matter what space charts and flight plans might say, no one questions the governor of an entire colony when he says he's never allowed a ship to land. Nobody wants that diplomatic nightmare on their hands."

He slowly shook his head in disgust.

"Most of the strangers coming to this planet are drifters. Like you. If they have any families or friends, no one seems to care enough to come looking for them."

"How long has this been going on?"

"Over two years now. At first, the colonists met in secret to talk about rebellion. Information was passed around about what was happening. That's how we initially figured out what was going on between Forrell and the slugs. But after the last mass plasma attack on the population, no one talks to anyone anymore. No one does anything to bring the wrath of Prometheus down on their heads."

"Help will come, Nova."

"Even if it does, it'll be too late. There are already too many dead. And nothing will bring my mother and father back. Nothing will bring back the man I would have married, my friends, or their families. I'll hate the enforcers forever for not inspecting this planet more closely, and for believing Forrell's lies. They've left us here to die."

Marcos couldn't explain the complexities of the political world to someone who was fighting for her life. He could have told her that enforcers couldn't forcibly invade a world and inspect its holdings without starting an interplanetary incident. His presence on Delta Seven was technically against the policies agreed to by many worlds. He was spying for his government.

But that information might just get him killed. And while he knew this woman was risking her life to help him, he didn't yet know just how far he could trust her. Especially if she found out what and who he was.

"I'm going to find a way off this planet," Nova told him. "Or I'll die trying."

"Maybe we can help each other."

She smiled. "I thought someone as brave as you would think the same thing. But I don't know much about you, Marcos. Except, of course, that you're certainly not one of Forrell's henchmen."

"In case I didn't say so when my condition was worse, my full name is … it's Marcos Orlandis. It's like you said. Not many who come here have much of a life, or they'd be bidding for better gems in other places and selling them to larger planets. I'm not a wealthy man or I'd have never come to this place. That's for sure!"

"But you have family. I heard you praying to your Creator when you were lying in the pit. I couldn't hear all you said, but most of it had to do with hoping you could see them again." She lowered her gaze for a moment. "I didn't mean to eavesdrop. But

I didn't even know you were alive when I went to find you. I … I went to pray for you."

Touched by her kind explanation, Marcos's guilt dug deep into his heart. For now, the lie about who he really was had to remain. He couldn't tell her everything about his family, or the truth about who he really was would become obvious. The number and names of all siblings must be withheld, with the exception of a very few family members whose names were so common as to be nondescript. His father and brother had monikers that were quite well used. But he *could* say enough about his ancestry and their zeal to see him back to assure her all wasn't lost. "I have a family. I didn't tell Forrell anything about them. And my brother will come looking for me, Nova. Count on it!"

"Is your brother a merchant, too? Were you in contact with him before you arrived? Will he know where you are?"

The anxious look on her face was almost heartbreaking. He knew she wanted to hear that someone might come and stop the madness. Though he hated to do so, he had to expand on the lie. There was no other choice. At least until such time as he could convince her that the Constellation League and his father hadn't neglected Delta Seven on purpose.

"My brother knows exactly where I am. He's in the same business as I."

Nova leaned forward and carefully hugged him. "Then, there's finally some hope. For both of us."

As she fed and tended him, he cursed himself for not telling her exactly why he was on the planet. But Nova might tell others, and he couldn't face the anger of a mob who felt the same as she. He'd never be able to explain the politics, or the fact that the enforcer fleet and its crews were at half force since the Warlord conflict had ended.

Losses of manpower and equipment couldn't be replaced overnight. It would take another year of building ships and training crews before things were back to normal.

Money wasn't the issue; time to resupply the fleet with trained crews *was*. And if news of *that* got out to certain inhospitable planets, those wishing to take advantage of the situation would do so. His father was in no position to offer a galactic defense against rogues, pirates, and any evil opposition that might want to take over every defenseless planet. Petty dictators had already warred with the planets that made up the Constellation League. For many years, battle had been a way of life. Peace had only come to the enforcers and the League planets a few years ago. And Delta Seven had been one of the outer-worlds that hadn't so much as sent one man or woman to train as an enforcer crewmember. It had preferred to stay neutral and had steadfastly remained so during the fights.

Now, the citizens of this small planet needed help. And while he could forget the past and yearn to aid this colony, there weren't enough ships and crews to do the situation justice, and the others belonging to the League equally needed help. And *they* were and always had been staunch allies. When help was allotted, they'd demand first call, and rightly so.

Still, Nova, and probably the other citizens of Delta Seven, wouldn't understand any of that. They were being brutally slaughtered, and a weapon was being used on them that had been universally banned. His father had suspected Delta Seven needed help and was doing what he could. And in such a way that no one would know.

Marcos felt sympathy for Nova and her world, but he also felt the need to defend what he knew to be the truth. To do so, he'd have to choose the time carefully. He knew Darius would come. All he had to do was survive until then.

His strength waned. He leaned back on his pallet of blankets. A small warm body cuddled next to him. He turned his head to see the white fuzzy creature Nova kept as a pet.

"Una likes you. She never left your side the whole time you were sleeping. Dogs sometimes know when someone needs help."

Marcos gazed at the little bundle curiously. "Are you sure that's a dog?"

Nova grinned. "She occasionally barks like one, so that's what I call her. But there are a lot of unusual species in the galaxy that no one has ever seen or classified. Maybe this is what dogs look like where she came from."

Somehow, he doubted the little animal was what Nova defined as something from the canine family. But the soft whirring noise Una made was comforting all the same. It made the pain of his open wounds diminish, at least for a time.

"Before you go to sleep, I have a question I need to ask."

Marcos shifted his gaze away from the strange little animal and toward his hostess.

"Was it you who slammed the window?"

Remembering the little thief in the street outside the inn, Marcos actually smiled, even though it hurt to do so. "So ... the little thief *was* you?"

She grinned back. "Thank you for alerting me. I guessed it must have been you. There were no other visitors staying at the inn but one lone gem merchant ... *you*. At least not that I was aware of."

He slowly shook his head. "I'm the one who should be thanking you. You saved my life, Nova. I won't ever forget it, though I don't know why you'd risk so much."

She thought for a moment. "My mother was Wiccan. So am I. We believe there's a reason for everything that happens. Maybe you were meant to save me ... so that I could save you."

"An odd set of circumstances, and an unusual reasoning for them," he jokingly replied. "The Creator of all things truly does work in mysterious ways."

She tucked the blankets around him, picked up a cloth to bathe his face, and smiled down at him. "You're my responsibility. So rest now. Let your mind be at peace."

Marcos let her soft words lull him into a deep sleep. Because of the gentle touch of her hands, her tranquil voice, and Una's comfortable rumbling, no nightmares invaded his sleep. He felt safe. The pain faded.

...

Adaman Forrell sat on the edge of his bed and grew cold with fright. He'd never trusted Prometheus Worthy. Limaxians were known to sell their own families into slavery if it meant their comfort and wealth would be increased by doing so. Even blood-sucking vampires feared them.

He stood and paced. The surveillance device he'd installed in Prometheus's chambers had proven its worth. The big slug leader was secretly searching for the man thought to be the prince of Luster. It was clear the Limaxian didn't want *him* finding the scorched merchant *first*. Seeing and hearing what he had, he knew he must act in his own defense; one that might eventually put him into a much better diplomatic position by doing so. He pressed a buzzer summoning his personal guards.

Two could play the game the putrid slug pursued. If it was true the prince of Luster survived, then Marcos Starlaw must be found by *his* constables first. The son of the king could become a powerful bargaining tool, a way to guarantee his own survival and possibly his position as governor.

When the guards arrived, Forrell opened the door and let the three of them into his room. When they stood before him, and he was sure he had their undivided attention, he began.

"I have a special assignment for you. There's a man I want you to search for. He'll be strong, young, and have green eyes. He'll be suffering profuse plasma burns. Find him and bring him to me at once. Tell no Limaxians. If the slugs see you and question your actions, refer them to me." He smiled craftily and continued giving orders. He saw the way his men responded; grinning like serpents when they thought they'd be given the chance to best slugs.

"Pretend you're hunting for replacement miners," Adaman suggested. "Arrest anyone caught harboring this person and lock him or her in a cell. In fact, it might be best if you searched at night. Since we've previously gone into homes after dark to look for workers, there should be no suspicion about your activities as long as slugs are nowhere near. Keep me informed of everything you do."

The guards nodded and would have left, but Adaman stopped them.

"One more thing. During the daylight hours, go to the marketplace and watch all the merchants who might be selling medicinals in any form. That means herbs, poultices, bandaging, and whatever a burn victim might need to survive. If anyone matching the description of this green-eyed man shows up, or if anyone seems to be purchasing more medicinals than usual, follow them to their residence. Once again ... make any arrests after dark, while all the Limaxians are drinking in the tavern. I can't put too fine a point on it—no one is to be given any reason for your search other than you're conscripting new miners." Forrell added an incentive: "I'll pay triple the wages to the man who can succeed in finding this burned, green-eyed stranger and whomever he calls friend."

The guards smiled even more broadly.

One of them stepped forward. "Is this the same man I saw the slug leader burn in the marketplace? That poor brute can't have survived, sir. Not after what Prometheus did."

Forrell nodded in confirmation. "He's a gem merchant who should have been thoroughly interrogated. That Limaxian idiot let his temper get the better of him, as usual, and never thought to do so."

The lead guard held out his hand in a questioning gesture. "Why would he need to be interrogated, sir? I still say the man can't be alive."

"I'll explain," Forrell congenially offered, and sat down in a nearby chair. "If you were there and witnessed the incident, you realize this merchant's assertive behavior wasn't common. Prometheus told me this man openly challenged his authority and even killed one of his best brawlers.

"That's true, sir. I was there and saw it all."

"You make my point," Forrell gushingly told him. "Given that kind of hostility, any prudent person would have suspected this visitor wasn't who he pretended to be. This stranger should have been brought in immediately and questioned." He shot the guards a sly smile. "But I say all this because we might still have that chance. Despite your assertions to the contrary, my good fellow, I have reason to believe the merchant certainly *did* live. Prometheus told me there were several human constables and Limaxian brawlers who went missing. Uh … they were sent to make sure the merchant's body was thrown into the pit. That body, as far as I know, hasn't turned up. And our constables and the slug brawlers sent to find it never returned to their duties. They are still unaccounted for."

Adaman slyly lowered his head. The lie concerning his ignorance of those missing brawlers and guards was meant to keep his own bribed men from knowing how expendable they really were. The unspoken but obvious suggestion was that the gem merchant the guards were to search for might have friends who'd helped him survive—that the merchant's allies somehow got rid of comrades of the very men who now stood before him.

He played to the loyalty of his constables to him, to each other, even while hiding the truth. As always, he'd placate his men and let them believe everything he did was for the good of the colony. They'd fall in with his wishes only as long as he could maintain his innocent guise and provide them monetary incentives.

The men he now ordered to go look for the Starlaw prince—assuming that's who the burned gem merchant really was—mustn't think of their target as anything other than another dissenting malcontent whose compatriots might have hurt their fellow employees. The more calmly and quietly he gave orders, the more likely his guards would obey without question. Especially since he was offering this new set of men such a magnificent reward for finding their prey before the hated Limaxians did. That alone was enough to energize them. Besting the slugs was just icing on the cake to these clueless, underpaid civil servants standing before him.

The guards looked at each other in clueless disarray. Adaman just pasted on a much practiced, gentle-looking smile.

The most senior of the three guards spoke his thoughts. "But why would anyone help a stranger ... especially to the point of taking out guards and brawlers? They'd be risking their lives by doing so."

The governor sighed and feigned a bored shrug. "Perhaps someone hopes this merchant can pay them for his rescue. Who knows? The reasons could be endless. We can only find out what's going on by locating the man. But we'll have to be more cunning, quieter, and a great deal more alert than the slugs. Left to them, we'll never get to the bottom of where your fellow guards really are."

"This assignment won't be hard, Governor. Limaxian brawlers aren't blessed with a great deal of intelligence," the first guard quipped.

The other two guards laughed in agreement.

Forrell patiently smiled. "I must agree with your keen sense of the situation," he liberally complimented. "I can add that I trust these slugs no further than I can piss. I'm sure you'll concur?"

The guards nodded, asserting their mutual accord on the subject.

"If he survived, let's find this gem merchant. That, gentlemen, is your assignment. I bid you goodnight."

The guards quickly left, to be about their task.

A few minutes later, Forrell sat on the edge of his bed, pulled his robe off, and prepared to rest. He chuckled at his shrewd handling of his minions.

Like all humans of Delta Seven, there was one thing they had in common—their hatred of the Limaxians. It didn't matter what the assignment was, he knew his guards were always willing to take on any task that bested or belittled the slugs.

Thinking the matter over, he shook his head at Prometheus's incredible stupidity when dealing with underlings. The differences between himself and that feckless creature were vast and went beyond species diversity. Chief among those variances was intelligence and the use of tact. Adaman knew he could get more by bribing his men than Prometheus could by threatening *his*. And that would be the reason *he'd* survive and the slug leader *wouldn't*.

He fell back into his sumptuous pillows and thought about the hidden cache of jewels Prometheus had in his quarters. The lot that the putrid, slimy creature intended to keep and never mention.

Adaman congratulated himself again for the foresight to install good surveillance equipment in the Limaxian's quarters. Using it during hours the slug leader thought he wouldn't be disturbed,

Adaman also had heard Prometheus discussing plans with his minions. Not satisfied with his share of the gems being mined, the big, gray, worm-like entity meant to use Adaman's gems as *extra* booty to buy arms and ships. Those purchased ships and weapons would then be wielded against any perceived enemies in the entire sector. It was the slug leader's intent to rule this parsec of space, but *that* was the way a thug used a veritable treasure trove of priceless jewels. Prometheus thought small.

One could rule far better using one's wit, diplomatic chicanery, and under-the-table bribery. He'd done it all his life and meant to finally rise to the position and honor he knew he deserved.

To that end, he'd have his share of stones *and* Prometheus's. He fantasized about ruling this world and setting himself up in a castle to rival that of Luster's king. Then the aides and embassy minions of others would come seeking *his* hand to kiss. Above all he had no intention of sharing such booty with ignorant miners who wouldn't know what to do with it except drink and whore themselves into witless stupors. Simply put, his goal was to rule and to make his way into power through the use of the endless wealth he saw before him. First, he had to get by Prometheus. If he could find the prince of Luster before the slugs got to him, he'd have a chance to play the rescuer and gain a very powerful ally in the form of the prince's father—Dar Starlaw.

"We'll see how the game plays out, Prometheus. We'll see who lives, who dies, and who gets to the prince first."

Chapter 6

Marcos finished urinating and limped back toward the cave.

It'd been two weeks since his salvation, but his entire body still hurt. When the plasma had hit him, he hadn't had even the protection of a shirt to cover his torso. But that was exactly why Prometheus, or whoever the slug really was, had torn it off.

As he carefully crawled through the space into the inner chamber, he saw two small, booted feet before him. He looked up and smiled.

Nova stood before him with her hands on her hips and an angry expression pasted on her face. Her striking amethyst eyes flashed in fury.

"What the blazes did you think you were doing? Why did you leave the cave? I was only asleep for a few moments when you turned up missing. I looked for you and was worried when you didn't answer my calls."

He slowly stood when the ceiling within the cave allowed. It was one of the more excruciating things he'd done recently, but he managed to stand to his full height of just over six-and-a-half feet. "I had to … nature called. I heard you, but I was a bit busy."

"I've been helping you take care of that."

Marcos smiled. "I know. You've been rolling me off the soiled sheets and replacing them. I'm always in clean bedding when I awaken. But there'll be no more of that. I have to start moving around much more. My joints will stiffen if I don't, and you shouldn't have to wait on me hand and foot. Not any longer."

She stepped closer to him and dropped her angry façade. "I know that having someone take care of such a personal need isn't palatable to a man like you. But it's very cold outside. You're only wrapped in a blanket."

"The cold isn't actually all that bad. In fact, it feels good on my skin. And I *will* take care of my personal needs on my own from now on. So, don't panic if I don't respond back when you call. I'll probably be behind a rock or tree."

"Well … you've slept and eaten well these last few days. A couple of weeks have gone by, and it is time you were moving about. But tonight, I'll bring you some clothes. Please don't leave the protection of the cave again without proper garments. You could make yourself ill."

Marcos sat on a flat rock and stared at her for a moment. "There's a curfew after dark. Exactly what did you mean when you said you'd bring me clothes tonight?"

She smiled. "I have to replenish my supplies. I go out after dark to steal because it's safer than meeting up with the slugs in the marketplace during the daylight hours."

"No! Absolutely not. There's no need for you to creep about at night and risk what will happen if you're caught." He walked toward his cloak, which was neatly draped over the back of an old chair. "I have money and some of the gemstones I bought sewn into the lining of this." He ripped open one seam and handed her a pouch with some coins. "Use this to buy what you need."

Nova slowly opened the leather pouch and saw the coins inside. "Marcos, this might be enough to bribe a ship's captain to get us off Delta Seven the next time a supply vessel lands."

"Do you really think that slug leader is going to let any citizen near a transport?"

She briefly bowed her head in agreement.

"It'll be better used to buy supplies and clothing. Whatever you need to survive."

"But I can steal what we need and save this."

He sighed. "Nova, what you're doing isn't worth the risk. Help will come, I know it. My brother and the rest of my family won't leave me here. And you can buy more and better supplies than what you can steal while running."

She considered this. "I guess I could get a better supply of herbs for my ointments. You'll need salves and poultices when the air turns colder."

"And you can walk right into the marketplace and never be suspected of anything."

She glanced down at the pouch. "Only if I don't make a show of having this much money. If anyone sees this purse, they'll question how a citizen of such a poor planet got it."

Marcos didn't consider his stash a good amount. He regularly spent more on drinks at Lusterian entertainment venues. To Nova, the sum must seem like a great deal indeed. She had very little in the way of personal property. Only what he'd seen in the cave. And that amounted to a few pots and pans, and some bottles of herbs and ointments, most of which she'd used on him.

"Why don't I go with you?"

Her mouth dropped open.

"Why are you looking at me like that?" he asked. "After you buy me some clothing, I'll put my cloak on, hunch over, and pretend I'm one of a hundred people in the marketplace."

"Are you *insane*? Do you know what the slugs will do if they find out you're still alive? Can you imagine?"

"Nova, I'm so badly scarred my own mother wouldn't recognize me."

"If your mother has seen those unusual green eyes she would."

The quip wasn't lost on him, but he persisted. "If you go, I go with you. You won't be buying supplies for me, risking your safety by stealing, or going into the marketplace alone."

"I've been doing a damned good job of taking care of myself, Marcos."

"Nova—"

"No and that's final," she angrily responded. "I'll get warm clothing for you. Buying it is best because no one will recognize their stolen clothing on you if you should ever be seen. But that's the extent of my compromise. You will *not* go back to the marketplace. Not ever."

He watched her stalk to the fire to throw on more wood with a force that wasn't necessary, and smiled. She was no bigger than a young girl. And if she knew that only members of the royal family and his closest friends were allowed to speak to him in such an argumentative way, she'd probably still use the same tone of voice. But she didn't know who he was. Their conversations had been about very general topics, tending to sidetrack anything that might anger one of them or cause a painful reminder of Nova's past.

He slowly walked to where she sat and took a seat beside her. "Could I ask a personal question?"

She glanced at him. "Depends."

"I just want to know how old you are. You look very young."

She gazed up at him. "Wiccans ... those from the planet Wyrdan that is ... appear younger than they really are. And the scars on my face hide a few lines." She tried not to smile at him when his brows arched in disbelief. "I'm twenty-seven years this past summer."

"You're lying," he blurted.

She chuckled and nodded. "It's true."

"You're so tiny. You haven't a waist as big as my lower thigh."

"And how would you know that? Been looking me over, have you?"

Her joking tone made him grin broader. "Well, I did look and was wondering about your age."

"So how old are you, Green Eyes?"

"Thirty-six this upcoming spring. At least the spring on my home world."

"And where is your home world? You've said nothing about it."

He didn't want to add to the heap of lies he'd already told, but there was something in him that feared her hatred. And she *would* hate him with a vengeance if she knew who he really was. "It's far from here. Close to the Lusterian realm."

"What's it like?" She turned to him, pulled her legs under her, and leaned forward to listen.

"It's bright. Very colorful. Not dull like it is here."

"I was born here," she quietly told him. "All I've ever known are the dull, sepia tones of this world. Even the people here dress as though they're already dead. But my mother used to tell me stories of her home planet of Wyrdan. She said there were forests and mountains as far as the eye could see. Everything was green and beautiful." She gazed into the distance. "Someday, I'm going to go someplace where there's lots of color. And there'll be tall trees with lovely birds living among the branches. I want to live in a place just the exact opposite of Delta Seven. And when I find a way to leave here, I'm never coming back. Not ever."

"My world has every color of the rainbow. People dress as if there's always a festival. Why, some of the women even walk around baring their breasts. On my world it's common."

She turned to him. "I think it would be wonderful to feel so free, even though I'm not certain I could do such a thing." She adjusted her position so she was sitting very close to him. "Tell me about the colors of your planet and the people there. I want to know its name and all the names of the people in your family."

Now he was in trouble. "I-I have a very large family."

"How wonderful. It must be grand to come home to a lot of people who've missed you."

He nodded. "It is."

"Tell me more," she encouraged.

"My … my planet has been called Avalon by the ancients." That much was true. It was a very old name, and only the historians ever spoke of it.

"I've never heard of such a place."

The eagerness in her face was beguiling. Starved for news, familial affection, and a simple desire to see other than the dull regimen of colors of her home world for the first time, she practically hung on every word. So this much, at least, he wouldn't lie about. "The streets on my world sparkle. Mines of white marble provide our building materials. And quartz crystal decorates the outside of some of the homes."

Nova gasped. "How wonderful! Why did you ever leave?"

"I-I had a job to complete. I would have gone back when my work was done."

"But it sounds like a wealthy place. Why would you need to scavenge the galaxy for poor-grade gems?"

"It was something I had to do. I can't explain." He threw some wood onto the fire and hoped she wouldn't ask more on that subject.

"I think I understand."

He looked at her. "You do?"

She touched his cheek lightly. "You wanted to forge a path for yourself. You're that kind of man, I think."

"That was part of it. I won't live off my family, that's for sure."

"I knew it was something like that. The way you stood up to Prometheus led me to believe you're a man who craves a challenge. Someone who takes action. And occasionally bites off more than he can chew. A *lot* more!"

He saw the twinkle in her eyes and knew she meant the last part as a compliment, despite how it sounded. "Do you want to hear more about my world or not?"

She looped her hands around his bicep. "Yes, please."

The gesture warmed him even if it smarted a bit. But the pain of her small hands on his arm wasn't so much as it might have been just a few days earlier. In any case, he didn't want her to pull away.

The contact was one of the first signs he was healing faster than he'd have thought. He happily continued with his description.

"There are many on my world who're wealthy. Commerce is very good. A man or woman can make a very decent living. I guess you could say I chose a harder path … because it was there."

"Tell me more about colors. What's it like to wake up every day and surround yourself with them?"

"It's breathtaking," he quietly told her. "I never knew how much until now. I won't ever take it for granted again."

She sighed and leaned her head against his arm. "Maybe one day I can see it."

Marcos put one arm over her slender shoulders. The gesture didn't hurt so much at all, so he kept it where it was and hoped she wouldn't shy away. When she didn't, he smiled broader. Even his face was healing.

"I'll take you, Nova. I swear it. We'll get out of here. My brother *will* find me."

She stayed quiet for a few moments. Finally, she spoke her thoughts aloud. "I sometimes wish my mother hadn't left her planet when she met my father and agreed to be his wife. I wish I'd been born someplace else. It's always been a struggle here. But my father always told us we'd be wealthy beyond our wildest dreams … someday. And we would have been much better off had the slugs not attacked that merchant vessel and besieged this planet. But the only reason I care about the gemstones now is because they could buy me a way off this horrible, wretched rock. All I want is enough to get out of here. Let everyone else keep the wealth of Delta Seven. I've seen what it can do, and it's not worth it. And I don't even care if I ever get healed of the scars, either. You and I could leave, go to your world, and you could show me all those beautiful colors. I'll bet they're grander than the shade of any gemstone you can imagine."

For the first time, Marcos realized that if the women he'd bedded could see the second-born prince of Luster now, they'd only reluctantly keep company with him. Even his position and title couldn't entice them into his quarters if his hideously scarred body was the only offering. But they would still come to him for money and his place in society.

That life now seemed very shallow. Maybe that's why he'd always craved action at the helm of an enforcer ship. That was the only place where he'd mattered to anyone outside his own family circle.

But he was sure if someone were to offer this little Wiccan a bag of gold, she'd rush to the first off-world vessel she could. She'd give it all to some captain who might kill her after taking it. All for a chance at freedom.

"Nova, I don't want to hurt you by asking, but I'm curious about something."

She tilted her head and nodded. "Go on, ask."

"You spoke of a man you might have married, and that he was killed. Can you talk about him?"

"Why?"

"Well … my brother lost his first wife and child when Warlords attacked their transport ship. When the war raged between the Constellation League and the Warlords, I lost a lot of friends as everyone did. But never someone I loved so dearly. My brother never talked about his wife and little girl after they were killed. I … I could never ask him what he was feeling for fear of the pain my questions might cause."

"How terrible for him … and for you," she whispered.

"He has another wife and child now. All that happened long ago. But sometimes, I see him looking up into the night sky, and I wonder if he's thinking of them. Is it like that with this man you loved? Do you think of him often?"

"Honestly … this may sound horrible, but I don't know if I really loved him so much as I thought of him as a very good friend. I think … I think that's why I put him off so many times when he asked me to marry him. I always made some excuse or another. Aeson and I grew up together. I think our families expected we'd make an agreement. And I believe I might have come to love him with more passion eventually. He was an honest man. But he died with all the others who tried to stand against Prometheus. All because of a pile of cold stones wealthy people wear for jewelry. All because some king on a distant planet, and his enforcers, wouldn't help us."

"It wasn't the king or the enforcers who killed your man, or your parents and friends, Nova. It was Prometheus and Adaman Forrell's greed that did it."

"I hear your words, Marcos. But the pain is all the same to me. The king and his people are among those who lust after gems of rare quality. If they loved their families more and their luxuries less, we'd all be better off." She stood and walked to her pallet of blankets. "I think I'll get some sleep. Tomorrow, I'll go to the marketplace and find you some clothing."

Marcos watched her stretch out on the neatly arranged blankets and felt pettier than at any other time in his life. When she finally slept, he stared into the fire and began to think about his predicament and his next move.

To keep Nova safe, he'd have to stay dead. If Forrell or the slugs ever found out she was the one who helped him out of the pit and nursed him, they'd slaughter her. And he wondered how many of the women he'd slept with would have done as much.

The answer to that silent query left him feeling barren. As if she sensed his tension, Una got up from a small bed Nova kept for her and waddled to where he sat. She hopped into his lap as though she belonged there, and began making those strange whirring sounds. He picked up the peculiar animal, held her to his chest, and eventually made his way to his own bed.

• • •

Nova looked over her meager supplies and made a mental list of what she'd need. As she did once each month, she opened the jar of white pills her mother had insisted she have on hand and swallowed one of them.

"Those are birth control units, aren't they?"

Nova quickly turned at the sound of his voice and blushed. "Yes. How did you know?"

"I have a lot of sisters." Marcos wrapped a blanket around his body and moved closer to the fire. "When you get up each morning, I know. It's cold as deep space when you aren't lying near."

She laughed. "I'll add more blankets to the list of supplies."

Marcos stared at the bottle she carefully placed back on a small rock jutting out of the wall. "Isn't that a rather large supply of those?"

She stared at the bottle a moment before turning to him and answering. "When the slugs first arrived, my father found this cave and made it habitable. He knew my mother and I would be reasonably safe here. And the birth control monthlies were one of the first medicinals he bought at the market." She paused. "Maybe you've heard stories about what Limaxians sometimes do to women. Getting pregnant with one of their spawn will cause a humanoid woman to die. There were plenty of women who were raped at first. My mother even tried to save a few of them when they conceived. But the species are incompatible, and death was inevitable. My father wanted me protected as well as my mother. I still have this large supply of monthlies, from their efforts. And

I never miss taking one. Not ever. Even though I know my scars would scare even the drunkest slug away, I take them just in case."

"Nova, buy my clothing and come straight back here."

His commanding tone made her stare at him for a moment. "Don't order me around. I'll do as I see fit."

He walked determinedly toward her and put his hands on her shoulders. "I-I want to come with you. Please, Nova. I'll keep my head lowered and stoop over like I've seen others do. I'll pretend to be a relative. If no one knows or recognizes you, it could work."

"No."

"Once I have the clothing, there's nothing you can do to keep me from following you the next time."

She arched one brow. "Then you'll stay nude."

He took a deep breath and exhaled it slowly. "I'll sneak out some night and steal clothing for myself."

She put her hands on her hips. "You will not."

"I will."

"You'll be caught and tortured worse than anything you've already experienced," she countered.

"It's up to you. You've used up the supplies you had by helping me. It's only right that I be there to help you."

Nova chewed on her lower lip. "So, you only want to protect me out of gratitude?"

"I feel the two of us would be able to protect each other much better. Please try to understand."

She considered his demand. "Are you well enough to walk far? Can you even make it to the marketplace?"

He hesitated.

"You'd be hampering me if you can't run. It could cost us both."

He took a deep breath and stared down at her. "Can we compromise?"

"How?"

"Buy what you need to see us through a week or two. I'll work on my strength and stamina. The next time you go out, I go with you. All right?"

She thought it over. "You can regain enough of your strength in such a short time?"

"Watch me."

The stoic expression on his face told her what she wanted to know. He'd do it or die trying. "All right. But we'll have to work on how you act, the way you talk and walk. You stand out like a diamond in a barrel of coal." She continued gathering her things for the long walk to the market.

When she threw on her cloak and pulled the hood up, he put one hand on her shoulder.

"Please, be very careful," he told her.

The way he said it and looked at her made Nova want to melt. He really was concerned. She quickly covered his hand with hers. "I'll be back before nightfall. I promise."

"If you aren't, clothes or not … cold or not … I'm coming after you."

She believed he would. And that thought kept her movements efficient and swift.

• • •

"I'm sorry, Governor." The guard took his helmet off and placed it on Forrell's desk. "There have been no unusual sales of medical supplies, and we simply can't find any man with eyes the color you've described. And if a healer helped the merchant, that person isn't making an appearance."

Forrell leaned forward, placed his hands on his desk, and thought for a moment. "It's quite possible we're looking for a man who has been dead for weeks. Even if someone helped him out of the damned pits, he might have died in some hovel or other. The key is whether there's even one person on this miserable planet who could or would have helped him. Someone with enough knowledge to hide from both us and the Limaxians. That party is still a threat if they're a dissenter. We still have missing guards. Who know what happened to them?" he boldly lied.

"Is there anything else we can do, Governor? Anything we haven't tried?"

Forrell stood and slowly walked the length of his office while pondering the situation. "There was a woman … a Wiccan healer who I know for a fact is dead. I saw her corpse myself," he muttered more to himself more than the guard.

He quickly sat back down and pushed a button on his desk computer that caused his vid-screen to rise from a secret compartment. He punched a few buttons and did a search of the general population before the slugs came.

"Of course! How stupid of me. I knew there was something I should have remembered."

"Governor?"

"There are community records filed within what served as the old census bureau. If I can access those records, I might be able to find out if a healer exists; one who might have been able to help this merchant."

The guard nodded. "But you'd have to go through the entire population."

"Not necessarily. I'll start with those I know had medical knowledge, then expand my search to their neighbors, friends, and anyone with whom they consorted. Make yourself comfortable. This could take a while."

He motioned toward his private stock of spirits and fixed his attention on the task at hand.

The fearful query he lived with presently had to do with the missing merchant's survival. What if someone had helped him— still assuming that merchant turned out to be a Starlaw. If that helper likely knew they had a prince of Luster in their abode—and the prince's savior spilled his or her guts about *his* governance of the colony—then what?

That he couldn't have. Whether the Starlaw son lived or not, whoever had moved his remains or helped him had to be found, and before Prometheus did. There was still a chance he could save his hide and his official status if he could get to those missing/hiding parties first.

While the guard busied himself drinking, Forrell searched records for the next two hours until he found the part of the census that listed familial relations. He typed in Bellos Drayton's name, and pulled up the particulars of the miner's family history. As he read, a sense of discovery infused him.

"Well, well … my old nemesis seems to have been keeping secrets from me. But he knew I'd have killed his daughter, too, if I'd found her.

"Sir?" The guard finished off his drink and approached the governor's desk once more.

Adaman swung his vid-screen toward the guard. "This is the image of an old enemy. He's dead now, and I thought all those in his household died with him. But he was careful never to mention the fact that he had offspring. Of course, the fool didn't know I could access these records. And I never would have *wanted* to had this entire incident with the merchant not occurred."

"I'm afraid I don't understand, Governor."

Forrell stood, walked to his stock of ale, and poured himself a goblet. "Do you remember some co-op miners being rounded up and put to death while some were enslaved in the mines?"

"Of course. But that was well over two years ago. I don't think any of the enslaved ones are left alive. And even if there are, they're in the bottom of a mile-long shaft digging gems. Any human down there that long loses their eyesight. They can't even find their way back to the surface without help."

"Quite true." Forrell lifted his glass and sipped before speaking. "But back in those days, I was very new to this planet and had only been governor for a little over a year. Even though my term was short, I immediately met opposition. One of my chief rivals, a miner called Bellos Drayton, tried to stand against me in open elections."

"Indeed, sir. I recall the incident. It is Drayton's image on your screen."

"Yes, it is. His wife was a Wiccan healer, and the only one among the population with such skills. According to the census last taken in those days, Drayton's daughter was old enough to have learned some of the healing arts from her mother." Forrell rubbed one hand across his forehead. "I remember telling Prometheus about Bellos Drayton and that miner's incessant ridicule of my Limaxian associations. Because he needed me in power, the slug leader simply ordered his brawlers to kill Drayton and anyone who stood in the way."

"That tactic is still being employed by the slugs," the guard acknowledged.

"Yes. In Drayton's case, I thought that was the end of that particular problem. And now I'm faced with putting myself in his shoes."

The guard shook his head in bemusement. "And that means?"

"What I'm trying to say is that if I had a child living under the threat of death and wanted her to survive, I'd hide her. In the confusion back then, there were a lot of men being dragged into the night. And while Drayton and his wife certainly did end up in the pit and were incinerated, their daughter seems to have just vanished. There's no census entry about her that dates later than a few months before her parents' deaths."

"And you think the girl is still out there somewhere, and that she could have something to do with the merchant's body disappearing?"

Forrell shrugged. "I don't know. But let's find out, shall we? Perhaps that swaggering merchant—a man we know had enough gall to confront Prometheus—had friends on this world who're looking to overthrow me," he said, while pushing his lies yet again. "If that happens, funds I've generously filtered into the constabulary will cease. We could all end up facing accusations of theft, collusion and various other serious charges from the Constellation League and its interminable bevy of solicitors. Things won't go well with any of us if you get my meaning, and I think you do."

"Yes, sir." The guard said. "Just give me information that I can use to search out some miner's girl who could have hidden from us for over two years. Let me know where she might hide, and how she survived, and it'll be my pleasure to find her."

"Look for a Wyrdan girl in her mid to late twenties. Though they're now considered human, most Wyrdans descended from a compatible alien race. They've bred with us for centuries. But most still possess some strange physical peculiarities. This girl's mother certainly did."

"Sir?"

Forrell sighed heavily and tried to explain better. "While her father was human, it's quite possible that a few ancient Wyrdan differences were passed on to the daughter. Things like unusual purple eye color, elongated and pointed ears, diminutive size, and a certain graceful air. Her hair would likely bear the sparkling quality you might have seen the town whores attempting to emulate by applying glittering hair gloss." He walked toward the vid-screen, punched some buttons, and brought up a new image. He then swung the monitor back toward the guard so the man could view an image of Bellos Drayton *and* his Wiccan wife. "Records say Bellos brought his bride here from Wyrdan. Take a look at this old image, originating from the time when they first arrived here. All immigrants back then were required to register.

All you have to do is look for a girl who might have characteristics like her Wyrdan mother. Even if she's been badly burned, if she still has eyes to see with they may be oddly colored."

The guard walked forward, looked down at the screen, and smiled broadly. If she survives, we'll find her. And we'll do it before the Limaxians can figure us out."

"Good. I'll add a substantial bonus if you can bring her to me without anyone knowing. I need to question her about her healing abilities, and any knowledge she may have of the merchant's missing body. She's not to be harmed in any way. Not until I'm done with her."

"Count on me, Governor. If she lives and looks anything like *this* she'll stand out," he said as he pointed toward the image of a beautiful woman with breast-length hair of frosted blonde and all the other characteristics that'd just been described.

Chapter 7

To keep himself busy and his mind off his missing hostess, Marcos began a regimen of a few, less-taxing calisthenics. His skin ached with the effort, but he gritted his teeth and kept going. As the day wore on, he grew tired of being cooped up in the cave with nothing more useful to occupy his time. Finally, he set about cleaning.

By the time he finished, everything was spotless. He even arranged a few metal crates, used for stools and tables, to best advantage. Then, he washed all the clothing and blankets he could find, hung up the laundry on a makeshift line stretched from one side of the small cave to the other, and reviewed his efforts. No matter what he did, he couldn't help feeling frightened for the girl who'd saved his life. Common sense told him she'd survived for a long time without his help. But things were different now.

Feeling the biting cold, he managed to hang one of the heaviest of the drying blankets across the opening. The heat in the cave rose, so he considered his efforts a success.

After that, he pulled the blanket used to clothe him more tightly around his healing body and made his way just outside the cave's entrance to collect more firewood. He noted how the trees of Delta Seven amounted to little more than saplings, and most in this barren part of the planet were dead or dying. It was easy to find branches and sticks to haul back inside the cave without revealing he'd done so.

When the wood was neatly stacked against one wall, he found the blankets were finally dry and warm. He neatly folded them and awaited Nova's return. But as the day waned, he feared something had happened. Surely she never stayed gone so long? Even little Una seemed anxious and turned to him for comfort. He sat on one of the metal crates, holding the animal and making sure the fire stayed lit.

Oddly, watching the fire burn and stoking it wasn't frightening as some might think, given his recent encounter with that element. But while one fire was used for cooking and warmth, the other had been quite different. He had no trouble watching and sitting next to that which mankind had used for centuries to survive. The very mention of anything remotely having to do with plasma, however, made his gut ache horrifically.

As time went on, he paced. Surely something was wrong, or she'd be back by now. With the small amount of coins he'd given her, she couldn't have made purchases to account for the time she'd been absent.

"Where the blazes is she?" he asked the little ball of fur at his feet.

Una turned toward the entrance to the cave, bounced up and down excitedly, and produced what passed for a bark.

"What is it, girl?"

"It's just me," came a soft voice from the entrance. "Oh, you've put a blanket up. Very good thinking. I think it will probably snow tonight, and the temperature is going to get much lower."

Marcos breathed a sigh of relief when the small, heavily clothed figure appeared from the other side of the blanket. She was carrying several cloth bags full of goods, which he quickly took from her and set to one side.

"Where have you been?" he angrily blurted.

She blinked and stared at him. "What's wrong with you?"

"You've been gone for hours. I was … Una and I were worried. Anything could have happened. It's almost dark and you could have been caught out after curfew. It shouldn't have taken you so long."

"Were you worried about me?"

"Of course I was."

She smiled and shrugged. "I couldn't just buy from one person. Someone might think the coins I had were in excess of what's usually spent. I had to go from one street to the next, spending just a tiny bit in different places. But I got very good deals by doing so, and more than enough to keep us fed and warm for another two weeks. That should give you time to recover enough to go with me. If you're able."

"I'll be able; there's no worry on that account," he assertively promised. "But I still don't understand. You only had one small bag of coins. There aren't that many places you could shop."

"I'll talk when I get the rest of our supplies in the cave."

"There's more?" Marcos stared at the bags she'd already brought in and shook his head in wonder. When he opened them and saw all the goods within, he got angry all over again.

Nova pushed the blanket aside and dragged in two more bags to place beside those already delivered. "There, that's the lot."

Marcos stared at her.

Nova briefly paused in her efforts to unpack and arrange everything she'd purchased. "All right … *now* what are you angry about? You look as though someone just spit on you."

"I told you not to steal anything."

"I didn't."

He waved a hand to encompass all the goods. "Then where did all this come from?"

She tilted her head and returned his stare. "You gave me twenty-two credits."

He shifted his stance and waited for an explanation.

"I don't know what the prices are like on Avalon, but things can be bargained for here."

"Such a small amount bought all this?"

"Yes. You just have to know how—" She stopped in mid-sentence and stared at the cave. "Why did you do all this?" She motioned toward all the laundry and all the supplies he'd already organized.

"I got bored and just started rearranging things.

She laughed outright. "What a good maid you're going to make someone."

"Very amusing," he dryly replied. "But you shouldn't have been gone so long."

She stopped unpacking, walked forward, and stood before him. "It took me a long time to carry all this here and make sure no one was following. I had to backtrack several times and be certain I wasn't leaving a trail."

"Carrying all that?" he asked as he pointed to the mountainous supply of goods.

"I'm stronger than I look."

Marcos expelled a long breath and began to help her unpack. "Luckily, you won't be going alone next time."

"I wish you wouldn't."

"I won't argue, Nova. We made a deal, and you're going to stick to it."

"Tell you what. Since you've cleaned and done all the laundry, and are arranging things so nicely, I'll start our meal. And it'll be a good one, too. Wait and see."

Marcos stopped in his efforts long enough to watch her scoop up Una and cuddle her. He was unpacking the last bag when a wonderful aroma floated from the small fire. "Something smells good."

"Hot leek soup. It'll do wonders for you. And I'll add in some herbs that will help you heal even faster. We even have some lemongrass tea."

"And no one noticed you with all these goods? The guards and Limaxians weren't alerted by all you carried?"

She shook her head and sighed heavily in frustration. "I know what I'm doing, Marcos! I've done it for several years now, and I'm good at it. That should be obvious since I'm still here. Besides, I don't go into town in the daylight if I can help it. This was the first time in quite a while. I kept my hood up, my movements subtle, and bought very little from each vendor. Just as I've explained. If anyone noticed me, there was no sign. But then, most of Forrell's guards are usually drunk or too distracted by whores, just as they were today."

He raised one brow, nodded at her explanation, then held up the men's clothing she'd bought and checked the items for size. "Looks like everything will fit. But I'll put it on tomorrow. Right now, I want to sit by the fire and watch the highly stealthy woman of the household cook."

She snorted. "Someone used to cooking had better. Something tells me you don't do it often."

"I'll have you know I'm a very good chef. When I'm in the mood to use my imagination."

Nova stirred her ingredients in a sparkling clean pot and watched as he sat near her. "Do they have leeks on Avalon?"

"Every conceivable vegetable you can every think of. And all fresh, too."

She pulled out a dry loaf of bread, broke it apart, and handed him a chunk. Then she sat closer to him and waited for the soup to cook. "Tell me more."

She had that immeasurably curious look on her face again. Marcos couldn't bring himself to tell her that she'd spent the exact amount on two weeks of food and supplies that he'd have spent on one drink in any Lusterian tavern. Yet she believed the small amount he'd brought into their relationship was a windfall. He slowly chewed on the bread and thought a moment before speaking.

"We have a marketplace that stretches as far as the eye can see. It's in the middle of the city proper, and all kinds of goods are sold there."

"Go on," she encouraged. "What kinds of things?"

"Cloth of all different kinds, from every port in the nearby sectors. Some of it is handwoven, but some is produced by mixing certain chemicals with natural fibers."

"And can the people sell their goods anytime? Is there a curfew?"

He reached out and touched her cheek. "No, little thief. There's no curfew. You can walk around the city streets on any night and find a plethora of shops open. Then, you can take a flying disc to the countryside, sit on a hill, and watch the stars all night if you want."

"*Really?*"

The expression on her face was both appealing and poignant. She should know such freedom, and he was determined she should. "You know, when my brother comes and I take you to my home world, I'll help you find an occupation and a place to live."

She looped one hand around his bicep and cuddled close to him.

Now the look on her face was absolutely endearing. He was overcome with the urge to help this woman see something better than what life presently offered.

"You'd do that for me?" she quietly whispered.

"Of course I would. You've not only saved my life, but you're my friend. I'd do anything for you."

She blinked back tears, fed him a small portion of her own bread, and smiled up at him. "Don't stop talking. Tell me more."

"How would you like a small plot of land all your own? You could grow your own herbs and sell them in the marketplace."

"H-how would I come by this miracle?"

"I have some land, little thief. And you could live there without anyone bothering you. Do as you please, and go where you will."

"Oh, Marcos … if you'd do that, I'd find a way to pay you any amount of rent. All I'd need is a small plot."

"And what if I gave the land to you?"

She pulled away from him slightly and stared into the fire. "I-I want nothing I can't work for. I only steal because I've had to. I'll owe nothing to anyone. Besides, you couldn't afford such a thing, I'm sure of it."

He put his arm around her. "Nova, never mind about whether I can afford it. It would be a gift from one grateful friend to another."

"I don't care," she insisted. "I'd only take it if I could give you something in return. And I have nothing of value to trade."

He thought for a moment and gently nudged her. "What if I could have some fresh herbs for my family's table? Or you could occasionally treat one of my rapidly growing brood of nieces and nephews when they fall down and scrape themselves? Most of them hate going to the physicians and getting into an incubation chamber. They're frightened of the confined space in the units."

She turned to him in relief. "I can do that. And I could help others, too." She chewed some more bread and leaned her head against his broad shoulder. "I can't wait." Then she frowned and turned to face him. "Marcos, you should know how dangerous it is for a merchant ship to approach this planet. Prometheus has a fleet of war vessels hidden behind Delta Seven's moons. Whores in the town have sometimes spoken about tactics gleaned from guards and Limaxian brawlers when they've been drinking too much. So I'm fairly certain the information is correct. Your brother and his crew could come under attack if they don't approach carefully. I wish there were a way to warn him."

Marcos put one finger under her chin and smiled down at her. "Don't you worry one whit about that. My brother will come armed with a full complement of artillery. He never goes anywhere without defenses."

"He must carry very precious cargo," she softly uttered.

"The most important thing to him is his crew. And he'll protect them at all costs. And he *will* find me. When he does, Prometheus and Forrell are going to wish they'd never been born."

That remark sent Nova back to tending the soup.

"Is it ready? I'm starving." He scooted forward and held up a bowl in readiness.

Nova nodded. "It's ready. We'll have a wonderful feast. And there's even some tinned meat for Una."

The little fluff ball waddled toward them and bounced up and down, anxious for its meal.

Marcos stared at the creature for a moment. "Are you *sure* she's a dog?"

"What else could she be?"

"I don't know, but something tells me that's the wrong species."

Nova handed Marcos a bowl of the soup, then opened a small tin of meat and gave it to Una before posing another question. "Marcos?"

"Hmmm?" he asked as he ladled the hot soup into his mouth.

"Can ... can Una come with us, too? Please?"

The pleading look in her pretty eyes almost did him in. She wanted nothing more than a small plot of earth and her pet. How many women of his acquaintance would be happy with so little? "I promise; we won't leave her behind. No matter what."

She shot him a brilliant smile. "Thank you."

For a moment, he gazed into her amethyst eyes and wondered what she'd look like without all the scars.

Then the truth hit him.

For the first time in his life, he really didn't care. But that was because the woman was his little thief. She was worth a million self-centered debutantes his parents' friends pushed his way. A man could have a wonderful life with such a companion.

•••

Prometheus threw open the chamber doors, stalked toward Adaman, and slammed his fists down on the table where the governor was eating. "So you thought you could outwit me, human?"

Adaman quickly scooted his chair back, intending to remove himself from the ugly slug's immediate proximity as well as keep his ale from spilling on his robes. "Wh-what the blazes is this about, Prometheus? Can't a man enjoy an evening meal in peace?"

"Did you think you could hide information from me? That you could find any clue about the Lusterian's whereabouts that I wouldn't know?"

Adaman swallowed hard and stood so he wouldn't be at such a disadvantaged posture. "You'll have to explain, my friend. I'm at a loss as to what this is about," he lied. He knew full well his men's covert activities in looking for the burned merchant had now come to full light, and the slug leader was outraged with the underhandedness.

Prometheus growled and leaned over the table. "You've been accessing the old computer database. Did you think my crew wasn't monitoring retrieval of information? They told me you've recently been into the old census records, and your search seems to have stopped with the family of Bellos Drayton. He had a daughter. But you'd remember that, wouldn't you?"

"I-I can explain."

"There's no need. I know what you were trying to do, fool. You meant to get to the prince first."

"Really, Prometheus … y-you're acting paranoid. The only thing I was doing was saving you work. You've taken on a great share of responsibility and I thought that I'd—"

"Enough!" Prometheus yelled as he waved one gloved appendage in the air. "You were trying to get to the prince first so you could either hold him for ransom and bargain your way out of the situation, or make a deal with him directly."

"You accuse *me*?" Adaman placed on hand over his heart. "I swear to you, on my word as a gentleman, that I was going to come to you with whatever information I gleaned. But if nothing can be found … if this girl doesn't exist … then why would I have bothered you with information that would have sent your people in the wrong direction? Besides, my men are better trusted by the population. This, you must admit."

The slug leader slowly walked around the table and moved closer.

Adaman backed up until he was against the far wall.

"If I didn't need you alive to make contact with whatever communication comes from deep space, I'd kill you on the spot."

"But you *do* need me," Adaman quickly pointed out. "Without my presence to respond to supply-ship captains and any unexpected messages from enforcers, this planet would be under siege by the Constellation League in months or even weeks. Aside from their scheduled visits, we don't know how close they might be. They surely suspect something is going on, or the king would never have sent his second-born."

Prometheus drew a long dagger from his belt and held it against Forrell's neck. "If this Wiccan girl is alive, I'll find her and kill her. And if the second-born son of the king still lives by her aid or anyone else's, he will disappear without a trace. The king would never barter for his child's return. That would make every member of his family a target. He knows this. But that won't keep him from unleashing his wrath. That's why this prince has to die, and his presence here eradicated. Any other action from you, and I'll take what gems my fleet can carry, scorch this planet and all who live here, then set a course for open space." He came even closer. "I'll make sure you're the last to die. It will be the most horrifying death you can imagine."

Adaman gulped. "I-I wasn't going to cross you, I swear."

"Then give me all the information you have. From now on, I command not only my men, but also yours. Those who disagree will end up in the pit. Make this clear to your people, Governor. Tell your constables and guards that if they want to see their families survive, they'll do exactly as I say. Do you understand?"

"Y-Yes. Completely."

Prometheus slowly placed the dagger back in its sheath, turned and stalked out of the room.

As soon as his surveillance equipment indicated the slug leader was gone, Adaman quickly called his most trusted assistants. When they were assembled before him, he issued his instructions.

"Do everything the slug leader and his brawlers tell you. He's threatened to take all the gems and kill us if we don't. And for the love of the Creator, don't get into the old computer records anymore. That damnable, slimy worm is watching us at every turn. He's a lunatic! I fear he'll eventually kill us all anyway."

The lead guard stepped forward. "Sir, what can we do? What chance do we have?"

"Only a slim one. But the next time any Constellation League ship is close enough for contact, I must get a message to them quickly, and hope they can respond before we're all slaughtered. I was insane to make a deal with that beastly savage."

Adaman put one finger to his lips, paced a few steps, then turned to his man again. "If ... if you can find the man I'm after and keep him safely hidden, all may not be lost. By working together, there might be a way for me to redeem our actions before Luster's king. Just keep looking for him and that girl." When several of the men simultaneously shot off questions asking who he was talking about, Adaman realized he couldn't keep the secret from them any longer. "Take your orders from my lead man." He gestured toward his most trusted minion. "He knows the description of the woman you'll be looking for. We're talking about Marcos Starlaw if anyone hasn't figured it out yet." He waited for the general, excited hubbub of his employees to die down before continuing. "Only by finding the prince alive and safely hiding him will we have any chance. Now get out and search as though your lives depend upon it, because they do. Bribe members of the population, tradesmen, or any human you can. Let them know we'll be destroyed if we can't convince the slugs that the prince still lives and that other enforcers are coming for him. Go now. I have to think."

Forrell watched the men hastily walk from his chambers even as they beleaguered his best guard with questions concerning the prince's presence on Delta Seven. The guard couldn't answer because no one, including himself or Prometheus, knew the real reason. The answers would only come with finding Marcos Starlaw.

He prayed the next communication from the Constellation League would come far ahead of schedule. If not, the only thing the enforcers would find on their next visit would be a charred chunk of rock. And his skewered, half-eaten body would be hanging in the village marketplace as Prometheus's last act of defiance.

•••

Marcos carefully hung a blanket in one corner of the cave where there was a small outcrop of rock. On the outcrop, he'd built a little fire and dragged a large metal tub near. This would serve as a private bathing area for Nova, and the fire would be close at hand so she could heat water from a kettle. "There, milady. Now, you'll have your privacy without worries. And you'll have all the hot water you want."

She smiled at him, and glanced at the makeshift bathing area. "That's very ingenious. But I haven't worried about privacy so far. I've always bathed while you slept."

"Now, you won't have to. And you can have a full bath instead of using a small basin and a cloth. You can undress instead of bathing yourself underneath that large robe you sleep in."

She gasped, picked up a cloth, and threw it at him. "You've been watching."

He laughed and ducked his head. "I must confess ... I did awaken on several occasions while you were seeing to those needs. As to watching you, there wasn't much to see. You cleanse while still clothed."

"I always keep something on in the event I have to run."

"I'll keep watch while you bathe. It isn't likely anyone would ever find you in this cave, but I can see where you'd be concerned. A woman on this planet can't be too careful. That's why I'm going with you to the market."

Hearing the water boil, Nova picked up a bar of soap and a washcloth and crept behind the blanket.

"How is it? Do you need more water? If you do just call out and I'll slip another kettle under the blanket."

"Thank you. It's wonderful," she happily replied. "You might want to go to the entrance and gather some snow for your bath."

"I'll do that. And I'll put our pallets closer to the fire. We should be quite warm."

When she eventually emerged from their new bathing area with a large towel wrapped around her slender body, hugging a damp little pup in her arms, something in Marcos's chest tightened. Even with the scars on her shoulders and head, Nova looked soft and inviting. She was a slender, tiny thing who looked so very vulnerable while holding her pet. But appearances could be deceiving. He knew her capabilities. She was a stealthy thief by necessity, a brave woman by choice. But she deserved so much more than she'd ever had on this rock in deep space.

When she saw him staring, Nova laughed. "I've never bathed Una before. Just brushed her. But the tub is all clean if you're wondering."

He shook his head in amusement. The little pup had been sleeping next to them for weeks. If Una bathed in the same tub it wasn't going to make any difference to him.

He picked up a large blanket, and walked forward. When he draped it around Nova's shoulders, she let Una jump from her arms. The little dog ran toward the fire and the pallets there and snuggled in for the night.

"I guess she'll be sleeping very close," Marcos jokingly replied.

Nova stood still while he wrapped the large blanket around her.

"You're such a small thing," he rambled as he pulled the blanket up to her neck.

"Marcos?"

He looped his arms around her body and held her for a long moment before responding. "Yes?"

"I know you'll be so tired of hearing me ask. But will you tell me more about Avalon and your family? And about your life there?"

Lying to her was wrong on every level. He felt it down to the last cell in his body. But he didn't want her to hate him. And she would if he told her who he really was.

He decided to take the coward's way out and keep describing things as if he were a normal citizen of Luster. When she knew him better, and understood the politics of the situation, maybe she'd accept who and what he was. For now, he wanted this closeness between them to continue. It seemed very important that she respect him for who he was right now.

"Ask a thousand times, and I'll talk about my home." Just so long as she'd keep talking to him and treating him as an equal, not an enforcer and the son of the king.

"I'll pass you water under the blanket if you'd like to bathe," she offered.

"I don't see the need to have the blanket hanging between us. You've seen every inch of me, little thief."

She shrugged. "That's true. I just thought you might like some privacy now that you're healing so well."

He shook his head, and pushed the hanging blanket separating their new bathing room to one side. "You can ask me questions, and pass me the buckets of snow at the same time. Then, when I'm done, we'll snuggle under the blankets and I'll tell you stories of Avalon until you fall asleep. You'll have pleasant dreams of freedom."

"What a wonderful thought," Nova said as she quickly handed him a bucket of snow he'd gathered and watched as he undressed.

He didn't miss the way she turned her face away when she believed she'd been caught staring.

As he soaped himself and finally rinsed, parts of his body began to tingle. Then the tingle became an outright itch as he dried.

By the time he pulled a blanket around his body and sat next to her again, he almost had to remove the heavy covering altogether. Everywhere the fabric touched, his skin burned and felt tight. He lifted his hand and began to scratch at the scars on his chest.

"Don't do that!" she told him as she covered his hands. "You'll open new wounds that could become infected."

"Can't help it. I'm starting to itch so badly that I don't think I'll get any sleep."

"That's a good sign. It means you're healing."

Holding her blanket around her, Nova walked to the area where her herbs and medicinals were neatly arranged. She pulled a small bowl from a stack and began to mix some ingredients. "The cold, dry air is irritating the newly formed scar tissue. But I'll mix something that will absorb into your skin and protect it. Until your exterior toughens, you'll have to keep applying it."

By now, Marcos had to toss the blanket aside entirely. The cold air from the cave's entrance hit his back while the fire in front of him kept that half warm. But neither the heat nor the cold were helping his physical situation any.

"Did this intense scratching sensation happen to you?" he asked as he rubbed one shoulder and the inside of his thigh.

"Yes. Obviously, there wasn't so much of my body that was burned."

She approached him with a small glass bowl in one hand, grasping her blanket around her with the other. Marcos put both his hands to his bald, scarred head and began to aggressively scratch.

Once more, Nova sat beside him, pulled his hands away, and began to apply the cream to his head first. "Stop it!"

"I tell you I can't help it," he complained.

"The warm bath you took might not have helped. The hot water could have dried your skin even more than the cold air. Especially as your skin is still healing. But you needed it." She began to lightly smooth the cream over his head, face, and neck as she spoke.

"Was I that rank?"

"No. Not any more than I was, I suppose. Living like this has some disadvantages. Now be still."

Marcos let her apply the herbed cream. It quickly absorbed into his flesh. He didn't think she could possibly have enough in that tiny bowl to do any good. At least not the way he was itching. But soon after she began to apply the remedy, the burning stopped. He sighed in relief, then did as she requested and kept his hands off his healing flesh.

Nova pulled the blanket away from his chest and began to smooth the mixture over his skin there as well as his arms and shoulders. "Turn around. I'll get your back."

He shifted his weight until his back faced her. The soothing ointment not only took away the painful tightness, but her hands were having an effect he hadn't planned on at all. Something in his posture must have alerted her because she stopped and leaned forward to look at him.

"What's wrong? This shouldn't be hurting. Is it?"

"No. It isn't … no."

"If you'll lie down I'll take care of your legs."

"Uh, I can do that myself," he said and simultaneously reached for the bowl.

She pulled it out of reach and arched one brow. "I'm the healer here. Is there something wrong with your limbs you don't want me to know about? Have you opened a wound?"

"No. It's nothing like that. It's just that you should be getting some rest. You walked all the way to the marketplace and back carrying supplies. You've got to be tired. I can start looking after myself now." He reached for the bowl again and frowned when Nova moved back, pulling his blanket with her.

She stared at his nude form and put the bowl down between them. "I-I see you are getting better."

Marcos tried to pull the blanket back over his erection, but she was sitting on most of the fabric. "For a time, I wasn't sure if I'd ever achieve an erection again."

She didn't take her eyes off his swollen cock. He sighed heavily in response and pulled another blanket toward his lower half.

"Do you mind?" he muttered.

At any other time in his life he'd have welcomed the steady gaze of a woman in such a situation. But this was different. She wasn't just any woman. And his opinions about life—at least his attitude about the way he'd led it—were quite different now. As he attempted to wrap the covering around himself, however, she put out her hand and stopped him. Then, her beautiful amethyst gaze roamed slowly over his body, finally meeting his.

There was hunger in her expression that quite astounded him. She'd seen him nude many times while tending his wounds. Her healing skills had probably required seeing a good many injured men whose clothing had been removed for one reason or another. "Nova?"

She simply blinked. "Th-the man I was to wed wasn't half so endowed." She briefly paused. "I'm sorry. I don't know what made me say that."

He stared at her for a moment. "You miss him? Being with him?" For some reason, that thought didn't sit well. He didn't want her looking at him and being reminded of some dead lover.

"I miss everyone I lost."

"What was his name again?" Marcos softly asked.

"Aeson."

Marcos put out one hand and placed his palm against her cheek. "He must have been a very good man for you to have cared so much."

She remained silent.

Marcos placed his index finger under her chin and forced her to look back again. "You miss having sexual relations. That would be quite understandable. You've been lonely a long time, Nova. I … I shouldn't mind you staring at me. In fact, it's only natural given the circumstances. After all, I'm much better now, and we aren't exactly in the position of healer and patient any longer. Are we?"

"I understand all that. You just reminded me of something I'd rather not have remembered."

He moved closer. "You can tell me anything. Whatever it is I'll help if I can."

For a long moment, Nova chewed at her lower lip and twisted the edge of her blanket in her hands. "I-I don't think I can speak about it," she quietly told him.

Something in her eyes worried him. He placed both his hands on her shoulders to get her to talk. "Did this man ever do something that made you uncomfortable? Something that maybe you weren't ready for?"

She stared into his eyes. "No. He never did or would. It's just very personal. And you're right … from now on … y-you can put the cream on yourself. I should be getting some rest."

Marcos watched her turn away, pull the blankets around her small body more closely, and reach for Una.

For a long time, he watched her lying there, knowing she wasn't asleep. And while he finished smoothing the cream over his legs, time and the cold didn't diminish his erection one bit. Sad for him, it began to itch too. Though only tiny spots of his genitalia had been exposed to the plasma, what *was* burned needed the comfort of the cream even more.

There was nothing to do but spread the stuff over his cock and balls. To do it, he needed to stretch out on his back.

While he'd always known the healing properties of an incubation unit would eventually put him to rights again—as a man—it was still good to know that he was responsive *now*. The emotional drain wasn't nearly as bad as it could have been while wondering when he'd see rescue, a healing unit, or medical technician again.

He vowed that whatever happened under the blankets, after Nova fell asleep, would be his problem. He wouldn't ask her about her man again unless she broached the subject first. There was something in her gaze that made him believe talking about him was painful for a number of reasons not having to do with his death.

Long after he believed she was asleep, Marcos stroked and smoothed the cream over his testicles and inner thighs.

He closed his eyes and relished the feel of his ministrations; the warmth, and relief at being able to enjoy this simple pleasure was wonderful. He couldn't help a small moan that escaped his lips. The cessation of the burning and the effects of the cream were heavenly.

Too late, he realized that she wasn't asleep at all. The woman was only lying there quite still, keeping her breathing even and steady so as to mimic slumber. But the slow rotation of her hips beneath the blankets gave her away.

He watched as she slowly turned to face him, but he didn't stop what he was doing. It just felt too damned good.

"I ... I can't stand it," she whispered. "I ... I want to see you touch yourself."

He slowly smiled and nodded. "It's all right, Nova. If it pleases you, watch. If it pleases you *more* ... touch me."

She swallowed hard and crept on her hands and knees toward him. It was a small distance to cover but it seemed like such a long time until she was close to his body. Just a few inches more ... closer and closer still ...

Chapter 8

Marcos's heartbeat quickened. Nova's beautiful amethyst gaze swept over him and steadied on that part of his anatomy jutting straight up. Molten passion lit her features. He'd never seen a woman's eyes so hot with raw desire. All his previous encounters had been with women who easily chose their men on any random occasion. Nova, however, had been without any kind of male encounter for quite some time. At least that was the only conclusion he could glean from what she'd told him and from her current response.

He watched her move closer with excited expectation. In his heart he knew her caress would be different. Not only because of her enforced, lonely situation, but because instinct told him she wasn't that experienced, or that someone, probably the man known as Aeson, hadn't serviced her and seen to her needs in a way that captured her passion. He silently swore to do everything to satisfy her, and not just because she'd saved his life.

She had a strength to survive that intrigued him beyond any sexual interlude. She could make a home from a small cave and dare to dream. Her mind and heart held qualities that mesmerized him. He wanted to reach deep inside her and blend those qualities with his.

What he felt toward her was more than sexual need. It was a deep, intrinsic bonding he wanted. And he believed he could share it with no one else.

She'd seen him at his worst and still wanted him. He'd seen her at her best and now craved her. But more. He desired her respect and for her to see him as the new man he'd become. Gone was the self-centered egotist. That man had been burned away, and a new one had risen in his place.

He waited for the first touch of her small hands, and knew it'd be something special. He slightly thrust his hips up in expectation, but couldn't help a small moan escaping as her knees grazed his thigh.

No heaven would be any better. So sure her first touch would be fantastic, he held his breath in anticipation.

• • •

Nova knelt beside him. Her breathing came in small gasps. A desire so deep overtook common sense. Even scarred and burned nearly to death, this man had summoned the will to live, and he was still every bit the warrior she'd seen face down that slug in the marketplace. The muscle, brawn, and carriage of a fighter were all there. The fire hadn't burned that out of him. So many others she knew had never been touched by the plasma, but their will had turned to ash anyway. Not so with this man.

She'd long craved such a man but had given up hope of finding him among the sheep of Delta Seven. She now included herself among that lot. But the fear that'd kept her from speaking up, while watching him do so on everyone else's behalf, vanished. He'd given her hope for the first time in a very long while. Next to her was the nearest thing to a god she'd ever seen. If others had been as inspired by his act as she, then what he'd done might spark a new revolution.

Instinct told her he wasn't telling the truth—or all of it—but desire wouldn't be quelled. Whatever or whoever he claimed to be, the man had his reasons. She no longer cared what they were, if he'd just stay by her side and chase loneliness away.

Death was just outside the cave entrance and all around them. If it should come tomorrow, she vowed to know this man tonight, in any way he wished. He represented strength, pride, gentle kindness, and caring. He was a man to trust. And what beguiled her most was the fact that his striking green eyes flared with the same desire she felt. He didn't see her as so many had: just another scarred woman slinking about the fringes of society. He saw the real her despite the scars. And when he offered his hand, she eagerly took it.

She gently ran her palm up the inside of his leg. He briefly closed his eyes and nodded for her to continue. His words, like all his actions so far, were encouraging and tender.

"That's it. Touch me however you will. I'll do anything you ask, Nova. We've nothing to hide from one another. We can be one."

She gazed into his beautiful eyes and saw his soul. Emboldened, she took the advice her mother had given so long ago when the facts of life had been explained.

She took his erection in one hand, and caressed the length of it. His hips rotated and lifted as her fingers explored his body. The soft moan escaping from deep in his throat emboldened her.

"I was taught the loving ways of my mother's people. I've never had the chance to use that knowledge ... never wanted to. Not even with the man I would have wed. And not even when he tried to entice me into loving him. But I want to now, Marcos. I want that more than anything."

"Ask of me whatever you want, and it's as good as done."

She continued to slowly stroke him. "I ... I want to mount you."

"Take your time," he whispered.

Nova took a deep breath, released his erection, and quickly lifted her caftan over her head.

"Your body is so small," he murmured as his gaze wandered over her. "I swear to you I've never seen anything so beautiful in my entire life, Nova."

She smiled and blinked away tears. Then she slowly straddled his upper thighs, but just below his erection. He lifted his hands and palmed the outside of her calves. Her gaze never left his as she moved one of his hands toward the juncture of her thighs. Her head fell back when his fingertips touched the moist folds of skin there. Excitement claimed her, even as he gasped and his breathing quickened. She had to have him.

She felt his body shift as he sat halfway up. His palms were warm and soothing as his fingers spanned her waist. With her head back, the softest part of her throat was exposed to him. He leaned forward and greedily claimed that partially scarred area with his lips.

She moaned, and his hands moved to her back. He began a soft, slow stroking motion. With each kiss on her neck and each caress of his hands, her body grew more ready. She wanted to give him what she hadn't given Aeson—something from her Wyrdan heritage that, when used, was said to drive a man nearly insane. But this special gift could only be bestowed on one man. When her body recognized the soul that matched hers, only then could that power release. Never could it be given to another; it was his for the rest of her life. She'd been taught to make very sure this power was released wisely. Poor Aeson had never captured her heart as this man now did.

"Creator's blood!" he murmured against her throat. "You're the smallest, sweetest thing I've ever seen. I don't think I can stand much more. I have to have you, Nova."

His breathy declaration thrilled her. But she had to make sure her body was ready for his gift. She looped her arms around his shoulders and pulled him into a full sitting position. "Kiss me."

Marcos pressed his lips against hers. She accepted the hottest, most sultry kiss of her life. He moaned deeply as his hands grazed her body. Her mouth opened, and she met each thrust of his tongue with one of her own.

"No one else will ever have you. I swear it! No one. You're mine," he softly growled as he broke the kiss to murmur the words against her mouth.

The assertive vow was all she needed to hear. Her body prepared itself for the Wiccan mating. "Lie back quickly. Let me take you," she commanded.

He did as she ordered, but his hands never left her body. She felt sweet, burning passion born of promise and something more. Something a lifetime of looking could never accomplish. She loved this man. And she'd love no other.

As he lay back, he stared into her eyes and spoke with barely contained ardor. "I mean it, Nova. I'll never let you go. Never."

She raised her body until the juncture between her thighs was directly over his erection. Then she carefully grasped it in one hand. "Don't worry on that account, Marcos. I'll make sure you won't want to let me go. I'll make very sure."

• • •

Marcos placed his hands around her waist. Ever so slowly, she lowered herself onto his manhood. Tight heat surrounded, sheathed, and energized him. She moved his hands to her breasts. The silent but bold request wasn't hard to interpret. She wanted him to massage her breasts deeply. As he did so, he used the pads of his thumbs to tease her erect nipples. A strange tightening sensation began around his cock.

He fixed his gaze on hers.

"Wh-what is that gripping … w-what's happening?" he asked.

She didn't seem capable of speech. Her eyes began to glow, and deep vibrating, coupled with harder gripping, rocked his cock from inside out.

His deep moan of satisfaction and fulfillment echoed off the cave walls. The sound was dragged from the very bottom of his lungs. He could no more stop it than he could stop breathing. And in that moment, he was sorry to have ever begged for death.

How could he have wanted to die when such ecstasy existed in the universe?

He could no longer speak. Only feel. There was nothing and no one else in existence but her. The gripping, vibrating, and pulsing was almost too much. At one point, he knew his eyes rolled back, but the perfect union and all the sensations that went with it had to go on.

Finally, he was able to grasp her breasts, but feared the need to hang onto and caress them would cause pain. Instead, he gripped her hips and felt his own being drawn up to meet hers. The strength of her body was incredible. And the vibration that began as a soft tingling kept growing in intensity.

Deep clenching around his cock caused him to gasp for air. He could neither thrust nor withdraw. She owned him entirely. He dragged in air through clenched teeth, prepared to ride out this storm of sensuous pleasure to the end.

She cried out loudly, threw her head back, and grasped her own breasts once before running her hands over her body. Even with the overwhelming tightening and simultaneous stroking, he eventually found the strength to caress her body as she seemed to require. He focused on her breasts and gently pulled them toward his chest. She put her palms over his, letting him know his caresses were exactly what she craved.

Suddenly, Nova was literally impaled on him as his chest and hips arched upward. Her cries of unbelievable satisfaction joined his as he finally released, and felt her body suck his seed up and into her.

After the waves of rolling, gripping sensations left, she fell forward. Satisfaction couldn't begin to describe what he'd just experienced. He wrapped his arms around her tiny body as she drew in great gasps of air.

"That was only for me. Only me," he muttered as he held her possessively within his embrace.

"Y-yes." She panted before confirming, "Just y-you."

He closed his eyes and held her in a fiercely possessive embrace. For a long time he neither spoke nor moved. All he knew was Nova and the feel of her soft body against his. It was all he wanted. Nothing else in life mattered. Not the fame of heritage, the money he'd earned, nor the medals won. She was everything.

Eventually, she pushed her body up and gazed down at him. He saw the tears in her eyes and knew she'd never been with another like she'd been with him. He wasn't surprised when his own vision dimmed.

He put his hands on either side of her bald, scarred head and brought his forehead against hers. "Nothing in my life will make me give you up. From this moment on, you're my next breath. You are the blood that runs through my body and every dream I ever had. I don't know what just happened, Nova, but the Creator brought us together for one reason. I'm more certain of that than anything else in my entire life." He paused to make sure her gaze locked with his. The next words would never be uttered again. Not for anyone else. "I love you, little thief. No one anywhere in any universe is ever going to part us. We'll leave this place as one. I'll give you the life you deserve, and no one will get in our way. Not some petty, greedy dictator calling himself governor. Not some hostile race bent on killing everyone who opposes them. I swear it on my life and my honor, Nova. I swear it!"

She broke into a soft sobs, and he pulled her head his shoulder.

"I love you, Marcos. I… I was falling in love with you the first time I saw you in the marketplace. You're either the bravest man I've ever known, or you're seriously looking to get killed. Either way, my life is yours. I don't want it otherwise," she said as she pressed kisses against his chest.

He lifted her chin with his fingers and nuzzled his nose against hers. "The words are said. We're one. You will have my name and all that I own, Nova. We *are* one. You saved my life. But more than that, you saved my soul. You've shown me what real love is, and from this day forward, I'll never be parted from you. Never."

She wrapped her arms around him again and snuggled back into his embrace.

He knew then that he had to tell her the truth. But not just this moment. Not when they were so close.

That she'd be angry about his heritage was certain. But he'd make love to her and whisper apologies until she accepted him. With gentle words of love—done while begging forgiveness—all could be made whole.

Nova wasn't a hard person to understand. She just wanted to be free. She wanted to be loved and accepted for who and what she was. She wanted her pet and a small portion of land, no more.

He'd give her that and all the love she craved, equal to the powerful, magical gift her body had bestowed.

For this moment in time, all he desired was peace in her arms. Then he'd tell her everything. After that, all they had to do was stay safe until Darius arrived. They could then leave this cursed, colorless planet far behind and embrace the golden future ahead.

• • •

Prometheus and Adaman looked up when two human guards and one Limaxian warrior raced into the governor's chambers, breathless and agitated.

"What is it?" Prometheus snarled. "I thought I told you we weren't to be disturbed while dining."

"Our long-range scanners, sir. We've picked up an enforcer ship at the outer edges of this system. And it's the Lusterian flag ship … *Titan*."

Adaman stood quickly, knocking over the contents of his goblet as he did so. "W-Wasn't that once the name of the heir's battleship? Wasn't Darius Starlaw the former commander?"

One of the human guards nodded in agreement. "Some time ago, Commander Starlaw took up a commission as the chief enforcer over Luster's capitol city. But he's temporarily back in control of the *Titan* for some odd reason and has hailed us. He wants to speak with you immediately. I think he means to land and send a cadre of enforcers into the colony."

"H-He c-can't," Adaman stammered. "I've issued an edict against their landing."

"Sir—"

"He'll be looking for his brother," Adaman manically uttered. "That's why he's commanding a Lusterian battleship again. But when he can't find his sibling, he'll place anyone suspected of harming him under arrest. He'll t-take us before the k-king. And wh-what if his brother really *is* dead and the enforcers find his remains? We'll be put to death!" He raised shaking hands to his face.

"Shut up!" Prometheus commanded, then turned to the human guards. "Tell the commander of the *Titan* he'll have to wait to land; that we cannot guarantee his safety since we've experienced civil unrest among the colonists. Warn him that he and his men might get caught in the fray. Ask him for a three-week waiting period. He'll have to abide by this request. He's already risking an interplanetary incident just by showing up after Forrell forbade any enforcer landings. He won't wish to be labeled an invader."

"Th-then why let him land at all?" Adaman began.

"We need to acquiesce in some small way ... to deflect suspicion," Prometheus explained as he turned to his own warrior. "Has the *Titan* been able to detect our warships?"

"No, sir," his Limaxian brawler responded. "Our ships are still hiding behind the nearest two moons, and that position will keep us well out of scanner range. As always."

Prometheus stroked his jaw with one appendage. "Give the following orders: Tell our warriors here to hide themselves.

Command our crews to take all the precautions we normally would when an enforcer vessel is within orbit. Now go."

The Limaxian bowed his head and lumbered from the room.

Prometheus turned to the human guards. "Tell the captain of the *Titan* that the governor will respond with further instructions shortly. Keep your wits about you, or you and everyone on this planet will die before this day is over."

The guards glanced at their governor.

"He's not in command, I am," Prometheus bellowed. "And if you value your lives, and the lives of your families, you'll do exactly as I say."

The guards nodded and quickly left the room.

Adaman slowly sank back into his chair. "All your men and mine now know the second-born prince was the one you tortured in the marketplace. They've been searching for him for weeks, and haven't found a single scrap of evidence that he's alive or in the company of some Wiccan healer. We'll have to do as I originally intended and deny he was ever here; say that we know nothing of him at all. It's the only way I can keep from being taken into custody. As ruler here, I'll be held responsible."

Prometheus snorted in disgust. "Because of your human guards's tactlessness, I'll wager even some of the population now know we're looking for the man I burned and had thrown in the pit. My warriors tell me they've been asking too many questions."

Adaman picked up a napkin and wiped the sweat from his forehead. "I-I'll do as I planned once we found out who you so ignorantly confronted and attacked. I'll order my guards and constables to warn the citizens. They must keep their mouths shut. Even if he lands against our will ... and if our luck holds and no body is found ... the king will have to relent. After all, he isn't supposed to send his people ... especially not his son ... to spy on peaceful planets. Our agreement with the Constellation League makes such actions illegal."

Prometheus snarled at Adaman and waved an arm in complete dismissal. "You fool. Nothing you do will work once they can't find Marcos Starlaw. The king won't ever admit his offspring was actually spying. He'll say he was sent to trade for gems, just as the son claimed. Or that he came on his own accord, without any permission from his sire. There's no law against him using any name he chooses so long as he isn't a criminal. And even if the king and the heir are so stupid as to initially believe that the younger brother never landed here for some reason, Darius Starlaw will certainly return to the last place where his younger brother was *supposed* to be. And he'll want answers as to where his sibling went. The only thing we can do now is lure as many of the *Titan's* crew into the marketplace as we possibly can. I'll have my men hiding there. As soon as I give the command, the *Titan's* ground crew will be attacked at the same time the *Titan* itself comes under fire in space. All the enforcers will be taken out at once."

"Creator's blood!"

Prometheus nodded. "Yes ... the loss of his first *and* second son will devastate Dar Starlaw. It will put him at a complete mental disadvantage. He'll have a lot of explaining to do as to why either of his progeny was so far from his post. Especially since the enforcers weren't allowed to visit this sector for months."

Adaman gasped. "That's insanity! How will you explain the deaths of all those enforcers and the destruction of their vessel? The king and all the allied planets in our pact will hold me responsible. They'll s-send an entire fleet here to investigate. And *you* ... you'll be hiding in space, gathering your warriors. You'll be waiting to kill them and then *me*. You'll start a war and Delta Seven will be in the middle of it. I'll have nowhere to hide." He waved his hands in denial. "I-I won't do this, Prometheus. There has to be some other way."

"It's too late for alternatives, you human swill. I'll give you one last chance to save your worthless life and those of the other humans on this dung-heap of a planet."

"If there's a way to hide my relevance in this matter, name your price," Adaman whispered. "I'll do anything."

"After killing all the enforcers, I'll take the gems that have been mined and leave … for the time being. Let no one communicate from this world; let no one leave it. You spread the word that if one hint of a problem finds its way to Luster, I'll know. I'll destroy this planet and all its inhabitants." He paused and nodded. "If, however, we take out the *Titan* and its crew successfully, we'll establish orbit again, and things will be as they were. Your people get to survive. Deny that any enforcer ever set foot on this world or contacted you. Do this my way, or your world burns! It will be your word, and that of your people, against the League. What can they do?"

"The *Titan* will surely have time to send a distress signal, even if the ship and all its crew are destroyed. And the next enforcer ships to arrive will be ready for battle. They'll have perceived our actions as an act of war against the Constellation League. Have you never thought of that?"

"We'll attack before they can send any message."

"But if they do—"

"Assuming that happens, months will have passed until allied forces can rally. By that time, I'll have contacted my home world. I'll have gathered a fleet that's strong enough to withstand anything the Constellation League can put together." He snorted as he moved closer. "What did you think all those gems were paying for?"

"Great Creator … y-you eventually mean to attack Luster itself. That's what this was all about! You've just found an excuse to do it sooner."

Prometheus slowly nodded. "When it's over, only those who've shown me they're worth keeping will survive. Only those with a purpose."

Adaman put his head in his hands and wept.

"You see … though the king is desperately trying to hide the fact, I have it on very good authority that the League's fleet was decimated during the battles with the Warlords. While the League is very close to replenishing losses, it won't be back to full fighting force by the time I have my armada purchased, outfitted, and under command. Even now, Limaxian generals have been sent Delta Seven gems. The wealth from their sales is quickly building our military might to invincible status. No one will be able to stop us. Luster will be mine … and its throne as well. It's a race between the Constellation League and me. We'll see who builds their ships the fastest. But I intend to win."

"Humanity is doomed," Adaman whispered, "and it's my doing. A-All I wanted was money from the sale of the gems. I just wanted the respect I've worked for all these years. Not this!"

Prometheus shoved the man cruelly. "Don't be so pessimistic, Forrell. Give me what I want, and our deal will remain as it always has. I'll still need wealth to run my fleet and pay my warriors. I'll still need miners to find the gems and bring them to the surface. I refuse to inflict manual labor on one of my warriors when such tasks are better accomplished by the human subspecies."

"What must I do?" Adaman sadly asked.

"As I command. Be assured that Luster's present ruler, along with his allies and their families, will be destroyed. Limaxians will take their rightful place, and I will be the new king in this part of the galaxy. Serve me and survive."

"Your genius knows no bounds," Adaman groveled as he bowed his head. "You know that, to mitigate their presence against my wishes, the Lusterian ship will have come with no backup from allies. They'll surely be alone."

"Indeed! This has all worked out much better than I could have ever hoped. The deaths of Darius *and* Marcos Starlaw will put me on Luster's throne sooner than expected. Without their beloved heirs to bolster it, Luster will crumble." He shrugged. "At first, Starlaw's coming here greatly upset my plans, but fortune has a way of favoring the bold. All one must do is think and plan. There's always a way out of any dilemma."

Adaman stared at him for a moment. "And … if there's even a remote chance that Marcos Starlaw survived?"

"Instinct tells me he did. There was no reason for my men or yours to have lied when they couldn't find his remains. Still, he can't hide forever. It's likely he'll surface when he hears, from some source or another, that I've killed his brother."

"And then?"

"When he makes his presence known, I won't put him to the plasma again. Not here. I'll make an example of him, in front of the people of Luster. As the last survivor of his family—a family I'll destroy soon enough—his death will mark the fall of a very old empire. I'll make it a spectacle to be remembered."

"You will use the arrival of the *Titan* to lure him out," Adaman said as he nodded in understanding.

"Just remember … your people must do as I command or all will die horribly. Nothing they can say will save the *Titan* or her crew. Nothing will save Luster's ruling family. My home world readies for the attack even as I speak. So if your citizens mean to prove their fealty and assure their survival, now is the time for them to take sides. Do so wisely and *live*. Understand?"

"Yes, I-I understand. I will make sure my people do as well," Adaman meekly agreed and rose to do as Prometheus commanded.

• • •

"Greetings, Commander Starlaw. Or shall I address you as Your Highness?" Adaman smoothly asked.

"Governor … so good to see you in excellent health. The use of my rank is sufficient," Darius responded, as he stood in front of the *Titan*'s vid-screen.

"Very good, *Commander*. I hope your household finds fortune smiling upon them."

"They are exceedingly well, Governor."

"To what purpose may I serve?"

Darius took a deep breath and cautiously watched the man's eyes. "I was in this sector aiding a medical vessel in distress. Turns out a few days' repair set everything to rights. But since I happened to be near, I thought I might pay my respects. I was also wondering if members of my crew might enjoy a three-day respite on your planet. They've been in deep space for some time and would like to patronize your merchants."

"Despite my request for a few months of seclusion, our poor planet is yours," Adaman gushed. "I only put our world off limits so that we might quell a small outbreak of criminal behavior. None of us wanted League enforcers to become innocent targets."

"Understood, sir. And has that matter been safely addressed?"

"We are very near a peaceful existence once again, sir. If I may request you wait just a short time longer, I'll instruct our constables and alert the populace that you'll be among us. In this way, they may *all* participate in a safe shore leave, watching out for any malcontents. My business colleagues value League patronage and want no outbreaks against your crew. Such a thing wouldn't benefit our small colony."

"How long?" Darius asked.

"Would three weeks be sufficient, Commander? With tempers flaring, I wouldn't want weapons of the magnitude your crew carries on our surface. Some of our more hostile criminals might get the idea to relieve you of them. Other moderates, and there are more of them among us than those of the criminal element, want nothing but peace. A little more time will help us better prepare and assure your safety and that of your crew."

"Things are that violent in your so-called near-peaceful existence, Governor?"

"Not at all. As I've stated we are making progress in that regard. Our constables are more than equal to the task, Commander. But it would be better if our citizens and business owners know you'll be among us. We want our malcontents to understand that no violence will be tolerated. Unfortunately, our world is a very poor one. Certain factions have become desperate. Such is the norm when humanity is faced with poverty. We need to assure everyone of your peaceful intent, and that you'll be here only to enjoy shore leave. That you, in no way, will be replacing our own constables and were not requested here to renounce any faction. It's just a matter of calling separate meetings of all work unions concerned and getting them to cooperate for the time being. I'm sure you can understand."

"Governor, if our presence will cause too much of a problem, we can seek shore leave elsewhere."

"No, no," Adaman quickly denied. "The opportunity to have paying guests among us rarely comes. Indeed this is the exact point I shall put to all my disputing citizens. They'll miss the chance to earn a few extra credits if they won't behave themselves. As soon as that point is driven home, I'm sure you'll have no trouble. Had I known you were arriving, I'd have spoken to my people much sooner."

"My apologies," Darius offered. "We were simply in the neighborhood, so to speak."

"And you shall have your shore leave. To the limits of our humble abilities, we shall be honored to receive you and your crew … if you can but wait just a while longer. Our sensors tell us you're still some distance. Perhaps, by the time you're in orbit, all this petty bickering will have wound itself down at any rate. I'm only embarrassed that I must ask you to wait at all, sir. We are not normally as unreceptive as all this must seem."

"Very well, Governor. I shall contact you again when the *Titan* approaches orbit."

"My humble best to you and your entire crew, Commander. And may your leave be a memorable experience. We have little, but we will offer all we can."

Darius bowed slightly. "Until we make contact again, sir. My best wishes for a quick resolution to your … problem."

"Good journey, sir." Adaman quickly shut off the communicator with a trembling hand.

• • •

"As soon as my brother's short-range transponder is detected, contact me," Darius ordered his second-in-command. "It'll be faint, too irregular and inconsistent to mean anything to anyone else who might detect it."

"Yes, sir," the officer responded. "I'll let you know the instant we ascertain his location. You realize that if he's injured … or worse … the tracking device should still operate."

Darius shook his head in denial. "Not the device he has implanted. It will only operate if his heart is beating. That's how I'll know Marcos is still alive."

"I've never heard of such a tracking system, Commander."

"It's very new technology developed by our physicians and computer techs. It was not handed over to other allied planets."

His second-in-command grinned. "Against treaties, sir?"

"We aren't the only member of the League withholding such technology. Let's just say this is one of those tracking methods that's non-aggressive in nature and didn't, therefore, need to be revealed to the other planets in the alliance." Darius walked toward the vid-screen and stared into the blackness of space. "Creator help Forrell if any harm has come to my brother. That oily serpent was lying to me the entire time we communicated. He's up to something. I can feel it in my bones."

"But what can you do without provoking an incident, sir? As shifty as he is, Adaman Forrell is still unapproachable by any legal means. With or without proof of a criminal act, Marcos was still spying on his planet. On most worlds that could easily cost him his life."

Darius glanced at his trusted officer. "I'll have to ask for my crew's complete trust. I'll take responsibility for this entire mission. But my brother had *better* be all right. If he isn't … diplomacy aside … I'll make someone pay."

"We're behind you, sir. I had a cousin serving on the Corillian with Marcos Starlaw. And my kinsman told me many times how your brother saved his life and the crew's. You should know there isn't a man in the fleet who wouldn't gladly die for him or you. Whatever your orders … count on us."

Darius smiled and put his hand on the big man's shoulder. "Let's hope we don't have to start a war to find out what's going on with that blasted little rock. Marcos isn't expecting me for months yet. I'm relying on my wife to placate my parents. Especially since we took off without their knowledge, and only a few weeks after Marcos departed. But I believe surprise can sometimes yield answers where diplomacy won't. Still, I'll deny your or the crew's knowledge about my sudden desire to leave Luster. You only followed my orders, and that's the story I'll stick with. If my father wants to metaphorically hunt heads after this affair, mine will be at the top of the list."

His officer laughed heartily. "I've been with you too many years and know you wouldn't have done this without a very good reason."

"Well … don't stand too close. Upon our return to Luster, I'll have a very large political target on my back. I'm only sorry I needed the *Titan* to do this and couldn't come on my own. Just pray that coming after Marcos so abruptly was a good idea. Something tells me I should have made the decision to follow him *sooner*. I have a feeling he's in big trouble. And not the kind he engaged when he was a boy, stealing fruit from the neighbor's orchard. This is something else … something only one brother would feel for another when a situation is very wrong."

Chapter 9

Marcos kissed his way up the top of Nova's left thigh, then to her midriff. He lingered there before gently teasing her left nipple with his lips. She softly moaned and wrapped her arms around his shoulders. All they'd done for three days was eat, sleep, and make love. And he'd never been happier in his life.

When he moved further up her body, kissed her lips softly, and stretched out next to her, Una romped forward, her antennae sparkling with excitement.

"She wants you to pet her," Nova said as she smiled.

Marcos laughed at the puppy's antics, picked her up, and placed her in the middle of his chest. "I'll personally build you a little box so you can sleep right by the huge fireplace I'll design for your mistress. Would you like that, girl?" Una snuggled under his chin and began the rumbling, whirring sound that was either cat-like or predator-like. He was never sure which. But he knew she did it when exhibiting playful behavior. "Maybe we'll find out what you really are and locate a companion?"

"Oh, Marcos, that would be fun. Then she wouldn't be alone. Nothing and no one should ever be alone."

Holding Una close to his chest, Marcos turned on his side to look at Nova. The flickering firelight lit her lovely eyes so they took on an even more gemstone-brilliant color. "You're going to like Lus—I mean, Avalon so much." He had to be careful. Instinct said she wasn't ready to hear the truth about him. They'd have plenty of time. All winter. He'd let her know when Darius arrived. By then, she'd be so deeply in love with him that who he was wouldn't matter at all. He was that sure of the outcome.

"Tell me some more about Avalon."

He laughed. She never tired of hearing about his home. But in a world where light filtered through the atmosphere in such a way that there were only dull colors to view, it was only natural that she'd want to know about beautiful sunsets and starry nights. And the truth was, he loved talking to her about all the things he planned for them. "All right. Let's start with my family."

"You said you had a very large one. I'll love being part of a big family. It sounds so wonderful," she excitedly told him.

"My brother is a bit of a stuffed shirt. But he and I have always backed each other up in every venture. I know if anything ever happened to me, he'd make sure you were safe."

"Don't talk like that." She frowned and put the fingertips of one hand over his lips. "Only talk about good things, Marcos. I know about the bad. But from now on, everything will be better."

"You're right, love. I'm sorry, but I wanted you to know my family will always be yours. No matter what."

"Tell me more about your brother, then." She snuggled close and scratched Una's tiny tummy as the pup rolled on her back to play.

"Darius is a strong man. Very determined, and very good with his little girl. Her name is Cory." He grinned. "His wife keeps him in line. If you ask me, she's the real strength in that relationship. It took a while for her to adjust to three-hundred years of advancement, as she's from Earth."

Nova stopped petting Una and tilted her head. "Marcos, I thought Earth was off limits to anyone, by unilateral agreement of galactic planets. Isn't it one of those technologically delayed places that mustn't be introduced to weaponry until they can manage to make formal contact by themselves?"

He may have made a mistake mentioning Laurel—Darius's wife. But he wasn't used to lying; it didn't come easily. "You're right, of course. Earth's communications are being monitored, and they aren't ready for us to make contact with them as yet.

But Laurel is a special case. She was severely injured when my brother made an unexpected landing on her world. His visit was a dire emergency, and since his vessel's arrival on Earth was directly connected to Laurel's injury, he couldn't very well leave her to die. It's difficult to explain. The circumstances would make more sense coming from him. "

"But … he just took her?" Una boldly asked and stared at Marcos in confusion.

"She'd have died otherwise. Earth's physicians couldn't have saved her life. And though it took a while for her to acclimate, she's happy, Nova. Truly she is. And she understands the circumstances behind my brother's landing on her world in the first place. I'll let them explain their meeting when you get to Avalon. You'll understand everything then."

"You and your brother don't make a habit of going to Earth, do you? The penalty for traveling to banned planets is death."

"Nova, love, I've never been there. And Darius *had* to land. It was a sort of emergency. There was no other alternative, believe me."

She nodded. "I won't ever tell anyone, Marcos. I promise."

He smiled and stroked her cheek. He couldn't tell her that Darius's visit to Earth had been sanctioned by the Constellation League only because his brother had been tracking a killer who landed there. Laurel had been caught up in intrigue not of her making, and had almost died because of it.

"So then … what's this *Earth woman* like? My mother told me a story that explains why many of us have the same genetic makeup."

"You're speaking of the Expansion Theory, and it's probably true. We have archaeologists and anthropologists on Avalon that have found very ancient writing. When the writings were interpreted, they reinforced the notion that there was a group of very advanced beings called Elders. And these enlightened ones went from planet to planet taking inhabitants, plants, and animals from one world and depositing them on others where they could thrive. Sometimes they were supposed to have left different technologies with those who were moved. It was supposed to have been an experiment to see what would happen with varied species, and different cultures, if they were placed in other environments and allowed to advance faster or slower."

She nodded. "My mother taught me something similar. That's why we're more alike than we realize. Even our religions are very close. All because these Elders, as you call them, kept visiting different planets at different times in history." She suddenly frowned and shook her head. "I ... I don't believe it was right for an advanced race to take people against their will. Maybe that's why no one knows what happened to the Elders. It could be they were punished by the Creator Goddess for interfering in so many lives."

He shrugged. "Maybe. I don't know of any writings alluding to the Elders's demise. But you're right about one thing. If they ever took beings from any world against their will, they were interfering. People, even those less advanced, have a right to live as they please and without intrusion. And they shouldn't have various kinds of technology forced on them until they're willing or capable of being responsible for it." He paused for a moment stroking her head as he did so. "You know ... it's said these star-traveling forebears would visit the same places over and over again, adding advancements, and taking away those among the population who showed greater intelligence. If all that's true, they believed themselves gods."

"Well, whoever was put on Wyrdan long ago left my people with genetic traits that gave me my eye color and pointed ears. At least, my ears were pointed until the tips were burned off."

She'd made a joke of it, but he didn't find anything about her injuries amusing. Instead of bringing up the topic of slug presence in their lives, however, he simply kissed the tip of her nose. "You're still very compatible … with *me*."

"Very, very compatible," she murmured as she moved closer to briefly kiss him.

Una grumbled loudly at being squashed between two bodies. She got up off Marcos's chest, shook her herself, and found a new bed on a soft blanket by the fire.

"Maybe the Elders did something to alter the animals too," he said and smiled at Una's attempt to circle her bed and make it softer. "There are species on many planets that are similar. Una, however, seems quite unique. Just like you," he said as he touched the tip of her nose with one index finger.

"I can't wait to leave here and get to Avalon. I know I must have said that so many times that you're sick of hearing it. But it sounds so wonderful."

"It is, Nova." He pulled her close. "We'll build a cottage in the woods, just as I promised. And we'll have a garden where we can go outside at night and sit under the stars. You'll have flowers of every color growing there; shades that you can only imagine. And we'll have quiet evenings together." He grinned. "There'll also be those evenings where my entire family shows up and plants themselves in every room, space, and corner imaginable. You'll get quite tired of them."

"No. Never. Especially if I can be included with all the birthdays, holidays, and special events. I want that so much, Marcos. To be a part of a family and have all that love to share. I … I've missed it so."

The earnest tone of her voice made him want to hold her even tighter. Nova never asked for any material possession besides a home. That could be nothing more than a tiny cottage by a babbling brook. She craved the things that mattered most. Family, peace, safety, and a future. He so desperately wanted to give her all those things and more.

"I'll bet you've never been on a picnic, have you?" he blurted.

She pulled away from him stared for a long moment. "What's that?"

"It's where you pack up some food in a basket, walk until you find just the right place, then put down a blanket, and spend the afternoon eating and talking. Then, just before the stars come out, you lie back and plan the future."

"Have … have you done this with others? Planned a future?"

"No. And I've only been on picnics with members of my family. No one else. Not ever."

She sent him a brilliant smile. "Then, I'll be the first lover to go on this picnic with you."

"You'll be the *only* lover I'll ever do that or anything else with from here on. And I'll take you to the ocean and let you see the way the moon glows on the water at night. Or we'll walk in mountain meadows where wild herbs are said to grow."

Tears formed in her eyes. "I'll go anywhere with you. Just as long as we're together. And as long as you'll love me."

"How could I do otherwise?" He pulled her closer and draped one leg over her body. "You're the only woman I've ever met who cares for who I am *inside*, Nova. Not for what I can do for them. And certainly not for my looks."

"Why do you say that? Are those the kind of women you've known?"

"That was the kind of woman I attracted because I was shallow and banal. I … I was a rogue looking for a good time. Nothing else mattered to me."

She shook her head vehemently. "I don't believe that! You're a good man. You wouldn't have risked your life for total strangers if you weren't. I can't for a moment think of you as shallow."

"Well … look where my good intentions got me," he reminded her and motioned toward the burns on his body. "I don't know that I did that man and his granddaughter any good at all. For all

I know, Prometheus went back, found them, and did whatever he would have had I not interfered. Maybe I was a bombastic, pretentious fool who should have remembered that invoking a Limaxian's anger could have had consequences for others. Prometheus might very well have turned that plasma on everyone else. Just as he did when you were burned." He gently stroked her cheek and kissed her forehead. "But we can remedy all this. As soon as we're out of here, my brother has an incubation unit aboard his ship. He can lock us up in it, and we'll sleep together until we reach Avalon. By then, we'll probably be completely healed. Then, I'll get to see what you really look like."

She suppressed a smile. "I'm told I'm quite plain for a Wyrdan. You might not want me if you see the way I really am."

"What if Fate decrees we stay just like this?"

"I saw you from a distance. That day when you were … " Her voice trailed away before she spoke again. "I couldn't see you well, but you were magnificent. Just as you say, I don't care if either of us is healed of our scars. As long as we're together."

"Then we'll let Fate make that choice."

"What's inside you is what I value. That's what I love, Marcos. Not the beautiful black hair I saw or the anger in your gaze."

He'd never tell her the real reason he had confronted the slug leader. To do so might give his identity away before she was ready to know it.

Years ago, during the allied conflicts with the deadly faction calling themselves Warlords, he'd landed on planet after planet, witnessing what scavenging slugs had done. They'd killed countless men, women, and children because they were too injured, too old or too young to be taken as slaves by the slugs. And of those children he'd helped rescue, their innocence had been stolen.

When he'd seen that girl beg for her grandfather's life, it'd all come back with a vengeance, and he'd gone off mission in less than a heartbeat. But no one knew these things about him. Not even Darius knew, and Marcos could never speak of them. Words wouldn't come. But anger over those old events had surfaced in the marketplace. His much-vaunted control had left him for a brief moment, when he had seen the chance to avenge all those children. And it'd cost him.

When he saw her gazing at him with great intensity, as though she could almost hear his thoughts, he shook his head and dredged up another smile.

"If I couldn't be healed, you'd never see all the steeled muscle beneath these scars," he joked.

"I told you … I don't care. And something tells me you don't really care either. Something tells me you are far deeper than you let anyone know."

He gazed at her for a very long moment. "You have the ability to look at people and see more than they wish. That's why I can't ever let you go. I think you know me far better than anyone ever has."

She caressed his face, then his head. "Just love me. And together we'll heal whatever wounds we have."

He kissed her very tenderly and heard her softly moan in response. Then he broached the subject he'd most feared speaking of. "Nova … what if the enforcers aren't the adversaries you seem to think them?"

"Enforcers are only as good as their leader. The king of Luster doesn't care about some little spitball of a planet that doesn't do him any good. That's the reality of the situation, Marcos. We're alone here and always have been."

"But you *do* want justice done, don't you? Forrell should pay for his greed and the murders he committed."

She pulled away. "Yes, I want Forrell and the slugs to pay for what they've done." She sat up and shook her head in confusion. "M-my mother once told me that Wiccans don't believe in revenge. She said such negative feelings only come back to the wisher, threefold. And though I know it's wrong to hate, I can't help it." She pulled the blankets closer to her body. "The more I learned about the way politics work, the more I understood that someone else just like Forrell would take his place. All the brave men and women who ever lived here are dead. And the enforcers still leave him in charge. They blindly believe everything Forrell tells them. It suits them to do so. And that's why I've gone against my mother's own teachings. I can't help it," she repeated.

"Nova, just as your feelings are complicated, nothing having to do with politics is that simple. You're right about the intricacies of the situation. They go much deeper than you can imagine. Enforcers just can't land on someone else's world and take over. That's not what they're about. They battle when attacked and respond when asked. There are other issues I can't—"

"Please don't," she said as she raised one hand in refusal. "This is one topic on which we'll have to agree to disagree. The enforcers and Luster's king wouldn't be so complacent if all this were happening to their families, on their world. Delta Seven is nothing to them. The sooner we can get out of here, the better off we'll both be. I just pray your brother doesn't get held here by the slugs when he comes. If he asks too many questions, that could very well happen. And he might end up getting the same treatment you got." She put her fingertips over his lips when he would have spoken again. "Your focus would be better placed on *him* than with what enforcers will or won't do. All we have to do is two things. Get to your brother before the slugs do, and get off this planet safely. It can be done, but we'll have to know, almost to the hour, when your brother arrives. It may be the only way to save his life and ours."

He took a deep breath. This was the time he should reveal everything. But there would be months of living in this cave with her feeling she'd been betrayed. He'd become the object of scorn; someone who had lied to her all along. He pulled her close, tucked her head under his chin, and stared at the top of the cave. After he could get her to safety, everything would be different. He knew it would. Nova would understand why he hadn't revealed himself. He could make her understand, and they could live all the dreams they'd planned. It would just take time.

• • •

"We've been through this. I'm going to the marketplace with you and that's final."

Nova knew he'd recovered a great deal of his strength, and had already delayed the trip for a week hoping he'd relent and stay safely within the cave. Now, there was no choice. Their supplies were low.

"What if someone asks questions about you, Marcos? What should I say?"

"I'll do as we discussed. I'll stoop over and pretend to be so badly debilitated by the burns that I'll appear as many of those poor wretches milling about. You can say I'm a brother, cousin, father, or whatever. Or even just a neighbor. Surely anyone who's done business with you won't care as long as they get their money. You've said they don't even know who *you* are because of your scars and because you did your shopping mostly at night … as a thief. You haven't been to the marketplace all that much."

"That's all the more reason that *two* newer customers will stand out. Even if our faces are as scarred as everyone else's. Don't you see? While there are many people in the square, there aren't so many they'll ignore someone newly burned. Your scars are still raw. Why do you insist on doing this?"

"I won't let you go alone."

"How many times to I have to say this? I've been taking care of myself for a very long time, Marcos Orlandis—"

"Not with those slugs everywhere. I don't like the idea of them getting anywhere near you."

She put her hands on her hips and glared at him.

"We've argued this to death. Even Una hasn't enough food for another two days. You can't carry everything we need, and I'm not staying behind. Get it into your head."

"You're being foolish," she insisted.

"And you're not honoring the bargain you made. I'm as strong as I ever was. I can easily make the trip. I'm going and the subject is closed!"

"What if I went out tonight and stole what we need, just like I used to? Then neither of us would have to—"

"No! Do you know what would happen if you were caught after curfew? Had I not been standing by a window the last time, you'd have been some oversized worm's tasty little supper. Or *worse*."

She grabbed up her long cloak and impatiently pulled it around her shoulders. "I don't like this. I have a bad feeling about it."

"If we act like we belong, we'll be all right. Just keep that in mind."

"Thank you for the lesson in how to survive. I'll take notes," she sarcastically responded.

She watched as Marcos dressed in the woolen shirt, long pants, and boots she'd bought for him the last time she went to the marketplace. His anger was born out of a sense of possessiveness. She could have found it more charming and heartwarming if it hadn't also been belittling skills she'd taken so long to hone.

The final garment he donned was his brown hooded cloak, the same one in which the money was still kept. The cloaks were the quintessential outer garb of all the citizens. Perhaps he might look like them if he could manage to crouch low enough. Marcos was so tall as to make that seem impossible. Indeed, when he stood next to her, she felt like a recalcitrant child. His height and size were so much more pronounced because of her fears. She tried to breathe deeply and focus.

"There's a break in the snow, so it'll be colder tonight. Let's get this over with," he told her.

She nodded. "Stay close to me."

She stalked out of the cave knowing he was recovered enough to keep up with her quicker pace. It would be some distance before they got to the city limits. Until then, it wouldn't be necessary for him to bend over and act as though he was incapacitated.

Once they got near the city and he stooped to appear as so many of the citizens, they both kept their silence. To augment the perception of his being older, he'd added a long staff made of an old, dead branch.

Eventually, she felt the need to instruct him yet again, though he'd not take kindly to any suggestion of not yet looking like a colonist.

Nova put her hand around one of his biceps as he stooped lower to hear.

"I've decided you're a neighbor that I'm helping. But it might be better if I did the talking."

"I'll relent on that," he quietly returned. "But if there's trouble, get out of my way. You run; I'll do the fighting."

"We both run, and neither of us fights, damn you!"

He might have made some retort she wouldn't have liked, but they had approached the first place she wanted to stop. To her utter relief, he simply leaned heavily on his staff and lowered his gaze in what appeared to be a beaten, submissive posture.

"What may I do for you this day, little one? Pots, pans, or cutlery?" the elderly stall owner asked.

As the minutes flew by, she counted their sojourn so far as exceedingly fortunate. They seemed to garner no undue attention. But Marcos still kept his staff ready to use as a weapon. His grip on the branch told her as much.

They moved from one stall to another and bypassed children huddling near barrels where fires had been started to keep customers warm. Nova's empty bags began to fill, but she never really saw Marcos relax. Knowing him as she did, she noted how his muscles tensed, and how he appeared more rigid than he would have back in the cave. Of course, that was a normal response to their situation, but he had to loosen up or someone would surely notice.

She patted him on the shoulder and shot him a silent glare, hoping he'd get the message.

When they came to a stand where dried fruit was being sold, Nova surveyed the choices. The seller there eyed her companion critically, but said nothing. To cover for Marcos's presence, she made an offhand comment to him about how she'd look in on him tomorrow, after getting him back to his cottage. That tactically placed remark quelled any curiosity the stall owner had. The salesman went about helping her choose from his poor selection.

While she was paying for her purchase, a small girl approached the stall. The child was pitifully thin, and her brown curls were dirty and tangled. Her clothing was torn and hung too loose.

The child reached out her hand for one of the stray pieces of fruit that lay too close to the edge of the seller's cart.

"Be off with you, girl," the stall owner chastised. "I haven't enough for my own family, much less someone else's."

The child turned away, but Marcos put his hand in his cloak pocket and drew out a coin. He handed it to the waif, and she took it and stared up at him as if such a thing had never happened to her before. Slowly, as if she'd imagined the entire thing, the little girl turned to walk away. But she hesitated once to glance back at the stooped man in the cloak.

Nova's heart filled with love for him. It occurred to her then that any child of his would never ever go hungry or know fear. Not as long as he lived.

The stall owner shook his head in disgust. "You'll just teach her to beg, old man. If the slugs catch that little girl asking others for coins, they'll kill her. Better to keep what you have to yourself. You must have been confined for some time, or you'd know what I say is true."

"He has been," Nova eagerly responded on Marcos's behalf. "He's been very ill since he was burned."

She caught a glimpse of both the compassion in Marcos's expression and his anger, and quickly led him away, toward another stall. "That was a very kind thing you did," she whispered.

"Not if it gets that child killed," he solemnly muttered. "If that merchant was right, I might have given her reason to beg from others."

"She'll likely buy bread with the coin since it's the cheapest product sold. My guess is it'll be the first loaf she's had in days." She blinked back tears as she spoke.

"Don't cry," he softly instructed. "Someone will wonder what's wrong." He took one of her hands in his and squeezed it tightly.

"I love you," she whispered.

He lowered his head to hide his smile.

About an hour later, they were almost ready to leave but stopped at one last stall for canned goods. These were the heaviest to carry, so Nova chose to purchase them last.

As she turned to look at the other end of the goods displayed on the long cart before them, an elderly man slowly approached. She vaguely recognized the gentleman, but couldn't remember why.

"Sir … madam … may I speak with both of you?" the stranger softly asked.

"I'm with a friend and am, as you see, indisposed," Marcos replied.

"Highness, please … I'm the man whose life you saved. You were badly burned in my stead, and saved the life of my granddaughter as well. I am, therefore, deeply indebted and obligated to warn you."

Nova froze. Only long-practiced skills kept her from gasping aloud and staring wide-eyed at her lover.

"What did you call me?" Marcos asked.

"Sir … I know who you are. There aren't many here who would recognize the green eyes of the Starlaw purebloods. But I knew who you were by your bearing in the marketplace that day. You have your father's strength of character." The older man slowly nodded in acknowledgement. "I know you, sir. I have been to Luster and know who you are."

Nova felt her heart actually beat harder as she stared at the dirt in shock. A stranger had just acknowledged Marcos as a member of one of the most regal families to have ever existed—a family headed by a man to whom she'd shown virulent disrespect.

Surely she'd misheard. Or the stranger who'd approached them was addled. She waited, barely able to breathe. What possible explanation could there be but that some wild mistake had been made.

She waited to hear her lover's response. But rising gut instinct told her the elderly stranger had hit on a truth she hadn't wanted to see.

How utterly, ridiculously foolish I am. Of course he acted like a warrior. He is one!

If her life had depended on it, she wouldn't have been able to move. She just stood there, frozen, and waited to hear what he'd say even as her heart told her the truth. That he'd lied was clear. That she'd believed him was her own fault. But what now? What could she say or do with the enemy patrolling around them, only yards away?

She swallowed hard and let years of experience—where being a non-entity in a dangerous environment meant surviving—take over. No one must see how her reality had just been shattered.

It took everything she had to keep a calm posture and show no physical response.

...

Marcos quickly glanced at Nova. She was no more than ten feet away, and was clearly trying not to stare at him. "You've made a mistake, friend."

The elderly man shook his head. "No. I have not." Then he nodded at a stand across the street. "You must come to my stall. Come quickly before my absence at my place of business is noticed."

Marcos watched the older man walk away and tried to slow his racing pulse. Fear for his life wasn't at issue. He'd been in dangerous situations many times. But not with the woman he loved by his side. Not with slug brawlers prowling the streets like vermin.

There was no choice. He gripped the staff and saw Nova nod almost imperceptibly. She'd heard. She *knew*.

This was not how he'd wanted her to find out, but he had only himself to blame. He should have been honest with her from the start. Now, he couldn't read her emotions. She cast her gaze to the ground or toward the passing slug killers that walked by only several feet away.

He took her hand in his, and helped her hoist their parcels while edging closer to the stall the older man indicated. To anyone watching, they must appear as innocent shoppers, nothing more.

"We stay together. No matter what!" she whispered as they neared the stranger's stall.

The earnest way she muttered the words made him want to hold her. Whatever she felt at that moment, she was keeping it to herself. If she hated him for his deception, she was doing a good job of hiding it.

Marcos turned toward the elderly man. He kept his bent stance; his hand clutched Nova's much smaller palm as he waited.

Whatever the stranger might say, he'd been recognized. Who else might know his real identity, and why—when they were so close to turning back for their small cave—did this have to happen now?

"Let me speak quickly and bluntly," the vendor said as he eyed Marcos and Nova. "Time is running out. You must listen carefully."

Chapter 10

Marcos stood in front of his revealer's stall. It was filled with inexpensive, handcrafted jewelry that meant nothing to him at the moment. All he was concerned about was getting back to the cave safely, and explaining his duplicity to Nova.

"What do you want of me?" Marcos softly asked as he gripped Nova's hand tighter and glared at the older man who'd outed him.

"I assumed this girl with you knows of your identity."

Marcos glanced at Nova; she kept her face down and almost hidden by the folds of her hood. "Go on and be quick about it," he instructed.

"Sir, constables have been visiting the various businesses, asking if anyone has tried to buy large amounts of certain herbs or medicinals," the merchant said as he pretended to show Marcos a handful of jewelry. "Slugs are looking for someone who might be a healer. There was once one among us. She was a Wiccan woman. The lady you're with has the look of that culture. It's her eyes, sir. Despite her scars, no other planet but Wyrdan produces such remarkably colored eyes. There are many here who might not know such things, and might think her a spawn of many races, but I'm older. I have traveled throughout this sector. And if she's who I think she is, I knew her mother. Many of us thought the girl dead."

Marcos's blood ran cold. Nova was everything. His fear on her behalf tripled over any angst he'd experienced so far. He'd rather face fire plasma a thousand times over than see her caught for helping him. The powers that be were looking for her due to him. He had gotten her into this mess; it was up to him to see her safely out of it, no matter what. This would likely be the last time he could chance coming into the marketplace. With this news, they'd be lucky to make it back to the cave unnoticed. So great was his fear that he could feel himself physically shaking; something he'd never experienced in his life. No matter how bad circumstances got, he'd always reckoned there was a way out. But what way out was there for her? Apparently, even her scars couldn't hide who she was or the skills accredited to her.

"I'm afraid your eye color gives also gives you away, sir," the merchant said. "I'm certain Prometheus and Forrell have figured out who you are and are looking for you. My guess is they know you escaped death, likely with the help of this girl by your side," he explained. "I have kept my silence and will continue to do so. No Limaxian or guard Forrell sends will make me reveal what I know. But you must not come back to this place again. Stay hidden."

As in the past—when Marcos had been on such undercover operations—he'd decided to explain the unusual hue of his eyes by claiming Vegan ancestral ties. That race had eyes that were almost the exact same shade of green. No one had ever questioned his heritage. Not until now. Again, Nova's ancestry was particularly prevalent in the shade of her beautiful gaze. There was almost no way to explain it away except that she *was* of Wyrdan ancestry.

Had he kept his mouth shut that day he'd been burned, the ruse he'd always used would have worked. But then this good man—a stranger risking his life to warn the enforcer son of a distant king—would be dead. Along with a helpless girl.

"You should leave here," the merchant warned. "There are many who will turn you in, in order to save themselves."

Marcos nodded. "I thank you, my friend. You risk your life for us, and I won't forget it."

"As you risked yours for me and my granddaughter, good sir. I consider the debt as one I owed." The man then reached beneath his stall and beckoned Marcos closer. "Take this. We are not allowed to have such weapons on Delta Seven. I constructed it some years ago and would never part with it unless I saw a chance of escaping. Now … I see you as that chance. If you can get away, do so. Tell the king how we fare and bring help."

Marcos took a heavy sword the old man brought from beneath a display table. He quickly hid it beneath his cloak, and badly wanted to tell his benefactor that help would most certainly come. But that knowledge had to remain with him and Nova for the time being.

Still, his heart soared over the hope gleaming from the elderly man's eyes. It was the first time since coming to this damned planet that he'd witnessed such an expression, except when alone with Nova.

The vendor would conclude that enforcers were coming to look for the second-born prince of Luster. Even without anyone saying so.

"I thank you," Marcos whispered. "If I'm caught, you and I never spoke. I never saw you or heard your warning, and I never obtained any weapon from you."

"If you should need other help, sir, I will gladly be of service," the merchant said. "My name is—"

"No. Don't tell me. That way, I can never be forced to give you up," Marcos insisted.

The elderly man bowed. "You are of old blood and would never do so, sir. My best wishes for your speedy trip home."

"Thank you."

Marcos gripped Nova's hand harder, then turned and slowly lumbered away.

To her credit, she kept her head down and her mouth completely closed.

He knew a confrontation was coming. But she was far too intelligent to broach the subject here, in the middle of a marketplace crawling with slugs and Forrell's butchers.

They had to move quickly.

If what the old man said was true—and there was no reason to believe he'd risk his life by speaking of such subjects if it wasn't—they could be watched from any building on any street.

He was horribly afraid for Nova, especially if she were caught in the open with him.

There was one possible solution, one ploy he might use to negotiate for her life if anything happened. It was a slim chance at best, but he'd take it if nothing else could be offered.

He kept the merchant's sword well hidden but within easy reach.

Nova kept her expression flat and her gaze directly ahead. She took very long and indirect path back to the cave, but did so with stealth that would have surprised any master spy. But then, she'd only survived by cunning and skill learned at an age when most girls are enjoying social life, parties, and the attention of fawning lovers. In every way, she was superior to every woman he'd known. And no matter how angry she was over his deceit, he meant to keep her. Forever.

• • •

"Are you sure?" Adaman asked without turning his head toward the guard by his side.

"I'm certain, Governor. I saw a girl with eyes the color you've described, and a man that seemed very badly burned. I think it highly unlikely that either of them could be who you're looking for. Neither looked to be a threat."

"That's *exactly* how they'd appear. Which direction did they take?"

"I lost track of them outside of town. I had to follow from some distance to keep from alerting either them or any slugs."

"Good job. I shall make sure you receive triple your normal pay this month. But tell no one what you've seen. If these are the two we're looking for, it's likely they'll be living in the barrens. Perhaps in the hills somewhere."

"If I go alone, I might be able to find a trail, Governor. But the snow is picking up. I could only start as soon as I know I'm not watched."

Adaman nodded. "Do so. But report to no one but me. As with today, don't come to my residence or any official place of business. Remember, we communicate only on the street and only where it will look as though we're exchanging pleasantries."

"That might mean my report could be held up until such time as I can find you in the marketplace," the guard advised.

"So be it. Better to get late news than to risk Prometheus finding out what we know. It may be our only chance to save ourselves. Remember that."

"Yes, Governor, I will," the guard assertively agreed.

Adaman took a deep breath, pretended to examine the rest of the stalls, and noted the looks of hatred on the faces of the humans around him. "The slug leader will kill me and all my staff, including you, when the time suits him. No matter what he's said about making us useful within his new empire, he most certainly will rid himself of us as soon as he can find someone to take our places."

"I don't like those stinking, damned slugs. Never have," the guard muttered. "But it was better to deal with them than to die."

"It might be that we can keep our positions and rid ourselves of the vermin if we're careful. Just find that girl and the man she's with. If they're who we're looking for, I might be able to salvage the mess Prometheus put us in."

"I'll find them, Governor. If I have to walk every hill, valley, and trail in the barrens to do it."

Adaman glanced both ways before continuing. "We've been together long enough now. Tell those slug warriors at the end of the street to accompany me on my shopping trip. Tell them I only trust *them* to guard my life since none of the citizens would dare accost a noble Limaxian warrior to get to me."

The guard smiled. "Yes, sir."

Adaman watched his trusted guard walk away and pasted on a welcoming expression when the two slug warriors approached.

• • •

"That man was the one you rescued. Even as far away as I was, I remember seeing him only moments before you confronted Prometheus. That's how he knew who you were ... *Your Highness.*"

Marcos put his bundles down when Nova did, rolled his eyes, and shook his head. "Will you let me explain?"

She rounded on him with ferocity. "You must think I'm the most inane creature you've ever come across. How could I not know who you were?"

"Nova—"

"But in my defense," she interrupted, "I never really paid much attention to the names of the king's offspring, let alone their physical appearance. There was no reason when the man let us wallow in misery while he enjoyed life, so safe and well fed on Luster!"

"Will you let me expl—"

"Of course, I *should* have recalled the legendary green eyes of Luster's royalty. It's a wonder you didn't have the color changed to match the rest of your ill-conceived disguise." She snorted in disdain. "I must have heard of all of you at one time or another. I must have heard the name *Marcos Starlaw* ... but then, I was too busy tending my wounds, mourning my dead, and trying to stay alive." She paced and slowly shook her head. "What was I thinking? I knew you were no merchant. I *knew* it. No simple gem buyer is built like a warrior, nor do they wield ancient weapons

… like swords … with such ease. And you did it as if born to it, which is even more reason I should have figured you out.”

Marcos simply stared at her, wondering what words she'd hear that would put things right again.

“Goddess's blood! I stupidly believed what I wanted to, what was most convenient.” She stopped in front of him and put her hands on her hips. “How far did you think you'd get with your ruse, while playing the hero so dramatically and with such little regard for your cover? And why did *I* fall for your lies? I know better. I'm not some silly child.”

“Will you *please* let me—”

“How could you let me go on as I did, believing you were someone else? Did you really not care for me at all? Was I only an escape venue, and did you really think I'd go to Forrell or those damned slugs to turn you in if I found out?”

“Listen to me!” he insisted as he put his hands on her shoulder to stop her agitated gyrations and gestures. “There was a slight chance you might not be held responsible for saving me if you didn't know who I was.” When she lifted her chin to argue once more, he put the finger of one hand over her lips to silence her. “I don't know what I thought at first. I was in so much pain that your kind words, soft voice, and tender mercies were all I clung to. Afterward … afterward I should have told you everything. You're right about that. But I adhered to the idea that if I were caught, I'd never tell anyone you'd helped me. I knew my brother would come. He'd see you rescued and off this planet in the event I couldn't speak on your behalf. I'd have found a way to let him know about you, Nova. You'd have been safe no matter what. And your planet would be freed. I vowed that long ago.”

She lowered her face and stared at the floor.

“I swear to you … on my love of you … I'd have seen you free from the pits of death itself. My father has known about Forrell's chicanery for some time, but to land on this planet without authorization could be deemed an act of war or, at the very least, a total disrespect of pacts signed with other planets under similar circumstances. The news of fire plasma being stockpiled changed everything. When my father received highly reliable information about its existence on Delta Seven, we ignored all treaties and quite a few laws to get here and check things out. If you're fair about this, you'll recall that other worlds, much closer to this one, had similar agreements to help in the event of an emergency. But with Forrell calling the shots, telling everyone in this sector of space that everything was all right, and that he needed no help, what could anyone do? *Think*, Nova! My being here now is cause for Forrell to kill me. He'd have that right because he could deem me a spy."

She lifted her gaze to his. "Y-You're doing this at your father's request?"

"Yes."

"He s-sent his son?"

"He'd send no one else. My father wouldn't issue orders to others he'd not give to his own flesh and blood. Besides, I'm very good at what I do. At least I … I usually am."

She swallowed hard and moved closer to him. "Wh-why did you make yourself such a target by confronting Prometheus? You could have been in deep space, asking for help and revealing Forrell for what he is."

He took a long moment to gather his thoughts and words. What could he say about something he'd never spoken of, not to any other soul? But Nova wasn't just anyone. She was the woman he wanted to spend the rest of his life loving. "I … I saw what slugs did to children during battles with the Warlord factions. Their innocence was stolen away. Those that survived slug occupation of various worlds will never be the same. Not ever." He almost choked on words that finally refused to come out. "I-I can't talk about it, Nova," he whispered. "As bad as things are here, you don't know and I can't … I can't say it … " His words drifted away.

"Goddess above, Marcos. You saw that young girl begging for her grandfather's life and you just—"

"For the first time in my life as an enforcer, I lost it. I wanted nothing more than to peel that slug leader's hide from his bones and watch him suffer the way I'd seen … y-you can't imagine what they did to the children of anyone deemed enemies. I just snapped. I can't explain … "

She reached out, touched his face, and then pulled him into her arms. "It's all right, Marcos. I think I owe your father an apology. And you as an enforcer." She pulled away slightly and blinked back tears. "It's just that I've wanted to be free of this place for so long. All that matters is that you stood up when no one else did. For having done it, you were burned as badly or worse than anyone I've ever seen. I just … everything's just so wrong and I … I wanted someone to blame … "

He held onto her and rocked her back and forth. "I swear this will end. I swear it on my life, or I'll forfeit it to see you free."

"I do love you, Marcos. No matter who you are, I do l-love y-you," she said as she wept. "I could never hate you. You're not the man I thought I could hate. You're d-different than what I … I love you so much."

"Then stop crying and hold on to me," he comforted. "Help is coming. Just as I've promised. But we have to be very careful now. If that man in the marketplace or his granddaughter are caught or we're found … but that won't happen. We'll hide the cave entrance even better, and we won't leave it again, not unless we absolutely have to. If they knew where we were, we'd have been set upon by now. Just keep that in mind. We're still safe. That means we have time for my brother to find me. Even Prometheus didn't know who I was when he was burning me, so the ruse lasted and worked for at least that long. That elderly man figured me out because he's had time to think about that day, long and hard. But that damned slug leader isn't as smart as he thinks he is. My openly confronting him has to have infuriated him no end. He had me in his grasp and could have made much more of an example of me with his minions and those of his home world. Imagine what his superiors will do to him when they find out he had a prince of Luster in his clutches," he said as he tried to assure her. "If he has any enemies among his people, they'll make use of the information."

"That's if they find out, and he'll search every dust pile to make sure they don't," she whispered. "You're a humiliation above and beyond anything he's experienced here."

"And in his desperation he'll get clumsy. So will Forrell. I promise you, Nova, we'll see this end together. At least, I know you'll see an end to it."

She hugged him even harder. "That won't mean anything without you. F-forgive me for what I said about your father a-and enforcers. Please? I don't want to hate anyone anymore. I just want out of this nightmare."

"Creator's blood, little thief, how can I blame you for feeling deserted after what you've been through? I should have told you sooner. I'm the one who should be asking forgiveness. But the coward in me where your loving regard is concerned ... that's my undoing."

"Coward? No, never. And I'll forgive you anything. Just don't die on me, Marcos Starlaw. Don't you dare die!"

• • •

"I understand you wish to speak with me," Darius said, as he stood front of the vid-screen aboard his vessel.

"Greetings to you, Commander," Adaman said. "I bring you official welcome from my planet. You now have permission to land a small contingent from your vessel. I trust you'll be among them? I would like to offer personal felicitations at my residence tomorrow evening. Would you be kind enough to join me?"

Darius bowed his head. "I'd be honored, Governor. Expect a small landing party at sunset tomorrow."

"I'll be at the landing port to meet you myself. I bid you welcome once more on behalf of my planet and its inhabitants. They, I might add, have taken to heart all warnings to behave themselves."

"I'm assured of our safety," Darius told him with a raised brow. "Until tomorrow, Governor."

Adaman clicked the communication device off and let the placid smile slip from his face. He turned to his most-trusted guard. Without speaking, he nodded, and the guard left on his nightly mission of searching the barren lands outside the city limits.

The buzzer on his communication console blared, and he viciously punched it, knowing who would be on the vid-screen. "Good day, Prometheus. We're on a secure line. The *Titan* can't monitor what we're saying."

"Good."

"The *Titan* will remain in orbit. I've invited Captain Starlaw to my residence tomorrow evening. He'll be on the landing port at sunset. I'll bring him straight here."

"My personal war-bird will take out the *Titan* just after he leaves the landing port. We'll surprise her before her crew can respond, and then I'll land and take Darius Starlaw into my custody. Make sure you keep him with you. I don't care what you must do, short of killing him. I reserve that pleasure for myself."

"There's still no sign of Marcos Starlaw or this woman healer who might have helped him."

Prometheus grunted. "It doesn't matter. We'll find them. If I have to alter plans, there'll be little lost but a few days at the most. I'm quite used to changing conditions. Experience during the war years stands me in good stead, in that regard." He leaned forward and glared into the vid-screen. "I always have a plan for *any* contingency."

"I'll keep that in mind, Prometheus. You'll get no trouble from me."

"Until tomorrow then."

• • •

Marcos slept until early dawn. Nova was in his embrace, and he wanted the peace between them to last forever. Grateful she'd so readily forgiven him, all his thoughts now were on when and how he could get a hold of Darius. His brother was near. He could feel it as he always had when they'd played hiding games deep in the woods on Luster. Despite the on-and-off bickering sometimes shared between siblings, their bond went very deep. Years of fighting Warlords and their savage hordes had intensified their sibling instincts. One corner of his mouth lifted as he held Nova closer. Soon, she'd be free, and he'd see his foes pay for the suffering they'd caused.

He slept a little longer but awakened quickly when something tapped into his slumber and shot a warning through his brain.

When he opened his eyes, Una was facing the entrance of the cave. Her stillness, unusual for her when they awakened from slumber, alerted them as nothing else would have.

He pushed himself into a standing position just as Nova did. They quickly dressed, without a making a sound.

Una's stance never varied. Her antennae stood straight up. Her black little nose pointed toward the cave entrance. She didn't growl or make a sound. But the stiffness in her body was ominous. She'd never behaved that way before. She was acting on instinct, which propelled Marcos to do the same. Unlike most sentient creatures who believed themselves above wildlife, there was one thing animals never, ever did. They never lied.

He gently squeezed Nova's right hand, then found and gripped the hilt of the sword the elderly merchant in the marketplace had covertly provided. It was the only weapon they had. And as Nova had already seen him use it, he wasn't averse to taking a head if some enemy stupidly popped one through the opening of their hiding place.

For a very long time, nothing happened. When Una didn't move, neither did they.

Then, in the distance, the sound of an engine broke the stillness.

"Get behind me," he softly ordered.

Without arguing, Nova grabbed up Una and did as he'd commanded. The only weapon she had, save him, was a small paring knife she grabbed up and hid within the folds of the cloak she'd donned.

Voices sounded.

He glanced at her and whispered, "No matter what happens, we stay together."

She swallowed hard, nodded, and held Una against her chest.

Chapter 11

The sound of talking filtered toward the cave entrance.

Marcos stepped directly in front of Nova, wondering at the foolhardiness of anyone on a search making such noise.

"They'll have to come through the small crawlspace one at a time," he whispered. "I'll take them out as they do."

He put his full attention on the cave entrance and took a stance, ready to wield the sword as his trainer had taught him to many years ago. That was the good part about ancient martial artistry. He could drop someone with one silent blow. The sword's edge was quite sharp enough to do so, and he was strong enough. If an intruder were searching alone, separated from his comrades, they might still have a chance to avoid detection.

The sound of voices grew closer; then, there was complete quiet.

"Marcos Starlaw? If you're in there you may as well surrender. You've no place left to run, and I'm your only chance of getting away from the slugs."

Marcos gripped the sword hilt tighter and kept his mouth closed. Whoever called out, though they were idiot enough to make so much noise during a search, they weren't quite so inane as to poke their head through the cave entrance without knowing what waited inside.

He sensed Nova's nearness.

"I could send my man in to get you, sir, but that would result in a fight. Neither of us has time for such foolishness. I could deploy tranquilizing, gaseous agents into your cave and take you when you're unconscious. But, again, such things take time, and we have little to spare. So come out and stop this nonsense before Prometheus's minions find I'm missing from my residence and trace me here. They'll have no qualms about taking your life in ways that will make the plasma seem gentle. Spare the girl further anxiety, if she's with you. Come out and let's speak like men who are both in dire circumstances."

Nova put her hand on his shoulder. "That's Adaman Forrell. I recognize his voice," she softly warned. "Don't trust him, Marcos."

"Please hurry," Forrell called out. "If I'd wanted you dead, you would be."

Marcos used one hand to push Nova further backward and behind him. "There's no one here but me," he responded.

"Marcos Starlaw … your brother's ship is in orbit. He will be at my residence later tonight. I'll hand you over to him. Whoever pulled you from the pit will likely die in your stead if you do not save them. Come out and let me see you safely to your brother. I wish to bargain for conditions."

"I don't know what you're talking about," Marcos lied yet again.

"You are wasting time we do not have, sir. There's only me and one guard. We've been searching for you for a very long time. It was only by accident that our ambient heat sensors picked up a trace of fire coming from this cave. We had to be right on top of you to do so, but Prometheus has many more minions and much more equipment at his disposal. If I found you, his brawlers will. You're in no position to bargain, and I won't be either if any slugs catch us here."

Marcos recognized desperation in the man's voice that, rang true. If those outside the cave had wanted him dead, they could have blasted the side of the hill and killed him and Nova instantly. They had at least that much fire power at their disposal.

"I'll come out," he agreed. "But the girl who helped me is dead. She died from an infection over a month ago." Better to lie about that than try to deny someone's obvious assistance in getting his body out of the trash pit.

"By your pleasure, sir … please be quick, or I can't guarantee our safety."

Marcos turned to Nova. There was a shocked look on her face.

"Stay put. Make no sound," he whispered. If I can get him out of here, you'll have to hide elsewhere. You can survive. I know you can."

He kissed her hard, gazed into her shocked eyes one more time, and turned toward the cave entrance. After maneuvering through the crawlspace, he emerged outside to see Governor Adaman Forrell and one guard at the cave's entrance. The man had actually told the truth. The two of them were standing on large, silver hovercraft undoubtedly causing the noise that had alerted little Una from a distance.

As soon as Marcos was outside the cave and stood to his full height, the guard quickly leaped from the transport's surface and faced him. The burly man aimed a laser at his head, but Marcos gripped the hilt of the sword he'd hidden beneath his hastily donned cloak.

"I know the girl is in there," Forrell severely addressed him. "You'd better tell her to come out, Highness, or she'll surely be found by the slugs. You know what they'll do to her."

"I wasn't lying. She's dead. She was a healer but I wasn't. I couldn't help her."

Forrell rolled his eyes. "Come out, Wiccan healer. You've no choice. The prince is a bad liar, and you know what will happen if Prometheus gets his hands on you. I'm your only chance now. I'll say it again though time is against us … if I'd wanted you dead, you would be! It's clear you mean something to Prince Marcos. Your presence will assist me in bargaining for Darius Starlaw's protection."

• • •

Nova swallowed hard, briefly closed her eyes, and slowly nodded. There was nothing else for her to do. And something in the way Forrell's voice shook made her think he might, for once in his greedy miserable life, be telling the truth.

Then she stopped.

Una was still in her arms. Tears filled her eyes as she considered what to do next.

It was best to take her pet's life humanely so the pup wouldn't starve in the cave or be horribly tortured over an open flame and then eaten by slugs. She slowly lifted her paring knife, but Una gazed up at her with all the trust in the universe in her soft black eyes.

She sniffed back tears, raised her hand, and gripped the knife harder.

Una tilted her little head and softly whimpered.

Goddess, Creator of all things, help me.

She simply couldn't. She hadn't the strength.

Even as she considered a second try, Una barreled into the cloth of her cloak and almost disappeared within the folds.

Nova wiped her tears away with her left sleeve, tucked Una securely within a pocket in the folds of her cloak, and stuck the little paring knife in the top of her right boot.

Una's body was completely hidden. There might still be a chance to set the pup free someplace safer, though doing so wouldn't be charitable with the cold months ahead. But some kind soul *might* find her. Maybe a burned and scarred child would locate the dog and might know comfort in the little pup's happy antics.

That was the only part of hope left to her now. Nova took a deep breath, held her head up, and walked out of the cave.

Marcos hung his head, his eyes briefly closed in apparent defeat.

The guard quickly assisted her onto the transport even as Forrell leapt from it and onto the ground.

"If you have a weapon, you'd better hand it over," Forrell advised. "Though I know you don't think so at this moment, I *am* trying to save your life, young Starlaw. I don't wish to die for my efforts."

Marcos glared at the man, then slowly brought his sword from beneath his cloak. He angrily threw it to the ground and put his face only inches from the governor's.

"If you hurt her, I'll kill you."

Nova couldn't look at her beloved. Her heart actually felt like it'd just broken into a thousand pieces. She'd never again know the warmth of his arms, or his soft voice in the night. But she'd had to come out of the cave. It made no sense to have the guard come in after her, engendering further anger and possible torture right then and there. Best to put that off until later. It would surely come. And maybe, just maybe, she and Marcos could die together. The Goddess might see them into the afterlife as one.

"We'll all be dead if we don't leave here right now." Forrell took a deep, shaking breath. "Luck still holds," he said as he turned toward his guard. "Put the prince in restraints so he won't try something idiotic. Release him only after we're at my residence," Forrell ordered, then gave a few more commands as he remounted the transport. "Pick up the sword, take the same exact route back. Cover as much of our engine's trail as possible."

"Yes, sir," the guard said.

Nova knelt to keep from falling as the transport moved swiftly away from the cave entrance. She looked back, believing she'd never see her home again.

She could get no closer to Marcos, as Forrell's body blocked her way. She couldn't even see her princely lover due to Forrell's robes blowing in the breeze as they sped away, closer to his residence and the city proper.

"I've had to disable half a dozen of Prometheus's contraptions in my own home just to make one room safe from spying," Forrell complained. "His minions would have likely found us were it not for the fact that they are occupied elsewhere. Their slug leader is on his ship, planning to ambush your brother when he lands with a small part of his crew tonight."

"What's your game?" Marcos asked. "I won't ask how you eventually figured out who I was; it no longer matters. Why don't you just kill me and get it over with?"

"I tell you, your brother *is* here. He's come looking for you though he's made every conceivable attempt to make it appear otherwise. But we can discuss all this when we get to my residence. We'll have to fly fast and sneak into my domicile through underground tunnels as it is," Forrell warned. "When we get to the city limits, sit down and pull the hoods of your cloaks up. If we're lucky, we might just get to my home without being seen. We're already fortunate enough that the slugs, inclusive of all their craft, have been told to hide. This was done so your brother and his crew will not locate them using an enforcer ship's close-range sensors, or by sight upon landing. If the slugs fail to keep hidden, I can easily see your sibling raining hell down on Delta Seven's uninhabited mining areas, since he'd assume you are dead and would be looking to make a very harsh point!"

"Sucks to be you," Marcos muttered with a disdainful snort.

Forrell's guard slowed their transport's pace when they eventually got behind the governor's official dwelling.

"Take this vehicle and resume patrol duties as if nothing has happened," Forrell said to the guard. "You know what to do."

"Yes, sir," the guard responded, then sped away after his passengers exited.

"If you want to live, give me no grief and follow me … quickly," the governor commanded as he swiftly moved to an old cellar door behind the large, granite building in which he lived.

"Why should we trust you?" Marcos asked.

"Because I'm as deep in this as you are. The slug leader will have me killed as soon as he's sure I'm of no use. Indeed, everything I did was to try to contain his violence," Forrell gushed. "We'll talk further when we're upstairs, in quarters more suited to such a discussion, and away from prying ears and eyes."

Some minutes later, the governor motioned them into an old cargo lift alongside him. The man pushed a lever that raised them upward.

The lift soon stopped, and they got out. The room they exited into was resplendent. Nova frowned thinking of how many of the colony's citizens went without many kinds of necessities while Forrell lived like some greasy potentate.

Nova gazed at a large space where candles glowed, food was laid out, and luxurious round sofas with cushions dotted the area. Tapestries hung everywhere. Forrell's quarters were a great deal warmer than the cave she and Marcos shared. And far more sumptuous than the man deserved. Everything there belied his effusive claims of victimization.

"Now I know what you used the gems for," she accused. "To buy yourself the comfort our people have been denied."

"You have me wrong, dear lady. I've only been trying to survive the slugs's siege as everyone else has."

She rounded on him. "You lying, murdering savage!"

When she charged the man, Marcos pulled her back. He heard Una whimper within Nova's robe. The little pup had only been able to keep her hidden spot due to the depth of the pocket in which she was situated. "He's got a laser in his robes," he warned. "He wasn't stupid enough to let that guard go and stay here unarmed … with you and me to hold him accountable."

Nova took a deep breath and stalked away, but not far enough that she couldn't hear what Marcos said to Forrell.

"You want to talk about my brother now?" Marcos angrily asked. "You didn't bring us all this way, risking your own neck for nothing. What do you want?"

"The *Titan* is in orbit," Forrell told him. "In a few hours, your brother and a small cadre of enforcers will land. I've offered the prince and his men hospitality at my residence. I'm supposed to hold them hostage here and await Prometheus's arrival."

Marcos lurched toward the man but stopped when Forrell aimed a small sidearm at Nova.

"Listen to me, you fool. I don't have time to repeat myself," Forrell said.

"If you're lying … "

"I'm *not*, Prince Marcos. While Commander Starlaw is being held here, Prometheus will order his warships to attack the *Titan* and kill the crew. Then the slug leader is supposed to land again and kill all the rest of the enforcers. The slimy bastard is singularly obsessed with the notion that he be the one allowed to take out the next ruler of Luster."

"And why should I believe you'd bring me here for any other reason than to have me killed along with Darius?" Marcos accused. "With him dead, I become ruler."

Forrell sighed. "Do I have your word, on your father's honor and yours, that you won't have me killed if I help you and Prince Darius?"

"I can't speak on my father's behalf. And certainly not on my brother's when he finds out what's happened to me."

Forrell looked over the hideous scars on Marcos's face and audibly gulped. "The confrontation i-in the marketplace was P-Prometheus's doing, not m-mine. I had no idea that incident h-happened until after it was over. You must believe me, Highness."

"We can talk about this later. What about warning my brother?"

"Y-You must let me explain, first," Forrell begged.

"There is no explanation you can give," Nova uttered.

Marcos clenched his hands. "I have to make contact with my brother. He suspects you and won't believe anything you say is the truth."

"O-of course. I understand. But it must be at the last possible moment. I've heard of Darius Starlaw's tactics and his capabilities. The *Titan* is one of the best ships in the enforcer fleet," Forrell affirmed. "I think it'll have a chance with the slug warships. But, if you warn your brother now, Prometheus will overhear your transmission, and he'll kill us all. He'll incinerate everyone on this planet, and your brother would likely die as well. We must wait until tonight and find a way to transmit from my private communication center. At the last possible second."

"And you want protection for your … *help*?" Marcos sarcastically asked.

"I know you'll keep your word if you give it. It isn't just my life we're talking about. It's everyone's in the colony. The entire planet will be burned to oblivion if the slugs find us out."

"He's lying," Nova growled. "Every word he utters is a lie."

Marcos stared at Forrell, took a deep breath, and nodded. "I can promise the slugs won't lay their hands on you while I live. I'm in no position to give my word on anything else."

Nova turned away. She knew exactly what Marcos meant. He wasn't saying he'd protect Forrell from the slugs. He was using semantics to promise *he'd* kill the governor himself, before the Limaxians could do it. The governor kept pleading his cause, not even guessing Marcos's intent.

"I-I know having possession of fire plasma is a violation invoking the death penalty. But you must believe me, Highness. I never had use of that chemical. The slugs found someone with the formula, forced him to hand it over, and then killed the man. I had to deal with them or they would have killed everyone here."

Nova lunged for him yet again. Once more Una whimpered as she huddled in her deep pocket hiding spot.

Marcos quickly pulled her back and held her against his body.

"You had him kill my father because he stood against you. You left us to suffer without incubation chambers or any way to heal our wounded," she accused.

"What's your answer to that?" Marcos demanded.

"It was Prometheus who wanted control of the planet and the miners … for the gems. He was the one who gave orders concerning whom to kill and when. He's trying to build a fleet to destroy the enforcers. He needed the gems to do it." Forrell put out one hand in supplication while still holding his weapon in the other. "Several times, I left the civilian communication center unguarded and hoped someone might be able to get a message through. I couldn't because my every move was being watched. But someone *did* do it, or you wouldn't be here, Marcos Starlaw. And, as far as interplanetary law goes, you could be put to death for being a spy on a planet within the Constellation League's jurisdiction. Your father doesn't own this world or any other. The Constellation League he administers simply dispenses justice when and as allied rulers and dignities ask for it. That's the nature of our agreement. You are not here with legal documentation, and have taken on an alias. I could have had you killed at the cave with complete impunity. Yet, here you stand. And I'm giving you such protection and hospitality as is mine to give until your brother can save us all from this horrifying nightmare."

"You killed my mother and father," Nova said as she swiped at tears falling down her cheeks. Marcos held her tighter.

"I've told you I'll keep you safe from the slugs," Marcos promised once more. "That's only provided I stay alive to do it, that you send a warning to my brother, and as long as Nova isn't hurt."

"I give you my word, Prince Marcos. And to seal the bargain, I give you my weapon." He turned the laser over to Marcos and stared at him. "I'm in your protection now. I trust you to keep *your* word."

"Why should Marcos do that? You never did," Nova cried.

"Your father might have been my rival, my dear. I do know who you are, and I remember Bellos Drayton and your mother, Risa, as pitting themselves against me on numerous occasions. But I can assure you … Prometheus wanted them dead and would have killed them no matter what. It was Prometheus who used the plasma during the insurrections. Not me."

"Then why didn't the slugs just kill you, too, if you're so noble? Why didn't he just take the gems and leave?" Nova asked.

Forrell shook his head and ran shaking his hands over his face. "*Because*, my girl. Slugs won't do manual labor. They needed humans to enslave. You should know this by now. And Prometheus needed someone on our planet's surface to answer calls from deep space. Someone human who could appear on a vid-screen as an elected official and not raise suspicions. He was trying to keep his presence here as secret as possible. All so he could gain the wealth needed to attack Luster. He believes the king, queen, and the entire Constellation League will never recover from such a horrible, decimating blow to their morale if Darius dies later tonight. He wants to take Marcos back to Luster, kill him there, and make an example of him. Without any other heirs old enough to take the throne, the king will be forced to man a warship himself and fight for his planet's safety. In that event, King Dar will likely be killed. Prometheus knows how reduced the league fleet is. Any losses now will almost crush their chances for a galactic defense. He hopes to win himself the empire. Even if his own losses are substantial."

"He means to kill my entire family," Marcos uttered more to himself than anyone else.

"You see how it is, sir. It's to my benefit to keep you and your brother alive. Prometheus won't have use for any human once he can attack and destroy your planet's defenses. He'll find other races to enslave. And with our gems, even if he doesn't have a ready fleet of warships now, he has an almost unlimited supply of wealth to buy off those of the criminal element to help him; criminals who'd glory in killing any enforcer they could get their hands on. And there are many such lawbreakers since the wars have been over."

For a long moment, Marcos stared into the distance, then back at Forrell. "My brother can take any cadre of ships if he's warned in time. The *Titan* is fully equipped." He grabbed the governor by the front of his long robe and pulled him roughly forward. "If you've lied to me, I'll see you dead. And in such a way you'll have prayed the slugs had taken you. Do you understand?"

Adaman threw up his hands in defense. "I swear, Highness. This place will keep you safe so long as Prometheus doesn't have time to notice I've taken out the surveillance equipment he uses to watch me. At the last minute, you can warn your brother yourself. I'll take you to my communication console, and your brother will never set foot on the planet until he's defeated Prometheus, and it's safe to do so. In the meantime, all we have to do is keep *you* safe from slugs still hiding on the planet's surface."

"So we sit and wait," Marcos angrily said as he paced a few steps.

"We shall transmit just before sunset. Until then, please, be seated and eat. You're likely cold and hungry. I would have come to you sooner and offered help, but I didn't dare try to hide you until the circumstances were right. As I've said, I'm being watched constantly and must make excuses when I disappear. I have many justifications in my arsenal. Just as I have medicines should your burns require tending. The healer is welcome to use them," he liberally offered with one hand raised.

"The only thing that will help now us is an incubation chamber. But you managed to make sure we didn't have any," Nova shot back.

"Again, the slugs—"

Marcos hauled the man to a pile of cushions and forced him into them. "I don't want to hear any more excuses. I've given my word, so keep your mouth shut unless you're spoken to and until it's time for me to talk to my brother."

Adaman nodded and proceeded to pour himself some ale with a shaking hand.

Marcos kept the laser aimed at him, but addressed Nova. "You may as well get some food in you and stay warm yourself. Just in case we have to run. Make sure Forrell eats out of any dish first."

"I will," she softly told him as she sat on the other side of the room, as far away from Forrell as she could get.

She wasn't hungry, and none of the delicacies on the tables could possibly induce her to eat. But she slipped small portions of food to Una from plates Forrell had chosen. She wasn't losing her pet now that there might be some chance the governor was telling the truth.

To keep her anger at bay, she kept her attention on Marcos. She now witnessed the strong, staunch enforcer he'd always been. With Forrell's explanations, it was easier to forgive King Dar. She was sure now that the ruler of Luster had tried to help. And she was heartily ashamed of all the terrible accusations she'd made before knowing who Marcos was or what he did for a living. He, in return, hadn't hated her. Instead, he'd held her in his arms and made love to her once more.

If tonight went badly, she'd at least been with the one she loved. Many had died on Delta Seven who couldn't say the same.

• • •

Marcos willed himself to keep a cool head.

Fear over what the night would bring kept forcing him to plan options he'd never have considered.

If he couldn't warn Darius, the *Titan* might be surprised by slug warships hidden somewhere in this sector of space. And if the *Titan* went down and Darius with it, he would *have* to survive until help could come. He'd have to transmit a simultaneous message back to Luster, though it wouldn't get there for a very long time. And that meant running and hiding again. The population would likely be decimated, and his and Nova's chances for survival would be almost impossible. Before he'd let the slugs have her, he'd kill her himself. And that would be as low as he would ever sink.

He silently prayed to the Creator that if it came to that, he could do the deed quickly and painlessly.

Then he considered another dangerous aspect.

How many others like Prometheus had access to the knowledge that the League's fleet wasn't at full strength? The launch ports for Luster's fighting ships were highly restricted areas and guarded constantly. The crews knew their own safety depended upon keeping the rebuilding of the fleet secret. But he surmised that having so few ships on patrol might have been cause for gossip. That gossip might have spread to outer sectors where brutal savages like the Limaxians dwelled.

He glanced at Nova and prayed he'd never have to do what his heart told him he *might*. Taking her precious life to keep slugs from getting her was the last option. The thought was too horrifying. By the same token, he'd hope someone on Luster would never let the rest of his family perish at the hands of Limaxians. No one should have to die like that.

Finally, he sent a silent prayer forward for his brother's safety. Not just because Darius was the heir to the throne, but because he loved him fiercely and wanted to see him again. Darius would search every planet in the known universe to see *him* safely home. That was how close they were and always had been.

More than anything else in his life, Marcos wanted this over with as soon as possible. He wanted to be back on Luster, as far from this colorless planet and its horrors as he could get. And he wanted Nova with him. He wanted a chance to start over with her. But the dreams could only become reality if he was careful. It was all up to him. And that responsibility was the worst of his life.

He'd previously only had to consider himself while undercover. Now, his entire planet and what was left of Delta Seven depended on this night going as the traitorous Forrell claimed it might.

• • •

"I don't like it," Darius muttered as he scanned Delta Seven's dreary landscape from the *Titan*'s vid-screen. "I planned on taking five of you with me on a small transport and landing on the dock where Forrell is supposed to meet us. But something just doesn't feel right."

"When you get one of those urges, it's best to yield to it, sir. I've never known you to be wrong about a hunch," the second-in-command replied.

Darius rubbed his jaw thoughtfully and shook his head. "I want a long-range scan of everything within three days of Delta Seven. If you find the slightest anomaly, report it. I refuse to believe something has happened to Marcos. If he were dead, I'd know."

"It's possible his transponder isn't working, Commander."

"Let's pray that's so. This business with Forrell has the smell of rotting D'nubrian slime worms."

"Scanning now, sir."

Darius leaned forward in the commander's seat and trained his eyes on the large vid-screen in front of him.

"Sir, we're being hailed from the planet's surface."

"Open a view window," Darius ordered as he stood. A scrambled vid-message as well as an equally garbled vocal message came through.

"Darius … it's Marcos. This message is likely weak and may be blocked. You're being set up for an attack. There are at least six Limaxian warships—"

"Get him back!" Darius barked out as his brother's voice faded away.

"I heard the part about the Limaxian cruisers, sir."

"All hands to battle stations," Darius commanded as he took his seat in his chair again. "Keep trying that communication link again, and broaden the long-range scan."

• • •

"I'm sure he must have heard you," Forrell said as he watched the vid-screen go black.

"He'd better have," Marcos said. "I'd say Prometheus doesn't trust you, or he wouldn't have attempted to block any transmission from the surface."

"He's a Limaxian. They trust no one and will even kill their own kind on nothing more than a suspicion. I suspected he'd try, but hoped he'd not be able to block a transmission entirely."

"I'll keep trying until I'm certain Darius got the message. It probably won't work, but it's our only chance."

"Shall I go back to the healer?" Forrell asked.

Marcos adjusted the controls on the communication console in an attempt to boost the transmission signal. "Not without me. She's safer where she is than out on the streets trying to get to us. And if this communication center is blasted in order to stop us from warning the *Titan*, I don't want Nova anywhere near."

"Y-you think that will happen, Highness? Is that why you insisted on leaving the girl at my residence?"

Marcos smiled when he saw the man start to sweat. "That's exactly why I left her. And on the off chance that we survive an attack here, she'll be there to tell my brother where we are."

Explosions sounded in the distance. At least one Limaxian craft was strafing the surface, attempting to destroy the communication station but apparently satisfied to level every building on the way there.

Though Nova had glared at him when he'd ordered her to stay behind, she hadn't put up any objection. His original intent was that they should stay together. Then, it occurred to him that this very thing might happen; that one of the Limaxian ships would head straight for them to cut off their communication. He didn't want the only woman he'd ever loved anywhere near, just as he'd told Forrell.

"Th-they're coming closer," Forrell gasped as he grabbed his robes tightly around his body.

"What's wrong, Forrell? Don't want a taste of what you've been dishing out to these people for years?"

"If I'd known we'd be blasted, I wouldn't have come with you."

"Too late." He grabbed the man's cloak and hauled him into a chair beside the vid-screen. "You'll be staying with me until this is over. Until the very last second. There was no way I was leaving you alone with Nova. You're not going back to your residence now."

"But if slugs show up there—"

"That's the part I didn't like. But as Nova has so often reminded me, she knows how to get in and out of buildings. I didn't want to leave her behind, but this was the only way to make contact with the *Titan* and not put us both in danger to do so. Besides—I trust her. I have faith in her. Which is more than I can say for you."

"When Prometheus believes I've betrayed him, he'll strike my residence with a photon torpedo. That little healer will be dead before she can run a hundred yards. She'll never get the chance to get far enough away."

Too late, Marcos realized that Forrell might be right. He had the choice of staying at the console and continuing to contact the

Titan, or warning Nova. He grabbed Forrell by the front of his caftan and hauled him closer. "Is there any safe place we can go?"

"Under my residence, in the tunnels. It's the only place. I've had the underground doors reinforced to foil assassination attempts. There'll be no food or water, but we can close ourselves off and survive a day or two if necessary. If those doors hold through the blasts and your brother's ship isn't destroyed, Prince Darius might be able to get to us. But we have to go *now*."

Marcos glanced at the console once more. Putting the distress signal on auto wouldn't boost it at increments necessary to provide the best chance for contact. That should be done manually. But every instinct now told him to get to Nova.

"Hurry up," he commanded. "There's no time to lose."

• • •

On the top floor of Forrell's home, Nova heard the explosions and knew they were getting closer. She grabbed Una, held her pet close, and eyed the door. "So much for us staying together, Marcos Starlaw," she bitterly whispered.

She couldn't wait any longer. Too many times she'd heard those ships coming, and knew what would happen to anything being strafed on the ground. She decided not to wait for Marcos, but take her chances elsewhere.

She took the lift down to the first floor and ran through the foyer.

Out on the street, people clustered then moved to the west, attempting to get away from the Limaxian ground craft. But if she headed east, where the ships had already fired, there might be a way to escape. The tunnels under the city wouldn't help if Limaxians found survivors beneath wreckage and shot fire plasma in them to flush anyone out. That was what had happened the first time there'd been a colony-wide attack.

As several Limaxians stumbled past the door and shouted commands to their comrades, Nova hunched in the shadows and waited for them to pass. At the other end of the block, she heard their craft moving ever closer.

Parts of Forrell's roof were already beginning to crumble beneath the ferocity of the blasts. She threw off her cloak, reached into her boot, and grabbed the governor's small laser weapon. Marcos had given it to her before he'd left. She'd silently tried to refuse the sidearm, but her beloved enforcer had shoved it into her hands just before he told her he'd return.

Now, he never would. She realized these attacks were being employed to send the population into a panic, and in an attempt to destroy the buildings up to and including the communication center. The slugs must have heard Marcos's attempts to reach his brother's ship and were retaliating. That meant Prometheus had anticipated Forrell's trying that very thing. And, as she always had, she found herself alone except for Una, surviving the best she knew how.

Her heart sank. Tears stung her eyes, but she quickly wiped them away. She'd mourn Marcos later. For now, she had to run. He'd want her to live and try to escape.

With at least one vessel firing on the surface, there might be enough energy released for the *Titan*'s scanners to read what was happening. If that were true, Darius Starlaw would mount a defense, even if he didn't know who the enemy was.

A worse scenario came to mind.

The *Titan*'s crew might be under attack right now, or the enforcer ship might be destroyed. Whatever had happened in orbit, *her* only chance was far away, not in Forrell's residence. It was now a target.

Outside in the darkness, she felt more secure. This was how she'd lived for several years, finding her way through dim, night shadows.

When slugs ran in different directions, firing lasers at any of the human population they could, she hid. Directly in front of her, one slug brawler was left alone as his brethren chased after families who'd emerged from their homes and stores to escape the onslaught. That single slug stood with his back to her.

She saw her chance and took it.

Without thinking another instant, Nova fired at the back of that slug's head and watched him weave in a drunken fashion before he fell to the pavement. She held Una tightly against her body and ran. East was the safest place. People were running toward her, but she ducked behind columns, rocks, transport vehicles, or anything she could find to escape their stampede. And the Limaxians went after them. The foolish slugs on the ground either didn't realize or didn't care that their own ships would blast them along with the fleeing humans. But no one noticed her as she waited for the bulk of those fleeing to pass. Even as she ran, she blinked back tears. Marcos would have found her if he could. Or she'd have seen him by now if he'd escaped with others. But nothing resembling the tall, horribly scarred enforcer passed her hiding places. Even in the dark she'd have known him among hundreds.

One thing, more than any other, kept her moving.

If there were enforcer ships still fighting anywhere near Delta Seven, they'd surely send messages to Luster and outlying planets concerning the conflict. From now forward, unless all enforcer ships from any world were defeated, help would come. It was the only good thing to come from this night.

Chapter 12

Marcos half-pulled and half-pushed Forrell toward his residence.

Crowds fleeing in their direction forced them to duck behind whatever protective barrier they could, but he was determined to get back to the governor's residence. It was irrational to think she'd stand around, with explosives going off everywhere, and wait for him. But he couldn't stand the thought of her going through this onslaught alone. She'd endured enough in her young life; he had to find her.

Blasts from a single Limaxian ship strafed buildings on the opposite side of the street where he and Forrell huddled. When he got a good look through the smoke created by dozens of large fires from burning buildings, he knew the ship doing the most damage was Prometheus's own flag vessel. Bigger and better equipped than others in a fleet of Limaxian war ships, it hovered on the horizon destroying everything it could. And he wished there had been another way to warn Darius. But there was almost no chance Prometheus would have allowed this population of humans to go on living at any rate. At least they had the chance to run while Darius was hopefully engaging the other five ships in battle. And that was *if* the *Titan* had received any part of the message he'd attempted to send.

"There'll be more slugs on the surface now," Forrell croaked. "They'll find us."

"They will if you don't move your butt and get us to the governor's residence."

"I tell you the residence has been blasted already. The girl is dead."

Marcos pushed Forrell from behind a column when it was safe to do so. "You'd better pray not. Or I'll have no more use for you."

Forrell gasped as a whiff of acrid smoke filled the air. "You said you'd protect me. You're an enforcer, sworn to—"

"I said I wouldn't let the slugs get you," Marcos said as he pushed the man harder to make him pick up his pace. He could travel much faster if the oaf wasn't with him. But he wouldn't put it past Forrell to find a slug and try to save his own hide by turning him and Nova over to Prometheus. That seemed to have been the way things had worked on this planet for years, with Forrell pitting himself against the slugs, and the people of Delta Seven lost in between their elected official and the invaders.

When he rounded the corner and saw the roof of the governor's residence in flames, Marcos's heart shattered.

"I told you. Prometheus wanted me dead for betraying him. The girl is gone. We have to get to safety before we're blasted."

"We can't go into the tunnels now. Even if the slugs think we're there, the building will collapse, and we'll be caught under tons of wreckage."

"But there's no place else," Forrell shouted.

"Yes there is. We can go back to the cave where you found me. Unless you lied, no one knows about it."

"But if we use a transport, Prometheus will see it trying to leave the city. He could track any craft from his ship."

"That's why we're going to run."

"Run? I-I can't … "

"Pick up your feet or I'll break your neck," Marcos warned. When Forrell did as he was told and made for the city limits, Marcos stood for a moment and looked back at the residence. The roof collapsed, and the entire inside of the governor's home went up in flames. "She got out. I know she did," he whispered.

He had to believe that. Nova knew what to do. He kept telling himself that as he ran after Forrell.

• • •

Prometheus landed his vessel and keyed the communication device hanging from his uniform epaulet. "How fares the *Titan*?"

Nothing came back except static.

He cursed and lifted a hand to motion his crew forward. "I'll have that bastard's balls. Find Forrell," he ordered. "Find his remains if he's dead, and if he's with anyone who's still breathing, bring them to me. He couldn't have possibly been so bold on his own. He hasn't the courage."

One of the warriors placed a hand on his leader's shoulder. "Commander Prometheus, we should board our ship and join the fight in orbit. We can deal with this refuse on the ground later."

Prometheus pushed the man away, knocking him to the ground. "Fool! The *Titan* was warned too early. Before our ships could withdraw from the moon's orbit and engage her. She now has the upper hand. But she won't keep it if I can convince Darius Starlaw that I control the planet's surface. He'll want as little bloodshed as possible. I can ransom for the humans's safety. Go now. Find as many humans as you can and round them up at the mines."

"Yes, sir."

• • •

Nova saw Prometheus long before he got to her location. She held onto Una and wove through the shadows. The city skyline behind her was ablaze. The heat from it kept her from feeling the intense cold.

As Limaxians drew nearer, she hid herself among metal packing crates and barrels, hunched down, and gripped the handle of the laser weapon, not intending to fire. There was no way to do so and take them all out. So she waited.

Frightened by the running, the smell of smoke, and the fear she sensed in her mistress's body, Una began to wriggle fiercely.

Nova tried to hang onto the pup, but she broke loose and ran. As she saw the furry body scamper back toward town, her eyes filled with tears. Una would likely try to get back to the cave, but being so little, she wouldn't know how to get over so much debris, most of it burning. And Nova had to sit there quietly and let the slugs go by. Any attempt to retrieve her pet would get them both killed. The best she could hope for was that little Una found some safe place to hide until she could find her.

She sniffed back tears, ducked her head, and gripped the weapon harder.

. . .

At the outskirts of the city, Forrell paused and leaned against a destroyed transport vessel. "I-I simply can't go on. I c-can't."

"Then I'll kill you and save the slugs the trouble." Marcos shook his head and snorted in disdain. "I was damned near burned to death. Parts of me are still recovering, yet you can't seem to pick up your pampered feet!"

"All right, all right. I'll move."

Through the snow they trudged. Marcos knew if they were caught out in the open, there was no chance to survive. Not from a slug attack or from the freezing temperatures. Several times, he glanced back at the city and felt his gut tighten. Somewhere, Nova was in the middle of all the burning chaos.

He had to get back to her. His first concern was Forrell and making sure the governor didn't escape the justice that would surely be rendered back on Luster. But it felt like he was doing the worst thing in his life. Had it not been for his innate sense of duty, he'd have killed Forrell and gone after his beloved.

It took close to an hour to reach the cave. By then, Forrell was nearly frozen. Marcos took only a few moments to throw wood on the fire and light it.

"Stay put, and you might survive."

"Wh-where are you going? I can't stay here alone. Not in this filthy pit."

At his wit's end, Marcos grabbed the man and threw him against the hard cave wall. "You'll die if you try to leave. The cold will kill you if Prometheus's brawlers don't. I'm going back for Nova."

"The healer is dead."

Marcos stalked to the governor, who had to back into a corner to keep from being pushed to the ground. "If you say that one more time … "

"I'm sorry. Of course. She might have survived." Forrell put his hands up to fend Marcos off. "Just go. I'll stay here."

"You'd better. If you were lying about no one else finding this place but you and one guard, you can be sure the slugs will make me seem like your best friend. Keep quiet, and stay vigilant."

"I can assure you, Highness. I'll wait right here for your return. The slugs don't know about this cave. Or that you and the little healer are alive. I swear it."

Marcos grabbed up a blanket to use as an extra wrap now that his cloak was no longer keeping him warm. He gritted his teeth to prepare for another long march in the cold. At least he could travel faster now.

All he could think of was getting to Nova. Nothing else mattered. He cursed himself a thousand times for not letting her come with him.

Making sure he left no trail for Forrell to follow, should he be so brave, Marcos trudged his way back to the city. Everything was ablaze. He cursed himself over and over for not having found another way to warn Darius and stop the Limaxians.

As he pulled up the hood of his cloak, wrapped the blanket tighter around his body, and bent into the cold wind, he went over the sequence of events that had just transpired.

There was no right answer. Things couldn't have gone well when he was outnumbered and outgunned, and not while trudging around with a traitor, trying to save the man's life when it wasn't worth saving.

When he finally got back to the main marketplace, there were no people or slugs present. They'd apparently run and scattered in all directions.

Buildings on both sides of the road were severely damaged. All the roofs were burning, caving in, or gone entirely. The heat was intense, but he moved carefully forward, avoiding falling debris and the small fires blowing trash started.

As he searched for Nova and begged the Creator of all things for her safety, he also prayed for his brother. The *Titan* was several times larger and much better equipped than the average Limaxian warship. But Darius would've brought no backup since doing so would have appeared too hostile to an allied-planet's dignitaries. His older brother might have been far outnumbered, and the star of the Lusterian fleet might be nothing more than scrap metal by now.

But even if immediate salvation were lost, lack of communication from Darius would result in more allied ships being sent. If he and Nova could stay hidden until their arrival, they could survive.

He pulled the blanket over his head and shoulders to keep cinders off his upper body. If the blanket caught fire, it could be discarded. But he had to move forward, through the burning debris, no matter what.

Two walls of flame suddenly burst skyward from both sides of the street. He ran until he came to the remains of Forrell's home.

Like all buildings, the walls had been made of gray stone. The roof had been constructed of pressure-resistant glass and metal brought in on transport ships, probably at a time when trade vessels could still land without being restricted to the airfield. Still, the sturdier material hadn't kept the structure from collapsing. Only the bottom part of the stone wall remained intact. Everything within the residence was now exposed to the night air. There was nothing but tons of rubble left.

He had to take a chance. As small as the colony was, he could still search for a long time before finding the woman he loved. "Nova!" he shouted as he strained to see through the burning beams of melted metal and rock.

No one responded, and he knew he was taking a huge risk. But he couldn't have stopped calling for her if all the Limaxians in the galaxy were marching up the street behind him. Patience was lost. He couldn't fathom going on without her.

Finally, he turned away. His heart broke as he searched under debris and found bodies. Faces of the dead were burned away; any clothing left was equally blackened. If she was among the deceased, he couldn't tell.

Surely she'd made it. No one knew how to survive this planet's disasters better than she.

A scraping sound on the paved street made him spin around. He had no weapon, but he could and would fight until his body gave out. But no enemy approached.

Running toward him—at a speed he wouldn't have attributed to her—was little Una. She barked excitedly and launched herself into his arms.

Marcos hugged her to his chest. The poor little thing was shivering uncontrollably. Her once white fur was now sooty and scorched. As he held her, the pup licked his face and whined in a heart-wrenching fashion.

"Easy, little girl; it's all right now. You're okay."

He gazed in the direction from which Una ran, took two steps forward then froze. Eight Limaxian warriors rounded the corner;

Prometheus was in the middle of them. There was no mistaking the largest of the slugs or the one who'd dispensed the fire plasma so many months ago.

With no place to hide that wasn't burning, Marcos put Una on the ground behind him, stood to his full height, and squared his shoulders. Prometheus stopped, momentarily blinked in surprise, and then grinned maliciously.

It didn't take the evil creature long to recover his composure. The slug leader raised his laser and strode quickly forward. The distance between them was covered in seconds.

When the big slug was an arm's length away, he and his minions stopped and growled.

As badly burned as Marcos was, he knew he'd been recognized. The vicious glare in his enemy's bulbous eyes said it all.

"Marcos Starlaw. It *is* you, is it not?"

He lifted his chin, but said nothing in response.

"I knew you'd escaped death. I knew it in my bones," Prometheus said.

"Why don't we finish this here and now … just you and me? No brawlers, no fire plasma. Just us. As it should have been."

"And why shouldn't I just blast you and be done it?"

"Because you think my brother will bargain for my life."

"Your brother is fighting for his *own* life. My warships have him on the run."

Marcos's eyes narrowed. The *Titan* might be fighting, but since Prometheus wasn't there to witness the battle, then the conflict wasn't going well for him. He'd landed on Delta Seven again to get out of the fray; likely to keep from being blasted to oblivion.

"I've had enough," the slug leader angrily declared. "The trouble you and Forrell have caused will make your deaths sweet."

"Forrell is already dead," Marcos told him. "I killed him right after I made him lead me to the communication console."

Prometheus's lip curled, and his eyes glowed red. "I knew that worthless bastard would betray me. But I don't believe you killed him. An enforcer would take him into custody so that he could stand trial. You'd want to see him pay for having you burned."

Marcos moved closer to the slug and stared him down. "That was *your* doing. And I will see you dead for it. With or without a trial."

"What I'll do to you now will make all else seem trivial, Starlaw. While I would have preferred taking your life in front of all Luster, killing you and your brother on the same night will still leave a horrifying taste in the mouths of those creatures occupying your home world. And they'll soon know I'm coming for them." He raised his laser, grabbed Marcos by the front of his cloak, and shoved him hard.

Marcos stumbled back several steps and fell to the surface of the street. A hideous growl emanated from behind him, and before he could move or utter a sound, Una ran forward. His eyes widened by the sight she presented.

The little sweet ball of white fur was gone. In its place stood an animal whose head had expanded at least ten times. Her mouth was open. Protruding from gaping jaws was a set of razor-like teeth that were fully as long as his forearm. He froze, mesmerized by the unholy transformation.

Prometheus quickly aimed his laser.

With lightning-like speed and the strength of a jumping equine, Una leaped forward and up. She latched onto the Limaxian leader's throat.

Prometheus dropped his laser to pull Una away.

Seeing his chance, Marcos grabbed the weapon Prometheus had dropped, rolled to one side, and fired. Three slugs went down. The other four turned and ran, screaming in terror.

Marcos slowly stood, barely believing an event he was witnessing with his own eyes.

Precious little Una—the cuddly little pup he and Nova slept next to on so many nights—had her horrifyingly long fangs sunk into Prometheus's throat. She held on, vice-like, until the slug leader's eyes almost fell from their sockets. His enemy's face took on an unseemly pallor, and he soon became quite still. Grey matter finally ran from the slug leader's mouth, down his chest, and into the street. The dead creature's eyes began to glaze over. They were fixated on the stars overhead. By the light of the fires burning around them, Marcos saw the scene clearly enough. He'd witnessed the end to a tyrant. And by a very unlikely source.

Marcos took a deep breath and backed away as Una actually began to feed sparingly on slug parts. Eventually, she tore flesh away from Prometheus's throat, leaving a large hole where his trachea had been. Then the pup shook the tissue violently and flung it aside. When she turned, he swallowed hard but didn't move a muscle.

"*Una?*" he whispered as he stared at the furry, mega-toothed beast before him. She now seemed all mouth and fangs with no body or facial features at all. The site would have quelled the hardest warrior. He counted himself among their ranks, even as his hands shook.

Somehow, without showing any appendages used for ambulation, she waddled toward him. He held his breath.

When she was a few feet away, she shook herself rigorously, and her head immediately shrunk back down. The upper and lower fangs in her hideous mouth disappeared. In the matter of a few seconds, the cute little pet was there again. Her black little eyes shone brightly as she gazed up at him.

"I knew you weren't a damned dog," he softly murmured. "In fact, I'm not even sure you're a *she*. But I'll take Nova's word for it.'

Una barked once and jumped way up and into his arms again. It was all Marcos could do to shove the laser into the folds of his cloak so he could hold on to the fluffy ball. The last thing he wanted to do was drop her and set her off again. He surmised she wouldn't attack him since she'd never done so, but there was no sense taking chances.

"Guess you don't like slugs either," he said as she whimpered soulfully.

While holding her carefully, he grabbed up the dead slugs's weapons, shoving each of them into his cloak pockets to conceal them. "Come on. We've got to find Nova."

As he walked away, he slowly shook his head.

The deadliest enemy he'd ever run across had just been bested by a tiny creature whose instincts were obviously seeded to protect.

Who knew?

Never again would he look at a lower life form and consider it less worthy, as so many did. One had just saved his life. Even as he moved forward in his search, he fervently swore to show due respect in future, assuming he had one.

•••

Nova huddled behind rocks near the incineration pit. It would be the last place anyone would want to search now. Decay and remains of the long dead lay strewn about. Only on one occasion had she found something worth saving and that was here. Now, it would serve as a safe refuge.

With the fires of burning buildings far behind, she grew colder. She had discard her cloak when burning debris had fallen on it and threatened to char her as well. Having been burned once, feeling flames come close to her skin had made her opt for being cold. Sadly, her gloves had been within the pockets of her cloak. Her palms were now so numb she couldn't have fired the laser weapon Marcos gave her, even if her life depended on it.

Marcos.

Where was he? And where was little Una?

In her fear, she began to cry. Never in her whole life had she felt so alone. She couldn't even go back to her cave. If Forrell were alive, he'd save himself from the slugs by telling them where she lived, and offering her up as the one who'd saved Marcos.

All her medicines, including her birth control tablets, were there. If any steam tunnels still existed, the buildings over them would soon collapse and make them uninhabitable. No family would take her in, since everyone was fighting for their own lives and the lives of their children and kin. She was sure the mines were guarded. Slugs would have killed every human near them when the fighting broke out, even Forrell's guards. There'd be little or no food left after the stores were burned. When the cold worsened, people would fight each other to survive.

She looked to the horizon. There simply wasn't any choice but to go back to the cave and take her chances. If it was empty, she could salvage what she could and move to some other location. There'd be another cave in the barrens, though previous explorations in the hillsides had proven them to be fairly unsafe. But then what? What would life offer after that? When would help come?

As the monumental task of surviving one of the worst tragedies overwhelmed her, Nova put her face in her hands and wept even harder. What was the use in surviving without hope? If Marcos and even her pet were gone, there was nothing left for which to live. Even if a fleet of enforcers arrived tomorrow, what motivation would there be to get up each morning?

She swiped at her tears and shook her head. Self-pity wouldn't help. "I *won't* give up. I haven't yet; I won't now."

. . .

As the night went on, Marcos encountered no one still living. Not even slugs.

He put Una on the ground and encouraged her to find her mistress. It seemed the little animal understood. She put her attention on furiously scrambling from one side of the street to the other. Though her head was almost indistinguishable from the rest of her fuzzy little body, she appeared to be sniffing the ground.

Finally, a hazy dawn crept over the horizon. Exposed as he was, he had weapons now and could defend himself. All he had to do was find Nova and get her back to the cave. If Forrell was still there alone and hadn't contacted any of his thugs, the place might be safe. The governor wouldn't have been able to contact anyone, since he had no communication devices. Cowardice being his mainstay, he'd have likely heeded the warning to remain there and keep quiet.

But if even Una's intense searches revealed nothing of her beloved mistress, what would he do then?

He finally shook his head and screamed out her name, loud and long. Fear she'd never answer made him act in a way contrary to all instinct. He remained in the hazy light and kept yelling, even when he knew he should hide somewhere until darkness and keep quiet.

Either he was going insane, or a very familiar voice responded— one he hadn't expected.

"Marcos! I hear you. Where are you?"

Marcos took a deep, gasping breath as black enforcer uniforms appeared at the end of the street. Through the smoke and limited light, he'd have recognized them anywhere. On hearing his cries and recognizing his voice, a dozen uniformed officers ran toward him from the direction of the decimated marketplace.

Darius had won. His brother and his crew had to have made it through whatever battle took place in orbit, or there'd be no uniforms on the ground.

As hope renewed every cell in his body, he ran toward them. One towered above the rest and pushed himself forward. He recognized the hue of green eyes so very like his own.

Barely daring to believe the vision, he stopped just a few feet from his older brother and stood there panting.

"By the love of all that's h-holy … is that y-you, Marcos? What's happened to you?" Darius asked as his voice broke.

Marcos's burned appearance shocked the personnel standing before him. From the looks on their faces, he knew he must be barely recognizable. They'd all rightly assume he'd been a victim of fire plasma, but that didn't matter now. He took a shaky step forward, then wrapped his arms around Darius's shoulders and hugged him hard. It was over. The nightmare was over.

Darius held him a long silent moment, then gently pushed him away. His stare was poignant and horrified. "Who did this to you, little brother? You tell me who was responsible," he whispered.

Marcos shook his head in denial, and swallowed hard to speak. "Later. I have to find someone. She saved my life. We were separated when slugs scorched the town."

"We'll find anyone you want, but you're going back to the *Titan* right now. You need to have a med-tech check you out."

"I can't. I have to find her. Please … Darius … help me look." He glanced at the other enforcers. "I'll need everyone." The pure desperation in his voice couldn't be mistaken. He'd never spoken to anyone with such anxious appeal.

"All right," Darius said. "We'll help you. We need to search for survivors anyhow." He turned to his crewmembers and gave orders. "Keep your communicators clear. Spread out in case of Limaxian brawlers. Though their fleet is burning, any who escaped in life pods may have made it safely to the ground. They'll still attack Locals may not care who we are at this point; they're frantic to survive and protect their families. Don't assume anyone is safe."

"Their fleet is burning?" Marcos asked.

"Most of it. The rest surrendered after reports filtered from their negotiators. Seems some monstrous creature is wandering the streets. It attacked and killed their leader. Those slugs who survived and witnessed that event said the animal is a murderous carnivore; they begged their own fleet officers for surrender just so they could get off the surface."

Marcos pinched the bridge of his nose between his thumb and index finger. Then he began to laugh uncontrollably and sank to the ground against a nearby wall. The sound of it was a bit hysterical, even to his own ears. Darius put one arm around his shoulders and offered comforting words, obviously thinking him half mad.

"Marcos … you need to get to the *Titan*. I'll have my crew continue looking for whomever you want to find. But it's obvious you're not well. No wonder we couldn't find your transponder signal. If the rest of your body is as badly burned as your face and neck, your tracking device was probably incinerated by the heat of the plasma."

The device his brother spoke of had been embedded in his breast muscle. It had, indeed, been burned. The remains had fallen from his chest as the flesh had. He'd never told Nova about it, because he hadn't wanted her to know who he was.

Marcos put one hand on Darius's shoulder and tried to allay his brother's angst. "Una! Come here, girl."

The fuzzy little figure that'd been frantically digging through debris in search of her mistress, acknowledged. She came bouncing toward him, making whimpering pup-like sounds that in no way made her appear as the horrific carnivore Prometheus's surviving ground crew described.

"The reason I'm laughing is *this*!" he said as he held Una up for the enforcers to view. "This terrifyingly grotesque monster is what killed Prometheus."

Darius frowned. Then he shook his head in apparent disbelief. "That's it … you're going back to the *Titan* right now. You're not mentally any better than you look." He grabbed Marcos's arm and pulled him up, but Marcos gently disengaged himself.

"I'll explain as we search. *Please*, Darius … I have to find her. I can also tell you where Adaman Forrell is hiding. He needs to be taken into custody. Just keep searching with me, and I'll tell you everything, in excruciating detail. But we have to keep looking. It's getting colder as we speak. Survivors might not last long."

Darius nodded. "All right. But you don't get more than three feet from me. Understand?"

At one time Marcos would have resented the childish warning. But the horror over his burns was still reflected in the crew's expressions. They probably thought he was about to die, right there in the street. Without wasting more time, he cuddled Una close and led the way.

Their search led them back through the streets, toward Forrell's residence.

As the enforcers dug through rubble, finding only bodies, it became clear that anyone who had survived had run into the hillsides and away from any standing buildings.

They were about to move to another street when Una jumped from Marcos's arms and ran to the demolished entrance of the governor's residence. Limaxian remains were strewn about the foyer, as indicated by slug body parts that didn't remotely resemble any humanoid colonists. Persistently, Una circled the charred body parts and growled. Suddenly she stopped, lifted her head, and ran excitedly into the smoldering, upright support frames that were still falling.

Marcos ran after her, even as Darius shouted for him not to.

Una's sharp barking alerted him to a pile of boulders and steel that was strewn where the foyer would have been. He knelt beside Una. She dug furiously at a pile of hot debris, even though her little paws were being burned. He pulled her against him to keep her from further harming herself. But even as he picked her up, she grabbed at something with her mouth.

Up from the ash came one garment: a very small, tattered brown glove.

He'd have recognized it as he'd have known his own uniform gauntlet from dozens of others.

Everything faded around him. He heard Una whimpering loudly as she nuzzled the glove. If there was any uncertainty about who'd owned it, the pup removed all doubt.

"I shouldn't have left her," he bitterly whispered. "I shouldn't have left … "

"You've had enough," Darius gently told him as he stepped around spot fires, put his arms around his sibling, and led Marcos out of the building.

Marcos didn't resist his brother's help this time.

And when they were standing outside the debris and on the street again, Una jumped from Marcos's arms, stood in front of them, and faced the building. Her sudden movement surprised everyone into stillness, as did the low, soulful howl she emitted. The pup stared into the remains of the building as she howled a heart-wrenchingly sad tone not even the hardest heart could misunderstand. She was mourning someone she'd lost.

"Let's get you to the *Titan*," Darius softly urged.

• • •

As med-techs hovered around him making comments and completing tests, Marcos woodenly listened to Darius's debriefing regarding the immediate future of Delta Seven and its inhabitants. He tried to say something that'd sound intelligent; anything that would make it appear as though he was listening. But his heart hurt too badly.

How could she have come so close to rescue only to die in the last hours? After all her efforts to survive, he'd gotten her killed. Her death was his fault. He'd promised to get her to freedom. He should never have left her side. She'd wanted to come with him; he hadn't let her.

He'd barely managed to describe the cave location so that Forrell could be arrested. The words came, though he didn't know how. Duty made him respond even as pain demanded his silence.

"Marcos … I have to get a lot of Limaxians in stasis cells where they'll do no harm on the journey home. What's left of their ships will have to be destroyed." Darius moved closer and spoke more softly. "You've done your job. You've been through far more than duty demanded. I just thank the Creator that I had a bad feeling about this mission and came after you sooner than we'd planned." He paused for a long moment before adding. "Whoever this woman was … we'll talk later," he finished as he patted his brother on the shoulder. "Stay here in my quarters for now."

A few med-techs, summoned to check his immediate status, drifted away. They muttered something about putting him in an incubation unit so his body's own, enhanced immune system could put him back to normal. What did any of that matter?

Eventually, he put Una on the floor and simply stood there. He couldn't decide what to do or where to make his body move. Eventually, the need to relieve himself made him shuffle toward Darius's bathroom.

He passed his hand over the computer relay, and the lights went on. There, for the first time, he saw his image very clearly. A large mirror stretched from the deck to the overhead, making his entire form quite viewable.

There'd been nothing more than reflective surfaces of old pots and pans in the cave. Now, he saw why others on the ship had gasped in repulsion. The disfigurement was terrible. Assuming he'd heard them correctly, the med-techs kept saying he'd heal. But would he?

He slowly put a hand to the mirror and leaned forward. "That's not me," he softly murmured. "I'm not in there anymore. That man burned away. That shallow, self-centered bastard doesn't exist. And the one who should have survived … the truly pure soul who should have lived … she's … she's …" His words trailed away.

He stood there because of Nova.

As he slowly undressed and saw the rest of the damage done to his body, he couldn't believe she'd ever let him touch her. He was monstrous. Some of the damage wasn't healed as well as he'd thought. He just couldn't feel it anymore.

Nova's love was for the man inside; the one he'd become and not the narcissistic lover women lusted after.

What he'd shared with a little thief was born in the soul. What they'd had would never die. Every soft word spoken in the night, and every touch, was so close and always would be. She was everything good and wonderful, everything no other woman would ever come close to matching.

Then he stopped and stared into the mirror again.

"I can still feel her. She's still with me," he whispered. Then anger overtook self-pity. "What, by all the gods in the universe, is wrong with me? She never gave up. When I lay there dying, she helped me. She knew how to survive. She knew better than I did! Even Una could be wrong."

With a newfound sense of strength, Marcos stepped into the shower and turned the water on. He cleaned his body even as his mind worked on a plan. And when little Una barked at him from outside the small shower stall, he almost joyously picked her up and soaped her as well.

"We're getting you something to eat. Then we're going after Nova. You hear me, girl? We're going back and we're going to find her. She's not dead. I was a fool for even thinking such a thing."

An hour later, Marcos donned one of Darius's uniforms and made his way to the galley. Una needed food and water, but he wouldn't partake of anything until Nova was safe. He refused everything offered and ignored orders from the med-tech to report to sickbay and an incubation unit. The crew would have to put up with how he looked for a while longer.

• • •

"Why aren't you resting in my quarters? And is that my uniform?" Darius demanded as he stared at Marcos.

"She's not dead. I'm going after her. And in case you're interested, her name is Nova. And yes, it's your uniform," Marcos blathered as he checked the powerful side arm he'd requisitioned from the armory.

"You say this little thing killed Prometheus?" Darius asked as he pointed at Una.

"Yes. Now ... I'm leaving *Titan*, with or without your permission."

"Marcos, if this girl is alive, don't you think she'd have seen our people out on patrol? They've been assessing the situation and doing a street-by-street search since the slugs surrendered. Surely she'd have made an appearance by now."

"It depends on where she is. But one way or the other ... I'm finding her," he insisted.

"Who is she to you? I know you said she saved your life but—"

"She's my future wife," he blurted.

"Your *what*?"

"Help me, Darius. If it were Laurel, you'd do anything in your power to find her. And I'd go with you."

"You're right," Darius acknowledged with a vehement nod. "I'll leave my bridge crew in command and get a wrist communicator. We'll sync communications in case we get separated."

When Darius quickly returned with two communication devices, he handed one to Marcos and snapped his on his wrist. "You'll be interested to know that one of our patrols just picked up Adaman Forrell. He was hiding in that cave, just where you told us he'd be."

"And there was no one with him?"

"Did you think she'd be there?" Darius asked.

"I-I don't know where she'd go. That was the place she called home for over two years. I only took that bastard there because it was the last safe place. I want him on Luster to get what's coming to him. You know all the rest; I've already told you," he finished with barely controlled impatience.

Darius put both hands on his brother's shoulders and gripped them hard. "We'll find your Nova. I promise. But the search will go faster if we use a transport. I'm having mine offloaded now."

Chapter 13

"Poor child. I ran here with my granddaughter to evade the slug's wrath. Seems you and I had similar thoughts about safe hiding places."

Nova slowly opened her eyes. Smells from the pit reminded her where she was. But some gentle soul wrapped a warm blanket around her as he kindly spoke.

As her vision cleared, the face of an elderly man floated before her. He was heavily cloaked, and a smaller figure hovered nearby.

"Don't worry, healer. I know who you are. I knew your father and mother. Don't you recognize me?" the man asked. "My name is Cornelius Pratt. And this is my granddaughter, Zia."

"Y-You're the man in the marketplace. The one w-who warned us. You gave Marcos the sword."

"Ah … you do remember." He put a hand on her shoulder. "Stay quiet now. We'll help you get warm."

She shivered despite the addition of the blanket. Her hands refused to move, and they'd taken on a strange, bluish hue. Frostbite could cause her to lose them. This man's help might save her life.

"Try to stay awake, healer. Uh … forgive me, but I forgot the name of Bellos and Risa Drayton's child. There've been so many children lost or hurt," Cornelius sadly said.

"N-Nova."

"Ah, yes … Nova. Well … I'll try to find help. I'll be back as soon as possible."

"No. The slugs—"

Cornelius glanced over his shoulder. "There hasn't been blasting for a while. And you need to get to a warm place. The temperatures will go much lower." He moved closer and tucked the blanket around her body more tightly.

Nova glanced at the young girl behind him. She frantically kept her eyes on the horizon, watching for any enemy. "Thank you for what you've done. But you have a granddaughter to help. You need to leave me, Cornelius."

"And what would that teach my granddaughter? Without compassion for others, you see where our population has sunk." He shook his head in denial. "It's time to fight back, just as Prince Marcos fought for me. Enforcers will help us. The ship I saw earlier today is a sign of rescue."

"E-Enforcers?"

"Yes. Zia and I were huddled beside some boulders here at the pits, the same as you. And when I heard an engine approach, I peeked up and saw an enforcer transport fly by. I couldn't get out of my hiding place in time to summon it, but if I can find some enforcers on the ground, I'll have you out of here in no time. I'll bet they even have an incubation unit that will fix you right up."

"M-maybe," she uttered, but not with much conviction. It was hard to believe help might be so close, especially when she was so very cold and after so much had happened.

"Now, stay put. I'll be back soon. Zia will look after you until I return."

Nova tried to smile but was too numb. "Whatever happens, I thank you for your kindness."

Cornelius nodded, and made his way up the side of the pit to the top.

Nova fearfully watched him go. She glanced at Zia, and the girl sat down beside her to share what little body heat she could.

"Your grandfather is a very brave man."

Zia nodded and looked to where he was just climbing over the edge of the pit. "When we saw you here, hiding so close to us, we knew we had to help. It was your man who saved our lives. If he hadn't stood up to the slug leader, we'd have died."

"Creator above! Marcos will think I'm dead! H-he might not have made it—"

"Not to worry, milady. All this will be over soon enough. Think bad thoughts no longer. We will be free," she excitedly said as she wrapped her arms around Nova's body.

• • •

For a full hour, Marcos searched. He called out Nova's name and had Darius stop his transport several times to let Una get to the ground and see what she could find. But there was simply no sign of his little thief anywhere. At the sound of a man crying out to them, they both turned.

"I wonder what he wants?" Darius mused as he saw a man running from one end of a destroyed city street.

Then Marcos recognized the stranger.

"Prince Marcos … you must help me. I am Cornelius Pratt. You remember me, I'm sure. I've found the healer … Nova. But she's in a very bad way. You must come," he called out to them.

From the depths of despair to the height of exaltation, Marcos's soul soared. The Creator of all things had answered his silent prayers, and he could barely contain his glee. His entire body shook with happiness. Though he registered the words implying Nova was hurt, she was still alive. For that brief moment, no words would come that could do the moment justice. He simply put his hand on his chest as if doing so could stop his heart from pounding so very hard.

"Do you know that man?" Darius asked.

Marcos blinked, took a deep breath and nodded. He forced himself to speak, though relief made it difficult. "He tried to help Nova and me before. I'll tell you about all that later." He pushed his older brother aside, grabbed the controls, and sent the transport racing to the other end of the street where the old man was slowly running toward them.

Cornelius stopped, and took a moment to catch his breath. "She's in the incineration pit. I'll show you."

"We were there earlier and saw nothing," Marcos replied.

"We've been there all night. Please … you must come!"

Marcos leapt from the surface of the transport, helped the man up to stand next to his brother, then got back on himself. "Show me where Nova is."

"Right away, Highness."

Marcos turned the transport back in the direction of the incineration pit and pushed the transport to its maximum speed. While the elderly man introduced himself to Darius, Marcos sped faster and faster away from the main part of the marketplace. And when he spotted two figures huddled together under a rock, he didn't even wait for the transport to come to a safe stop before jumping off and making his way to Nova.

He knelt beside the girl who was trying to keep Nova warm.

"She's very, very cold," Zia told him. "She was here all night without a cloak or anyone to warm her."

"Thank you for staying by her." Marcos smiled at the girl. "I'll take over now. You and your grandfather will be safe."

The girl smiled, moved aside, and let Marcos into the narrow crevice formed by two huge boulders.

"Nova? I'm here, love. Can you hear me?"

"M-Marcos?"

"I think she's getting worse by the minute, Highness. We should get her to someplace warm as quickly as possible," Cornelius warned.

Marcos noted the discoloration on Nova's small hands and quickly pulled her to him. As he lifted her up and let Darius maneuver the transport closer, Cornelius helped him put Nova on the platform. Then he and his daughter joined them.

In seconds, they were headed at breakneck speed back to the *Titan* and its physicians. But all the way there, he held Nova close and kept talking to her. She looked up at him with eyes that were too fixed, and it frightened him. An incubation unit could heal many things, but it couldn't bring the dead back. Still, he refused to think that even the hour they'd wasted bypassing her would make a difference. She had to live. She must.

• • •

The physicians told him she would recover. They were in the last stages of readying Nova for deep stasis in an incubation unit. While the injuries from the cold would heal more easily, the scars required a great deal more treatment than an overnight stay in the unit. It was designed to augment the body's immune system by boosting internal structures. And there were many things the unit couldn't heal if the patient had been too long from treatment. But the scars she bore were of no interest. He just wanted Nova to be safe and healthy.

He sensed a presence behind him as he stood and looked down into the incubation unit. The box-shaped apparatus was moments away from being activated, and he didn't want to take his attention away from Nova. Her clothing had been removed to effect maximum exposure to the unit's boosters, but a blue sheet was draped modestly over her body to cover her.

Darius put one hand on his brother's shoulder. "Marcos, the physician said he found a small knife and a laser weapon on Nova."

"I gave her the laser," he softly replied. "The knife probably came from the cave where we lived. She only had one." He stared down at her, hoping she'd awaken before the unit was activated.

"What was she going to do with a small paring blade?"

"Knowing her, she probably intended to use it on herself before letting the slugs get her."

"Your future wife is a brave woman, then."

"Yes, she is. Tell the physicians to spare no amount of power."

"They won't," Darius responded in a comforting tone. "And now you have to get into a chamber of your own. I'm sorry we don't have the newer models, or I'd have put you in with Nova. We traded the double units in lieu of smaller, single chambers that could more easily be located throughout the ship. We assumed there might be an overflow of patients for the med bay. Space there, after these kinds of situations, always comes at a premium as you well know."

Marcos nodded in understanding. "As long as she's all right."

"Come with me, little brother. Let's get you healed and back home."

Marcos took a deep breath and left Nova to be tended by med-techs already taking her vital signs. As he slowly walked away, a surreal sense of time hit him hard.

Was it really over? Was Nova really safe? Had they actually made it through the occupation of an allied planet, or was he dreaming?

"Before they put you in the incu-unit," Darius said as he applied the nickname many enforcers used for the healing chamber, "you should know that Adaman Forrell surrendered. And he won't get away with what he's done, Marcos. I'll see to that, even if you're still being healed and can't speak at his trial. In reality, we shouldn't need your testimony now. There're more than enough survivors willing to speak up. *Finally*. The population of Delta Seven is no longer held hostage."

"The situation was … it was … *bad*, Darius."

Darius put his hand on his brother's shoulder. "Don't talk about it anymore. Just heal and rest. I'll speak with you again when we get home."

"You think it'll take that long for me to recover?" Marcos asked.

"The med-techs do. But however long you're under, if Nova comes out first, I'll see her taken into the castle. She'll have your rooms and all the respect due a future family member. Laurel will help her."

"Good. And you'll see to Una? She's more than just a pet. She … she saved my life as much as her mistress did."

Darius smiled. "Whatever that little thing is, it's in my quarters, snuggled into my personal blankets. Don't worry. Everything will be fine. You just get in *this* and heal," he gently reiterated as they approached the incu-unit meant to house his younger brother.

Marcos gazed down into the incu-unit being readied for him. Before he got in and went into a deep, healing slumber that could well last months, he wanted to say a few things to his sibling. "Just so you know, Darius, I'm not the self-centered, womanizing twit who left Luster with delusions of grandeur. And … I think I want a quieter life. This has all been … it's … if not for you, I'd be dead. I know that. I just want you to know how much I … how very much you and the rest of the family means … I wanted so badly to get home … " His words drifted away. Tears blocked his vision and a lump formed in his throat.

Darius simply pulled Marcos into his embrace and whispered to him. "You don't have to say another word. I've had your back since you were born. And you'd have done the same for me. We're family. Now get inside the unit, and don't worry about one more thing. I'll take it from here, little brother. You did your job."

Marcos nodded as tears fell down his cheeks. Darius hugged him hard once more.

With his brother standing near him, Marcos finally got into the incubation unit and stared up at his sibling until the zerion mist in the silver, coffin-like box began to work. His last coherent thought was for Nova.

"Tell her I love her. Tell her for me every day."

"I will, Marcos. J-just get well. I l-love you," Darius stammered. "Love you too."

...

Ten months later

Nova sat in the semi-darkness of Marcos's bedroom. Stretched out on the bed in front of her was the man everyone waited for.

After being in a stasis situation for so long, even the med-techs who'd removed him and who'd let his family bring him home weren't sure exactly when he'd awaken. But they urged everyone to let him do so in his own time, outside the strictures of technology. He was healed now, but residual effects of the extraordinarily long incubation period were still at work. It'd taken time to see his scars diminish. No physician had ever treated a man burned so badly; at least none who survived. But the process was finally over, and he'd awaken sometime soon.

There were a thousand things to tell him. First and foremost, she'd missed him. He needed to know how loved he was. His family had taken her in as one of their own, just as he'd said they would. And every day, she received a message from some unknown source on her wrist communicator. It was just three words.

Marcos loves you!

She suspected Darius was behind the missives, but he simply smiled and said the words came from his brother. The delivery of such a note was one of the sweetest things she'd ever experienced in her life. Someone, whether it was the older brother or not, thought enough of Marcos to make sure his last words were ever in her memory.

Other sweet things kept her company while awaiting Marcos's return to consciousness.

The beauteous plants and animals of Luster—the very same ones he'd described back in that little cave—were breathtaking. The colors on her new home world had almost overwhelmed her senses when she'd taken her first look out a window. So amazed was she at the floral scents, the cool breezes, and the lush growth, she'd wept for almost an hour. Brilliant flowers of red, purple, orange, yellow, fuchsia, and every other hue imaginable were ever present on the hillsides near Marcos's family estate. Birds of all shapes, sizes, and colors flitted outside the windows as if they knew they'd not be harmed. And as she stayed by Marcos's side, his family visited en masse. They always made sure fresh floral arrangements were delivered to his quarters—now hers to share—and that a view of the Starlaw palatial gardens was very near, especially on days she couldn't bring herself to leave her lover's side.

Nova also had her fill of any food or drink she could possibly desire. Lovely clothing had been sent by Marcos's mother and sisters, all for her new wardrobe. Life was exactly opposite of what she'd known it to be. And she loved every moment of it. All that'd make living perfect was Marcos's reawakening from his healing slumber.

But there were other parts of life not so sweet.

Adaman Forrell had stood trial, had been found guilty, and had been sentenced to the icy prison planet of Denophri for the rest of his life. Defense attorneys had kept the courts busy for many of the months Marcos was unconscious. They'd argued their client was a victim of circumstance and that League enforcers, led by Darius Starlaw, had landed illegally. They'd used a myriad of technicalities in an attempt to get their client free. She'd stood witness as soon as her own three-month healing process in the incu-unit was done.

When Prometheus's body was found and rumors persisted concerning a strange beast tearing Limaxians apart on Delta Seven, Darius Starlaw, his crew, and family let the gossip flow where it would. Since no such attack had ever occurred before or since, the king himself advised letting the chatter wind its way down, without saying anything. The matter was deemed a rumor at best, hysteria at worst. Most people now thought Prometheus's own brawlers had turned on him when they realized they were doomed.

Then there was Una's new, delightful situation thereafter.

Marcos's mother, the queen, took it upon herself to contact zoologists. Though baffled by Una's species, they still managed to find three more of her kind living on an outlying moon of Uraxis. The queen brought the entire lot back to Luster since scientists hadn't found them any threat to Luster's environment.

Now, four of whatever Una was—all acting as though they were pups even though their ages were indeterminate—guarded the family's nursery with great love and fervor. They played with Marcos's nieces and nephews on the lawn each summer afternoon. Even the highly proficient and professional household High Guard laughed at their antics, with the result that Una was never alone. She flourished in the company of others of her kind, the adoration of adults and children, and with the grateful heart of her devoted mistress. The Starlaw clan had, for the want of a better name, dubbed the species *Novans*. The happy coincidence wasn't lost on *her*.

As with Forrell, those Limaxians who'd committed the attack on Delta Seven and the League ship Titan were firmly entrenched in prisons on Denophri. For her part, Nova vowed not to mourn if Forrell was ever found dead in his cell. Limaxians had long memories, short tempers, and ways to get around prison systems. The matter was out of her hands and the control of other surviving Delta Seven citizens. Forrell could do what he'd always done and fend for himself.

With the denizens of her world set free, the booty from the mines was now theirs to divide amongst themselves. And there was plenty to go around.

Nova had been receiving her allotment for months; it had been enough to buy the cottage of her dreams, start the herb garden Marcos had spoken about, and even invest in a highly successful natural herbal emporium in the heart of Luster's capitol city—Crystol. Her investments had done so well that she now employed several refugees who, like her, never wanted to see that dim mining colony of Delta Seven again.

If being an entrepreneur with a tidy bank account was something she'd once spurned, the freedom to hire others, donate to charities of her choice, and provide for herself for the rest of her life—and without asking anyone else's by-your-leave—quickly changed her mind. There were always two sides to an issue. In her cave, being hunted like an animal, she'd only been able to accept one viewpoint and none other. Things and minds changed. Her heart and perspective did as well.

She also understood the politics of Marcos's father and the Constellation League a great deal better. If there were remnants of anger left in her heart—from having spent two years living from hand-to-mouth in a cave and from seeing her parents, friends, and beau die—that pain also fled. The fault for those actions lay with those who were either dead or permanently incarcerated, not with the enforcers who had to walk so many political fine lines as to constantly be judged from all sides.

Since her staunch new friends, Cornelius Pratt and his granddaughter Zia, were now living quite close to the Starlaw family castle, she regarded the ins and outs of diplomatic difficulties in a whole new light.

Cornelius, with a firm handle on what'd happened on the mining colony, had recently been appointed as the first ambassador from Delta Seven. As such, he maintained constant contact with

Delta Seven and Luster's other ambassadorial partners. Indeed, Cornelius and Zia were frequent guests at the Starlaw castle and, like Marcos's family, they eagerly awaited the return to society of the badly injured second son of the royal family.

It was Cornelius's constant tutelage of protocol and consular tact that better educated Nova on just how difficult diplomacy could be. In fact, diplomacy had been made more arduous by Forrell's lying and stealing from his own people. Even now, she considered a very heartfelt offer to become one of Ambassador Pratt's liaison officers to Luster. After devoting time with her newly healed lover—whenever he eventually woke—she fully intended to accept the position.

In her heart she knew she'd wronged the Starlaw family by assuming they'd not wanted to help. Her shame mounted once she'd met them and understood the depths of empathy offered to her people as well as others. But she had no better evidence of their selflessness than that which resided in their son, Marcos.

In regards to setting things right, a position as an ambassadorial liaison might be a way of making amends for her attitude with Marcos. After all, as her mother had always taught her, it was wrong to criticize others for something you were unwilling to do yourself.

But first she wanted time alone with her beloved.

She'd missed him sorely but so had so many others. She'd have to learn to share him. They weren't in that small cave any longer, and those who needed to reconnect with him must have their chance. But she vowed the nights would be theirs and theirs alone.

If Marcos wanted to continue his career in enforcement, she'd accept it. He'd been in a position as a covert officer when she'd met him. How could she fear the occupation he loved when doing his duty had saved her and her world?

All matters could be sorted. There was only one thing to wait for, and that was Marcos's return to consciousness.

It was late one Lusterian summer night, but she'd stayed by Marcos's side as much as possible. She had been with him even more since he'd been brought home and put in his own bed by loving family members.

Occasionally, he'd move a hand or turn his head slightly. With his body healed of all scars and his immune system enhanced to do so, there should be few side effects from the incubation unit. She was told he'd be groggy, and his senses would need time to adjust. But this was minor in comparison to almost having lost him.

She sat on the side of his huge bed and pushed his long black hair back while thinking of all she'd have to tell him. There were all the plans they meant to enact. But would he even recognize her? She hadn't recognized herself when she'd first seen her reflection in a mirror.

One of the more lauded effects of the incubation-unit technology was that his hair *and* hers had all grown back with luxurious textures. In his case, Marcos also sported a very long beard when taken from the incu-unit. Previously, he'd not been able to grow even minimal facial hair through the scar tissue produced on Delta Seven. Since normal bodily functions were restored, the king and Darius had actually shaved off Marcos's beard and still shaved him each morning. Her job, as she saw it, was to sit with him each night so the rest of the Starlaw clan could get some sleep.

But Nova knew the score. If Marcos so much as looked like he might be coming around, and she didn't awaken everyone in the castle no matter what hour of the night or day, she'd catch every kind of hell for it. But that was a price she'd gladly pay for being part of a big family. There was always plenty of love to share.

Secretly, she hoped he'd awaken during one of her watches, so they could share just a few words alone. To that end, she always wore her prettiest dressing gowns and left her waist-length golden tresses flowing freely. She intended, as any girl with her lover would, to look her best when he saw her.

The evening grew darker and lovely; warm breezes filtered in through the balcony windows. Fresh scents from the castle gardens filled the room. She never tired of the smells or colors produced by the beautiful fauna. It was like living in a wonderland. She stood and wandered closer to the balcony, taking in the starlight and the ethereal beauty of the gardens far below.

She understood why Marcos had used the ancient name of Avalon when referring to Luster. He'd been trying to promise her what his heart wished to give, without causing pain over his heritage. Yes, she understood a lot of things these days. Mostly, she knew she'd never ever want another soul the way she wanted him. He'd saved her in every way imaginable. She was his and always would be.

• • •

Marcos felt the soft warmth of clean bedding around his body. Someone was with him. He sensed the presence and knew he wasn't alone. *This* time, he had to awaken. Whatever had kept him from reaching consciousness before wasn't going to stop him now.

Bits and pieces of conversations, held in low tones, meandered in and out of memory. Was he still in that cave on Delta Seven or somewhere else? Had he died and gone to the reward he believed all just and decent souls received? But if he was dead, then what gentle soul accompanied him? He felt that soul as one feels hope. It was something he couldn't see, but it was still there.

Finally, he mustered all his inner strength and opened his eyes. Semi-darkness surrounded him, but as he rested there, it seemed that starlight filtered through the room.

My room!

He was back home. Or he was dead and dreaming he was home.

He knew every curve of the arched, white marble of the roof over his bed. The walls were made of the same, sparkling substance.

Dark green curtains, ever the color of the Starlaw men, billowed into the room along with warm breezes.

There was someone standing in the starlight. The silhouette was sylph-like, dainty and so wonderfully beautiful. Long, golden strands of loose curls shimmered in the otherworldly light. They shifted up and down with each new draft of air.

If he'd been accompanied by some waif-like angel into the next life, nothing could have been lovelier.

In slow motion, she turned.

He heard his name called softly, but the syllables also rang in his head as coming out too slowly. His sylph bolted toward him. And when her hair lifted, he saw the pointed tips of her ears and truly knew he'd been blessed with a companion of fae legend.

As she came closer, his eyesight adjusted. The face of his sweet vision was familiar. Her eyes were the most luscious shade of amethyst, he'd ever seen. She wore a dressing gown of pale lavender. Even in the dim light, the colors were astonishing. The most intricate details would forever haunt his memory, like the bejeweled belt cinching her ridiculously small waist, and the lovely, graceful hands reaching for him.

He felt her warmth as she touched him and smiled so brilliantly that all the suns in the universe going nova at once couldn't reproduce the brightness.

Nova!

Of course. He knew her. He loved her. But the scars were missing. She'd either died with him, and they'd been healed and joined in the afterlife, or the miracle of being home again, *with her*, was real.

He felt her wrap her arms around his shoulders. Her tear-filled voice was soft but imbued with joy. She kept speaking to him over and over. As she did, syllables turned to words. And words ran into sentences he eventually understood. Then he remembered Darius rescuing them.

Floodgates opened as memory suddenly returned.

He tried to push himself off the bed to hold her, but she pressed him back and softly begged him to rest.

It took everything he had to open his mouth and get out a sound. When he did, it was hoarse and made no sense.

She gently helped him into a position to enjoy cool, clean water from a green glass tumbler. One sip wasn't enough. He drank more and more.

With dryness of tongue assuaged, he croaked out what he most wanted to say.

"I … l-love … y-you."

She pushed his long hair back off his shoulders, kissed him hard, and then held him again.

Dead or alive. Let this go on. Let it go on forever.

• • •

Many weeks later, Marcos stood on the balcony of his new residence. With training and hard work, his strength had returned and so had his physique. Instead of sharing it with women who cared little for the soul within the shell, however, he now shared his intense arousal with only one. Nova was all he needed.

The Autumnal Repast, to celebrate the changing of the seasons and the bounty produced from the summer, would soon begin. The love of his life was dressing in the next suite, but he decided they had plenty of time to travel to the castle and join beloved family and friends.

The decision to make love to her all over again was cemented when she walked toward him wearing a sparkling, halter-top gown of gold. Her soft, golden hair was piled on top of her head, leaving the pointed tips of her ears exposed. Her pert breasts were pushed high; the creamy skin above them was perfect. She smelled of flowers and fresh air. His lover looked like some kind of moon goddess.

He dropped his uniform gauntlets and pulled her into his embrace.

"We'll be late … *again*," she softly teased.

"I'll make excuses," he said as he began kissing her shoulder, then her neck.

"What will the king say when one of the princes doesn't show up on time?" she saucily asked as she helped him unbutton his dress uniform tunic.

"If he and mother want grandchildren from us, they'll have to get used to it."

She smiled coyly. "If we have a little time, will you do that thing you did the other night?"

He nuzzled his nose against hers. "Are you speaking of what we did in the large bathing tub? Is that the thing you're talking about, love?"

She slowly nodded.

"If we go that far, we won't get to the party at all. You know that, don't you?" he hopefully asked.

"My … that's too bad. What a shame. Stuff happens. I guess *I'll* have to make the excuses," Nova jokingly murmured as she walked backward toward the bathing area, pulling him with her.

The new love in his life was giving him ideas that'd last until late the next morning. But with a full life before them, and all traces of sadness and pain gone, there'd be plenty of time for enforcer parties, ambassadorial soirees, and formal dedications.

Tonight was theirs. And he wasn't wasting one more second of time. Let it not ever be said that a prince of Luster kept his lady waiting.

About the Author

Candace Sams (aka C.S. Chatterly) graduated from Texas A&M University with a BS in Agriculture, worked as a police officer with the State of Texas, did a brief stint with the Texas Department of Public Safety Undercover Narcotics Task force, and was also with the San Diego Police Department. She taught for the San Diego County Sheriff's Department and worked in law enforcement in Alabama.

She currently trains as the senior woman on the US Kung Fu Team (working on her fourth black belt), and has been awarded the Medal of Putien from China and the Statue of Tao for her work in martial arts. She is the holder of several international martial arts titles. In 2000, she was one of a fifteen-member team—authorized by act of Senate—to represent this country as a martial arts ambassador to mainland China. Her experiences in law enforcement and martial arts (Shaolin Kung Fu) are frequently used in her career as an author—she is known for writing fight scenes into her fictional works. As an added note, Ms. Sams is also a Master Gardener and loves working outdoors.

After publishing more than sixty titles in the fantasy, science fiction, paranormal, and action-adventure genres, she's received more than thirty awards from various organizations, including five National Readers' Choice Awards and a *USA Today* Best Book nomination. Her *Tales of The Order*™ series, as well as several other works, are now being vetted for movie options.

Hailing from Texas, Candace loves the country life. She and her husband of more than twenty-five years live in a rural area of the US. A plethora of dogs and cats have adopted them. She loves to hear from readers and can be contacted through her website at *www.candacesams.com*. Candace also writes erotica as C.S. Chatterly and can be contacted from *www.cschatterly.com*.

More from This Author
(From *Starlaw* by Candace Sams)

"Christ … it's frickin' eerie out here," Cory Martinez whispered.

"And colder than it was supposed to be," Laurel Blake added.

Along with what was normally on their belts, such as side arms, flashlights, extra ammo, and handcuffs, they had special radio equipment that only allowed certain shift members—including the dispatch supervisor—to hear what was going on. Besides all that, she and Cory were dressed in navy-blue jumpsuits with matching PD jackets and baseball caps. They'd added black gloves and combat boots to easily move through the park undergrowth. At the moment, their radios were silent, indicating the undercover detective pretending to be asleep in a clearing was all right so far. He was posing as a homeless man in order catch someone who'd been murdering them and literally draining their blood for the past three weeks.

"So where's the bachelorette party?" Cory asked as he nudged her.

"Why the hell are you asking about that? Pay attention, butt-munch!"

Cory grinned and ignored the reprimand. "Come on. Maria won't tell me."

"That's because she doesn't want you to know."

"But you'll tell your partner, right?" Cory prompted as he nudged her several more times.

Laurel pressed her lips together to keep from smiling. "I might be your partner but I'm *her* best friend and the maid of honor. And she asked me to keep my big mouth shut. So chew on that and keep your mind on the job."

"That's not fair. You guys know where I'm having my bachelor party—"

"That's because there's not a single man at the station who could keep his lips zipped. I swear … when it comes to gossip male cops are worse than any woman I've ever known."

"Laurel—"

"No! Shut up and pay attention."

She saw his scowl even in the dim light filtering through the trees.

"She didn't hire those male strippers, did she? You know … the ones who jerk their junk while movin' around in skimpy costumes and letting women stuff twenties down their G-strings?"

She simply smiled back, deciding to let him sweat the answer.

"Oh man … that's not right!" he groused.

"What's not right? The overstuffed G-strings, or a lot of turned-on women having a good time while tossing back enough tequila to go toxic?" she teased.

He moved closer. "Did you say tequila? Maria gets crazy when she drinks tequila. She gets horny as hell and doesn't remember anything—"

"Okay … that's enough information," Laurel advised as she held up one hand to stop him. "You need to talk to her, not me. And we need to keep our mouths shut … *really*," she insisted as she pulled the collar of her jacket higher.

They sat in mutual silence for another fifteen minutes. Cory finally broke it again with more commiserations concerning his upcoming nuptials.

"I hate the invitations. They suck."

"Then why didn't you help her pick 'em out?"

"I did. Her mother overrode my opinion. She wanted red roses all over everything. I can't stand red roses."

Laurel finally turned to look at him. "What in hell did you choose?"

He grinned. "Daisies."

She pressed her lips together. "In all the years we've known each other … I've never thought of you as a daisy kind of guy."

"Everybody does roses. I read in *Weddings Today* magazine that it's the most used flower in the world where weddings are concerned. I wanted something bright. Something uncommon. Something yellow and 'camera friendly in darkened churches,' like the magazine says."

"Which is why your wedding colors are burgundy and black," she responded while shaking her head in mirth.

The idea of Cory perusing a wedding magazine was too much. But he was all about marrying the girl he'd loved since high school. In the end it wouldn't matter *how* he got Maria down the aisle as long as he got her there.

"My future mother-in-law took every opinion I had and tossed it right in the crapper, like my ideas don't matter." He snorted in derision then let out a few curses in Spanish. "She and I are gonna have a long talk after the wedding. There's not gonna be any of that shit where she tells us how to live our lives, what to name our kids, and how to decorate our house."

"Says the man who likes daisies."

"Excuse me … daisies symbolize love, patience, purity, and simplicity. They're perfect for weddings," he insisted.

A scrambled message over their earpieces made them both sit up at the same time.

"Did you make that out?" he asked as he gently tapped his earpiece.

"Say again," Laurel requested as she keyed the microphone hanging from her jacket epaulet.

There was no sound.

Cory made a second attempt. "210 Adam from 115 King . . say again … over."

"*For the love of God … help.*"

Laurel and Cory stared at each other when the clear but panic-stricken voice of one of their comrades sounded through their earpieces.

Without waiting one second longer, Laurel relayed their need for backup as she stood and ran to their comrade's aid.

As she bolted forward, she put her hand on her weapon and mentally plotted the shortest distance between their spot and the assigned location of the caller.

Cory pounded through the brush behind her. She knew he had her back as she picked up the pace.

Through her earpiece, she heard orders being issued from the nearest officers including the dispatch supervisor. It didn't matter if the perp heard them coming now. If a cop was in need, scaring away an attacker might save a life.

Tonight's assignment should have been simple.

Moments later they crashed through the undergrowth into a nearby clearing.

Laurel stopped in her tracks as she saw a tall figure straighten. He'd been bending over someone lying on the ground.

The light wasn't that good but she knew damned well the man in the dirt was one of *theirs*. The old, patched clothing was the same as what he'd been wearing when tonight's assignment had been issued.

She pulled her weapon at the same time Cory did. Despite the cold of the night and the breeze blowing through the trees, sweat broke out on her forehead.

"Police! Put your hands on your head. Interlace your fingers and don't move," she loudly ordered as Cory repeated the message in Spanish.

The language repetition was something they did any time there was a chance for misunderstanding. It wasn't required by standard operating procedure, but it'd saved them a lot of trouble on numerous occasions. She simply waited to see if the man in front of them would comply whether he understood in English *or* Spanish. Her concern was less for his safety, more about the downed cop's injuries.

When the stranger slowly did as she ordered while turning toward them, Cory switched on his flashlight. Laurel gasped and felt her pounding heart lurch. Both of them backed away as Cory spit out a low, feral curse.

The illuminated figure before them was the most grotesque thing she'd ever seen. As Cory's flashlight kept their suspect clearly visible, the man gazing at them then presented a fanged grin. Blood dripped from his mouth as if he'd just cannibalized something. His face bore an unholy resemblance to a movie vampire. His body and even his skull seemed emaciated beyond explanation. There was no reason for how anyone could survive and look so horribly gaunt. His angular face personified evil. There was a wickedly hollow gleam spilling from his eyes. But if the man was insane and an escapee from some facility, he was at least cogent enough to know he'd be shot if he moved. He glared back at her and her blood almost ran cold. The savagery in his expression was palpable and the long, leather-looking duster he wore augmented his thin, tall appearance. Her brain reasoned he couldn't possibly look as bad in daylight.

From the full moon now gleaming through the clearing as clouds moved away, as well as the glow from the flashlight Cory held, their suspect's appearance looked damned hideous.

Cory slowly moved forward. "Watch this son-of-a-bitch!" he commanded. "I've gotta check Mac."

Laurel swallowed hard and tried not to gaze right in their suspect's eyes. Her training made her pivot to keep Cory out of her line of fire. That same training kept her rooted to the spot when her gut told her to run away.

"All right … Batman … or whoever the hell you are … if you move, one of us is gonna put a hole in you as big as a fuckin' house!" Cory tersely promised as he carefully moved toward the downed undercover officer.

Laurel noted there was no repetition in any second language this time. As with her, Cory's concern was for the undercover cop on the ground, not on the ghastly suspect and certainly not on using proper language when addressing what might very well be their killer.

She was aware of her partner kneeling but she still kept her attention on the monstrosity in front of her. What he was, why he looked the way he did, or whether this was the same murderer they'd been looking for wasn't as important as Mac's safety.

"Christ! He's *dead*. His throat is torn out!"

Other officers burst into the clearing.

Laurel heard them drawing weapons and letting loose a barrage of questions Cory tried to answer. Still, her attention was fixed on the horrible sight of what had to be a nightmare torn from her brain, a man with blood dripping from his jaws and down his pale neck.

He stared back and she actually started to shake. The voices of those around her dimmed as the suspect grinned sickeningly. She heard the rattle of handcuffs.

She and Cory had only been there a few seconds before help arrived but it seemed like hours. Their suspect's hands were still on his head but she saw his gaze shift. Before she could utter the warning instinct pulled from her gut, the corpse-like entity moved and was suddenly no longer there.

Shouts rang out as others tried to train their lights on the man, relocate and then subdue him. She knew it was too late. Terror filled her and almost cut off her air. She lifted the muzzle of her weapon, unable to fire in the ensuing mêlée. Fear she'd strike a comrade made her freeze.

In a split second that reminded her of an old movie reel, the perpetrator seemed to materialize and run from one side of the clearing to the other. Something shiny came from beneath his flying leather duster. Whatever the object was, it emitted a light beam and a high-pitched, vibrating sound.

The beam shot forward in a straight stream and struck Cory first. She saw his flashlight fly out of his hand and roll away.

More shouts and cries broke what should have been the calm of the midnight air. She finally responded. Nothing she did was fast enough. Nothing anyone did kept the wraith-like being from moving at a speed defying explanation.

Cory's body hit the dirt.

Two detectives tried to jump the suspect but they had no better chance than her partner. They were struck by the suspect's strange beam weapon and both slumped to the ground. Random shots were fired. She knew triggers were being pulled in panic. Logic was lost on the scene as she followed her compatriots' example and shot at the empty space left by the fast-moving suspect. She heard dull thuds as the bullets of other officers hit the man but nothing slowed him down.

Three other detectives fell near Cory. Her distress on their behalf was almost overwhelming. This was what it felt like to face death. She was next.

In the matter of a few seconds—in a scenario playing out in light speed—no one stood but the attacker and her. At least one cop was dead, according to Cory's shouted description.

"Stay back!" she yelled and knew the warning would do her no good, even as she made it. Her brain, body, and emotions were reacting to training. There wasn't anything left from which to draw. Nothing they'd fired slowed the monstrosity down. And when a person could move at some unholy, inhuman pace, and take a shitload of bullets while putting an entire undercover operation on the ground, he didn't have to follow her commands or anyone else's.

It suddenly occurred to her they'd been set up. The thing with her waited until every cop in the vicinity was there.

The dispatch supervisor had to have sent backup but all the yelling and shooting had kept her from hearing what happened through her earpiece. Surely there'd be sirens any moment. But passing seconds seemed like an eternity as their attacker slowly advanced.

"I will feast well tonight," the gruesome entity rasped out in a grinding, hissing voice.

Laurel swallowed hard.

She opened her mouth to warn him again, as her index finger felt the cold metal of her trigger. There was only one way she'd get out of this.

Warnings had done no good. Following the rules hadn't made a difference. She had no idea who on the ground might be unconscious or dead. And she desperately wanted to live.

"Fuck it!" she whispered as she emptied what was left of her ammo into the tall man.

When he kept strolling forward, grinning as her efforts were a game, she knew all her childhood nightmares concerning Halloween-like creatures were real. There really were things in the night that couldn't be stopped by the best weapons available. There really were otherworldly creatures.

He stopped only a few feet away, seemingly savoring his victory. His glowing eyes looked her over, assessing her. The brightness of them was terrible and menacing. This monstrosity had no fear of anything. If she ran, he'd drop her in the next beat of her heart.

She was out of her league, without any options. This thing was a beast of prey. He enjoyed the hunt and had set the entire scene to suit his taste. A thousand things went through her mind. Chief among these was the thought of her best friend lying a few feet on the ground, and her sorrow for his parents, who'd never really know the truth of what'd happened to their son.

"Very nice … pretty, pretty," he slowly whispered in broken English. Then he licked his lips and made a loud sucking sound as he did so. "I learn your human words so you will understand … because you are a woman and the flesh of such is always sweeter, I will take you slowly. I will slake my lust on your body as I eat. And it will be *good*, little enforcer. There may even be enough life left to feel me inside you. Perhaps I'll hear you scream in fear as you lie beneath me." He nodded. "That would be most pleasurable. Most pleasurable indeed!"

Under the bright light of a full moon, his raised weapon looked like something out of a science fiction movie. Laurel knew she had only seconds left to breathe. But there were ways to go that were preferable than letting this beast take her as he wanted.

She gathered her strength and prepared to lunge. She'd either knock him to the ground or take a chest shot from his space-age looking weapon and end it.

His long, bony finger curled around what looked like a trigger. It seemed like the darkness hid nothing now though she mentally begged for total blackness.

A low whining sound came from the brush. He jerked his head to the left, as if shocked by the sound. Then her would-be killer cried out loud and long; the sound of his feral scream echoed everywhere.

A burst of light sliced through the night. It was similar to the illumination created by the monster's weapon except it seemed far more powerful. Sudden glow lit everything around them almost as bright as noontime.

The horrible entity before her lurched sideways. Long, flowing hair she hadn't noticed before flew around his features as he fell forward yelling in fury.

The muzzle of his weapon was still aimed in her direction. As he dropped toward the dirt, silvery light shot from it and right at her. Sudden, white-hot pain made her cry out in agony. She heard her own voice mingle with that of her attacker's. The sound of her cry seemed strange, as if the outrage it represented belonged elsewhere.

Intense pain flooded every cell of her body.

In weird slow motion that punctuated the agonizing moment, her body flew backward and onto the ground.

Stars shimmered overhead. Except for the breeze coming off the nearby ocean, the night grew silent again. She took one shuddering gasp and pain destroyed her instincts to stay awake. Darkness closed in.

• • •

Darius Starlaw ran forward with his ground crew. Among them were his second-in-command, Barst K'rad, and his medical technician, Gemma Tocurus. All who'd landed on this small rock of a world were chosen because of their previous experience and the knowledge that they'd lay down their lives for one another. In this instance, the danger was most extreme; he'd take no chances.

His weapon was still aimed at his quarry; he didn't dare lower it. Because the criminal he'd just leveled was only stunned, the butcher might still be a threat.

"Hurry," he commanded. "Their technology is primitive but they'll still locate Goll's vessel soon. Barst, we know the general coordinates … find it and take it out. Sear everything indicating a craft was ever present. There's no time to waste."

As Barst hurried to do his bidding, Darius looked at the carnage around him. There was nothing to be done. It took none of Gemma's skill to deem everyone around them was dead. Blood and gore littered the area.

Gemma picked up a metal tube still rolling on the ground. Light came from one end. There were several such devices lying scattered across the dirt. Apparently, these objects were what provided the primitives light in darkness.

Another crewman knelt beside Goll. "He's unconscious, sir. The threat has been mitigated."

"Get that bastard aboard our light shuttle and back to the *Titan*," Darius commanded. "Make sure the decontamination units are on before you enter. Just as we didn't bring any microbes to this backward world, we can't bring as much as a speck of dirt back. Is that clear?"

"Yes, sir."

While the first crewman picked Goll up, threw him over his shoulder, and trudged to his ground transport with another officer assisting, Darius considered the damage. Barst arrived back in record time and made his report.

"Goll's small ship is history. Not so much as a bulkhead bolt is left. No one on this world will know it existed."

Darius nodded. "Good. Before we return, let's get a clear image of what happened here. It can all be used against the prisoner and I want it all to count."

Barst gazed around the clearing even as Darius knelt to get a closer look at the carnage.

"They never had a chance, did they, sir?"

"No … they didn't," Darius muttered. "At least Goll will do no more killing *this* night."

"These victims are physically like you, sir."

Darius's brow rose. What his crewman said was true enough. None of the dead had blue skin or shocking white hair like Gemma. None bore the round-headed and brown, furry countenance displayed by Barst. "Looks are deceiving. On my world they haven't the strength even a child could summon. At least that's what I've been told." He sighed heavily and shook his head in sadness. "Why, by Cronos's balls, would they attack an entity so obviously superior? Surely they must have seen he wasn't like them! Why didn't they back off?"

"Why are some of the victims in similar clothing?" Gemma asked.

Darius sadly shook his head. "I hate to say it, Gemma, but I think they're some kind of enforcers."

"What a terrible end to our quest," Barst offered sadly.

"Barst … follow the others back to the ship. Take personal responsibility for putting Goll in enviro-stasis. I want no mistakes," Darius ordered as he re-holstered his weapon.

Gemma still moved among the victims, making one last check for life signs. Assuming she might find a survivor, Darius knew they wouldn't last long. Earth's technology wasn't advanced enough to undo the damage Goll wrought. He silently cursed himself for not getting to Earth sooner.

"Two still live," Gemma announced. "But one is more seriously injured. If my communo-chip is translating properly, this tag on his clothing says … Martinez. The second one is a woman. Goll's weapon may have been drained by the time he shot her. She's not so badly burned as the others."

Darius moved and knelt beside the surviving male that Gemma identified as *Martinez*. The stricken enforcer opened his eyes and stared straight up at him. Moonlight in the small clearing was quite bright now. It was as if the darkness fled, coinciding with cessation of hostility and the capture of the one responsible for the slaughter.

The Martinez man grabbed the front of his uniform tunic and pulled him closer. Darius didn't fight what was likely to be a whispered last request. He simply gazed back into the dying man's eyes. Life was quickly leaving this injured fighter.

Darius let the man whisper into his ear. The croaked appeal was the same he'd have made to anyone if the situation had been reversed. He only understood the message because his communication chip was attuned to their current surroundings—Earth English, a place called Balboa Park.

Sadly, he couldn't say anything in comfort. The dying human had no such communication device embedded in his body. But he *could* hold the man's shoulders and upper body in such a way as to convey friendship. He wasn't even sure the tubular lighting devices lying on the ground or the moon overhead allowed the victim a good look at *his* face, but body language and gentle physical contact might offer some comfort.

Darius listened intently as a seemingly last request was made. After it was done, the man referred to as Martinez closed his eyes and went limp. He breathed his last.

Gemma tried to revive him, but she soon stared into the darkness, whispering her version of a prayer.

As commander of this sad scene, there was nothing Darius could say or do. He swallowed down a sudden knot that lodged in his throat, and gently lowered the dead man back to the ground. Gemma was the first to speak.

"Commander … what did he say?"

Darius sighed heavily, ran one weary hand across his face and the back of his neck. "He wanted me to 'look after my partner … the woman who was with me.' Those were his exact words."

"Assuming there are no other victims in these woods and that this is the female he spoke of … her life signs are barely stronger than his were," Gemma told him. "I don't know how much longer she can survive. I can barely read in the light from these primitive tube-illuminators, and we can't turn on our own ready beams without summoning every constabulary in the area, but I think the tag on her uniform says … *Blake*. Is that a name or some kind of unit designation?"

"I don't know. I think it's probably her name. Just like Martinez," he surmised.

Gemma glanced at her portable wrist bio scanner then moved closer to the one survivor. "The blast entered this woman's left shoulder and went all the way through. Her breathing has been compromised. She won't survive the night if the primitive physicians here cannot treat this kind of laser injury, and I find it inconceivable that they could."

Piercing alarms tore through the stillness.

"I think those are warnings coming from conveyances. If memory serves, they're called sirens," Darius said. "We're out of time. I don't want to encounter innocents not knowing if even stunners will do permanent damage." He looked down at the unconscious woman. "We need to go now, Gemma."

"Sir, we can't leave her. She'll die if we do," the medical technician insisted.

He slowly shook his head. "You know our orders. We've interfered all we dare."

"Sir … *please*. We can't leave her. You said she's probably an enforcer … like us."

Darius touched the unconscious human woman's face. She was shivering, indicating shock was taking hold.

"Sir? Let me try to help her," Gemma pled.

"Orion's blood!" He gazed down at the still figure before them and made a decision for which his entire crew might suffer.

A dying man had begged for this woman's life. If someone he cared for were lying there, what would he do to give them one more chance?

An old wound opened and he knew the answer to the question. His crew would understand. The punishment, if there was to be any, would be much less harsh for saving a life than if he'd taken Goll's. If he had his way, that penalty was to be his and his alone.

"Get moving. I'll take her aboard but I have one last duty to perform."

"Thank you, Commander!"

He watched as Gemma made her way out of the clearing.

Alone with naught but the dead and one injured human, he stood. Then he set his sidearm to maximum.

"I grieve with those who will never know what happened to you. But know your deaths were not in vain. Justice will be served … you will rest in peace," he murmured just before he fired and incinerated the bodies of the dead around him as well as all their weapons.

There could be no evidence as to the existence of an advanced race. Leaving dead behind—dead whose wounds were produced by highly unconventional weaponry—was in violation of supreme code. Let the local constabularies ponder the burned clearing and conclude what they might. There'd be any number of reasons for such a thing, but none rationally involving advanced races from other worlds.

Like the men he'd just incinerated, no one would ever know what happened to the girl. But if he took her aboard the *Titan* and she *did* live, she could never know this world again. Rules prohibited returning her.

He easily scooped up the injured girl's body then followed Gemma out of the clearing.

"Enough damage has been done this night," he called ahead toward Gemma's quickly retreating form. "We need to be aboard our shuttle, back on the *Titan*, and out of their atmosphere before we're detected."

"Understood. I'll relay the need for alacrity," Gemma said as she picked up her pace. "And I'll have a surgical team standing by for the Earther."

Only a few moments later, but what seemed like a lifetime after the evening's events, Darius entered their rescue shuttle craft with Gemma.

Barst looked up from the flight controls. "By your command, sir … Goll is in enviro-stasis. I saw to that parasite's incarceration myself and will make sure he's secured aboard the *Titan*. He won't be giving us any problems."

Darius saw his crewman's large head tilt in shock. Apparently Barst didn't believe his eyes. The man was staring down at the body in Darius's arms.

"In the name of the Creator of all things … who have you brought aboard?"

"She's an injured Earther," Gemma explained. "If you'll take her to the med lab, once we're aboard, Commander, I'll ready an incu-unit for her and inject a communo-chip."

Darius nodded while firing off another order for Barst. "Lift off as soon as possible or Earthers will be crawling all over us. I don't want any incidents."

"Yes, sir," Barst responded.

In moments, their rescue shuttle landed aboard their command craft—the *Titan*.

As landing bay crews scurried about to make sure the hull of the shuttle was decontaminated, Darius carried the unconscious woman to the med lab. Gemma rushed ahead to get her equipment ready.

By the time he entered the state-of-the art medical facility his technicians were so proud of, an almost imperceptible movement of the ship confirmed Barst had put the *Titan* into quasar drive.

He breathed a sigh of relief. Now they could head home. Their assignment was complete.

"Put her there, Commander." Gemma motioned to the incu-unit closest to her instrument cart.

He lowered the girl into the unit then straightened. His intent was to leave and head to the communication center. Someone needed to speak to the officers there, make sure they monitored Earth transmissions concerning unidentified flying objects. If they were lucky, they'd gotten away with nothing more than a few citizens transmitting news of some small, strange craft in the night sky. It was for that very reason the much smaller crew shuttle had been used as a landing unit.

Just as he was about to turn, something made him glance down. He hesitated then froze in place. Air actually left his lungs when he got his first good look at the woman whose life they'd saved.

There hadn't been enough time, nor enough distance from nearby homes and businesses to properly illuminate the clearing and get a closer look at a planet considered off limits. Nor had there been time for close scrutiny of anything other than who might or might not be breathing. Now, with pressure off, he took stock of the situation.

If anyone on the bridge needed him, they'd call. That part of him that *wasn't* on duty—the part below his waist—stirred at the sight of sudden, breathtaking loveliness. That first good look of the rescued victim was the very thing that froze him to the deck.

If a fusion bomb went off next to the ship, he'd have a hard time distinguishing between his response to that, or to this creature lying so still and pale in the incu-unit.

"She's exquisite," he murmured as Gemma and several of her assistants bustled and moved equipment.

Their injured Earthling had blood spattered over her clothing, neck, and face. Parts of her uniform were in shreds. All that notwithstanding, her skin was perfect, like the lovely smooth and white lunar stones of his home world. Her pinned-up hair was a soft brown color; golden lights shimmered within the strands. Her features were evenly aligned and delicate. Soft brows gently arched over each eye. Her very slightly upturned nose and high cheeks bore a small spattering of freckles. He noted she was more finely bred than half the debutantes his world presented for his perusal. Her body looked lean and toned. She'd probably be tall and athletic if she were standing. And *unlike* many spoiled and selfish beauties his family shoved at him ad nauseum, this woman had dared face a creature many times more powerful, one who'd killed on numerous worlds and who'd been chased to this end of the galaxy before finally being incarcerated.

Sadly, she hadn't been privy to that information but she'd bravely faced Goll down even as her comrades fell.

He leaned closer; curiosity over the color of her eyes gripped him.

"Shame," he softly murmured.

"Commander?" Gemma prompted as she readied her equipment.

"I … I was just thinking that it's a shame such a beautiful creature might die."

Gemma looked up from her work then briefly studied her patient. "My … she *is* attractive, isn't she? Even all that blood doesn't hide her attributes. For such a small waist and hips, her breasts appear generously ample. Wouldn't you say so?" she teased.

He straightened and cleared his throat. Now wasn't the time to indulge in flights of sensual fancy. Certainly not over an injured Earther.

"What news of her condition?" he gruffly asked.

"According to the data being correlated by the incu-unit, she has a good chance to recover. I'll need to close her off now so the zerion mist can do its job."

He backed slightly away and watched as Gemma flipped switches that automatically closed the lid to the box-like, silver unit. He stood in silence as the magnetic field modulators were affixed and attuned.

Gemma knew her job. There was no good reason for him to stand there gawking. For the life of him, he simply couldn't make his booted feet turn and leave the medical facility. But when the staff stared at him, as if his presence was no longer necessary, he knew he'd overstepped a few invisible boundaries. His need was showing.

"Uh ... I'd ... I'd better get back to the bridge," he loudly affirmed.

"I'll relay any changes in her condition," Gemma said as she grinned up at him. "If she looks so good lying there with a big laser hole in 'er, I'm sure she'll clean up *quite* prettily."

He squared his shoulders and glared down at the med-tech.

Good-natured snickers at his discomfort made their way around the space.

"That's of little to no consequence to me!" he declared, a little too forcibly. "Just ... just do what you can to help her. I'll speak with you about your lack of decorum later!"

He quickly turned and strode away.

•••

Hours later, Darius ran one hand across the back of his neck and rolled his shoulders in weariness. Since the bridge crew had no immediate need of him or his second-in-command, he and Barst walked to the detainment section. When they got there, they mutually considered their prisoner. Goll was quite thoroughly contained in the stasis cell before them.

"You need to rest," Barst recommended. "It's been many hours since we left Earth and you haven't taken a break."

Darius stared through the icy-looking clear pane of the unit. Through it Goll appeared even more gruesome than when he'd been awake. Hatred for his captive rose within him like morbid pestilence.

Goll couldn't see, hear, or move. He wouldn't need to be fed or removed from the cell for any reason, not until they landed back on Luster. That was the advantage of the stasis technology. A prisoner could be kept there for up to one year, without sustaining permanent injury. Yet, Darius wanted to turn the cell's controls off, jerk the malignant creature from his cryo-slumbering state, and beat him to death with his own two hands. Nothing would have given him greater pleasure than to tear the filthy murderer apart, bone by nasty bone. Something of his thoughts must have become obvious to Barst. His second-in-command kept trying to get him away from the cell before he acted on impulse.

"Commander, everyone in the Constellation League knows of your loss at the hands of Goll's sire, but we're enforcers. We must abide by the law or we become just like those we hunt." Barst paused and waited for a response. When none came, he tried again. "We've been together a long time. I'd hate to see you lose your freedom and your career over *this* bottom-feeding scum. And I'd hate to have to break in another commanding officer. It's hell on my nerves."

"I'll let him live, old friend. Only long enough to see him executed on Luster," Darius muttered.

"There's no doubt that will happen. He killed an ambassador, and we witnessed him destroying Earthers. The penalty for just contacting an isolation-class world is life in prison, never mind the murders."

"I want to be there when he dies," Darius blurted. "Forgive my callousness but I pray it's slower than usual."

"Darius, you need to rest," Barst reiterated as he dropped his superior's title. Perhaps you could stop by the med lab and have Gemma concoct some medication or other to help you sleep. Please, old friend … take my advice?" Barst placed his hand on the larger man's shoulder.

"All right. I'll do as you recommend." Darius turned with a sigh. "I want to see how our passenger is doing anyway. Creator only knows what I'm going to do with that one. I'll stand before High Council for taking her."

"Gemma will vouch for your reasoning. The woman's injury was caused by our prisoner. What can the admiral say? Were we supposed to let her lie there, suffering from a horrible wound before she eventually died? We certainly couldn't kill her, and she had a class one laser wound that could have never been explained to her contemporaries. Worse, she might have been accused of something when she couldn't rationally explain what happened."

"True enough," Darius agreed with a slow nod.

"Besides," Barst continued, "I popped in and took a look at her, just as Gemma was adjusting a communo-chip. Once the admiral sees that beauty he'll probably want her aboard *his* ship."

For some reason, that comment didn't settle Darius's nerves. The admiral's taste concerning young women was notorious. The man wouldn't give a flaming nova whether the girl in question was sexually compatible. A be-feathered, avian denizen from the outer rings of Moriar, Admiral Tel'duc't was nothing if not a hedonist. He liked designing new and exotic ways to pleasure himself, and with females from every conceivable species. Sadly, the bastard openly bragged about it. And though the ladies in his company were always quite willing to serve as arm candy for someone as powerful as a League admiral, those same females weren't well thought of after Tel'duc't was done with them. Darius slowly frowned, then turned away. His destination was the med lab.

Every muscle in his body yearned for rest. He'd been awake for three straight shifts. Thoughts of getting his hands around Goll's emaciated little neck kept him from sleep. Now, thanks to Barst's council, he was seeing things more clearly.

A short time later the med lab hatches opened automatically as he entered the white and silver pristine space. Gemma stood there with her back to him. She was studying a computer screen.

"How's the patient?" Darius asked as he glanced at incubation unit.

Gemma turned to chastise her superior. "When are you going to get some rest?"

He rolled his eyes and shot her a slanted grin. "I must look worse than I actually feel as everyone is so concerned about my sleeping habits! As soon as you brew some of that relaxation potion you have hidden away, I'll head to my quarters. Unfortunately … I've been awake so long I'm not sure I *can* sleep."

"That *potion* is called Turesian tea. It has to be steeped the old-fashioned way for its benefits to be of value." Gemma grinned and got up to heat some water.

He took the opportunity to move closer to the only occupied incubation unit in the lab. According to controls on the outside, the Earther's vital signs were not only stabilized, but they appeared to have dramatically improved from those previously listed on the unit's database. "You were right. She's recovering."

As he spoke, he gazed through the top view port and noted how the woman's color seemed healthier. At least it was better-looking by Lusterian standards. There was no other comparison to be made but to what he knew of other races within League jurisdiction.

The woman's clothing had been removed, as every patient's was when placed inside such units. Without it, the injured rested more comfortably. In its place, a ubiquitous blanket covered her slender form. The top of it rested just over her breasts.

He saw her wound closing. Thanks to the electro-magnetically zerion-altered field within the unit, the flesh was suturing before his eyes. Even the scar would disappear as healing progressed. As he stared, other thoughts took the place of curatives.

He took a small step back when mental meanderings caused his gaze to linger on her perfect, creamy flesh. Her fingers were long and slender. The tips had been meticulously manicured. Her body was athletically lean without being unappealingly thin. Muscle in her upper arms was evident. Her hair shimmered in the light from within the unit. There were streaks of red in it that he hadn't noticed earlier.

How would it feel to run his hands through the long tendrils and curl them around his wrists? What would her voice sound like when she eventually spoke? Again, he wondered about the color of her eyes.

Blue.

He decided they must be a deep, sparkling gem hue, the color of Lusterian midnight stones that were rare and prized.

How soft she looked. How very holdable.

It'd been a long time since he'd viewed a female with such striking, perfect features. Her flesh almost begged to be stroked. A man who could win this courageous creature's affections would live in a universe of passionate yearning. Whispered secrets would be shared in the night. She'd likely have any lover on his knees, begging to take her.

The sound of Gemma's activities brought him out of the delicious reverie.

He blinked quickly, lifted his chin, and tried to regain his composure.

What in the galaxy was wrong with him? The last thing a professional Constellation League supervisor should be doing was ogling some nude victim of a laser attack, even if she was so heartbreakingly lovely. and even if he had been without female companionship for such a long time. In all respects, from the top of her head to the tips of her toes, she appeared just as any woman of his own Lusterian race would. There were only two arms, two legs, two eyes, and two very finely shaped breasts.

"Here, Commander, this should help you get some rest. It's all herbal, nothing harmful."

Darius took the mug Gemma offered and moved away from the unit. He settled onto a nearby lab chair and watched as Gemma worked with the controls on it.

"You know, she'll regain consciousness soon. She's moving her fingertips," Gemma informed him as she carefully lifted the lid.

Darius placed his mug on a table and came to stand by their patient again. He wanted to see if his impression of her eye color was true. Gemma would never know about his interest in that regard, only surmising he was acting with concern.

• • •

Laurel fought her way out of the hazy darkness. Even through closed lids it was clear soft light surrounded her. She felt warm but lethargic, as if she'd been asleep too long. There was a minor twinge in her left temple, as though someone was gently pressing against it. After taking a deep breath and slowly letting it out, she opened her eyes and waited for them to focus. Throbbing in her left shoulder reminded her of the last thing she remembered. She and Cory were in Balboa Park. There was a stakeout and it'd gone bad.

She looked up and shook her head slightly to clear it.

The face of a pretty woman hovered above her own. This person might have been her own age, but who'd really know since the hoverer was a wonderful shade of *aqua-blue*.

Laurel assumed her caretaker *might* be a doctor, but lovely and exotically tilted dark eyes—coupled with pointed ears peeking through a mass of long, snow white hair—made her think twice. What she was seeing, blue skin inclusive, had less to do with any modern medical facility and more to do with Halloween or a little girl's fairy party. Someone was obviously playing a very weird practical joke. Or there was a better explanation.

I'm on some pretty damned good meds.

"Can you hear me?" the blue woman asked.

Laurel tried to speak but only managed a low moan.

"Here … give her some of this," a man's voice offered as the woman took a mug from him. "Are you sure her communo-chip is adjusted properly? One has never been placed in an Earthling as far as I'm aware. Maybe it's not working or something's wrong."

Laurel was helped into a semi-seated position. She tried to sip whatever was being offered. Blue skin girl seemed kind enough. The drink was warm. It was soothing on her throat and tasted like mint.

"Try to speak again," the woman encouraged as she set the mug aside then lowered her patient into a prone position again.

"My partner ... Cory ... is he all right?" Laurel whispered.

"The chip works," the woman said. "I'm happy to turn things over to you, Commander. I just save lives. Explanations are *your* job."

Someone else moved into Laurel's field of vision. Whoever blue girl spoke to was about to address her. She remained absolutely still and tried not to lose it. Something told her she wasn't in Kansas anymore, and that she wasn't going to like the answer to her question.

"Enforcer ... I assume that's your formal occupation ... can you remember anything that happened?"

Laurel stared at the new face hovering over hers. She registered his question, posed in a very deep baritone. Her vision was clearing by the moment but she wasn't prepared to believe anything she was seeing was real. The meds were still onboard. Perception of their presence made her hallucinatory state at least a bit more acceptable.

The man who'd just spoken was much taller than blue girl. He had long, dark hair that was pulled back at the nape of his neck. Strands of it were falling over one shoulder. He sported some kind of uniform. Epaulets on the shoulders of his dark tunic made him look as though he might be a member of some elite police group she'd never heard of. But the gentle kindness in the blue girl's tone wasn't in his. The clench of his tan square jaw, the dark green riveting eyes staring down at her, and the serious set of his handsome, godlike features were off-putting.

"I remember someone attacking us. What about Cory?" Laurel asked again as her voice cleared.

She waited as the two characters consulted. All she wanted was one simple answer. Why weren't they giving it?

"Here, Commander, I found this in her clothing. It appears to be identification of some sort."

That was the second time blue girl referred to tan guy as *commander*. What was that all about?

"This is your identification, isn't it? You *are* an enforcer, aren't you?" he asked.

She gazed at the black badge wallet tan guy had in his right hand. He'd opened it and her ID number and photograph were clearly visible. She was about to ask what idiot on the planet wouldn't recognize a police ID, but tact made her reel in the comment. She licked suddenly dry lips and tried a different angle. Tan guy quickly offered her more tea. She eagerly sipped it if only to gain more time to compose an answer.

For the first time, she noticed the very large, coffin-like box around her. The interior was lined with lights and soft, white padding.

She tamped down panic, swallowed more tea, and amped up her courage. Now wasn't the time to lose composure. Not if she wanted out of this damned container and back into reality. If she screamed or did anything that made them believe she was out of control, they'd likely load her with more drugs. What she had in her was too much as it was.

"I'm with San Diego PD. Please … tell me where my partner is. His name is Cory Martinez. We were ambushed on a stakeout. What happened to the men with me? Are they all right?"

Something was very wrong, aside from their not answering questions concerning Cory. A supervisor should be present. She saw no one remotely resembling another SDPD cop. Because of their absence, she wondered if anyone had contacted her parents.

Dad was ensconced somewhere in the northern part of the state with a wife two years younger than she was, expecting a baby anytime. Mom was at a law convention in New York with her live-in, architect lover.

As dysfunctional families went, they weren't strongly attached. Still, someone should have contacted them. They might not show up for any mundane reason but surely they'd come if their daughter had almost been killed.

How long had she been lying in the coffin-like box? How bad off was she that such a contrivance was necessary?

She barely turned her head, afraid to see what devices might have been attached to her body. There wasn't enough nerve in her entire arsenal of mettle to ask what hospital this was, and why she'd been placed in the big container. Someone would tell her soon. But she just couldn't ask about the medical side. Not yet.

With every passing moment fear crept into the smallest part of her soul; she was sure it invaded even the smallest cells. Dread made her lie absolutely still.

She clearly saw the faces of her attendants. Garish as blue girl was, big as tan guy seemed from her prone position, their expressions were pretty raw. Neither wanted to speak first. Theirs was the expression cops wore when they knew they had to deliver bad news.

She began to shake.

Stay strong. Don't break. It'll be all right.

• • •

The poignancy of the moment and the look on her face would forever linger in Darius's memory. He knew he'd never rid himself of the haunted gaze so fixed on him. Her eyes *were* a luxurious, gem-like blue that should have been shimmering with laughter. He got the impression she was much more acquainted with happiness than he. She had cared for her friends, they'd likely cared for her. Being as close to her comrades as the concern exhibited, how could she be anything other than contented? At least as long as they were present. But they weren't alive any longer and he needed to say so.

The man who'd died in his arms had asked for this woman's care. He recalled that last wish, even as that brave soul's life force sped into the universe and conjoined with others of equal valor. He owed that man's friend the truth.

He took a deep breath and exhaled before speaking. There was no easy way to tell her, but the responsibility for announcing deaths at the hands of criminals always fell to the most senior officer.

He uttered what was necessary, to dispatch news quickly and as painlessly as possible. "I'm sorry. Your friends didn't make it."

In her gaze he immediately recognized the signs of disbelief. She looked back at him. Then her eyes shifted to Gemma. He could almost hear her thoughts.

Suspicion surely prompted her to question what he'd just said. It was a normal process of denial he was well aware of, having delivered such messages far too many lifetimes in his thirty-three years. But sooner or later, like it or not, the woman lying there would have to come to terms with the truth. It'd been spoken. It was up to time and circumstance now to drive that harsh reality home.

"I *am* sorry," he softly repeated. "But there's no other way to say it. You're an enforcer. You know what can happen when you accept responsibility for defending others."

Laurel shook her head. "You've probably misunderstood. We shot at a man … me and some other officers had to have brought him down. That's who you're talking about. Our suspect is the one who's dead. Not Cory!"

Darius considered her response. Experience in these matters came to his rescue. Because of his communo-chip, he was able to read the primitive writing next to her picture ID. Gemma had already mentioned this woman's name when they'd found her lying on the ground. But he still needed to hear her say it. She needed to maintain a level of consciousness his explanations required. Answering mundane questions compulsory of any enforcer might buy her the time she needed to emotionally acclimate.

"What's your name?"

"Laurel Blake. What's this thing I'm in?" she asked as she glanced at rows of blinking lights inside her container.

"This is an incubation unit or simply an *incu-unit* as we refer to it. It generates energy fields that react with the body's cellular processes. It significantly shortens and augments healing." Then he got back to the meat of the discussion. He moved closer and simultaneously gestured for Gemma to drop the walls of the incubation unit away. Once that was done, he softly repeated the facts she needed to understand.

"The only two people left alive were you and the man who attacked you. I'm sorry."

She searched his face, looking for any break in his gaze. Even now, her instincts kicked in. She was processing as someone with experience in such matters.

He simply waited. There were no tears, no cries of protestation. Just silence.

She eventually turned away. Before she did, he caught the telltale look of even firmer denial. A bit of coldness entered her blue eyes. She wouldn't be convinced easily. But neither was she a collapsing heap of emotion. Primitive as he'd been led to believe her culture was, that was to her credit. He gently squeezed her hand then moved away.

Gemma followed him a short distance before adding an opinion.

"Her vital signs dropped when you told her, Commander."

"Watch her. Make sure she isn't left alone," he ordered.

"Yes, sir."

Darius walked out of the med bay and slowly headed toward his quarters. He unfastened his left shoulder epaulet and let the front of his tunic fall open. As he approached his quarters, the hatch separated to allow him access. He moved into his personal space and quickly pulled the fastener from his hair.

Stripping his clothing off without caring where the garments landed, he numbly stepped into the shower compartment and let the hot water wash away what was left of his emotions. He could only speculate as to what would happen to the woman.

There was one other truth yet to be told.

She could never go back to her world. He and his crew had been given special dispensation to chase Goll "wherever he ran." But Earth—as a world too technologically backward to know about other life forms—was a planet listed as unapproachable for any other reason. Life in prison or even the death penalty might be applied in any case where a violation existed; special permission to go back wasn't obtainable.

Gemma, Barst, and the rest of his crew knew about the *no association* edict. What *he* knew was that it couldn't be augmented for the purposes of returning Laurel. Gemma believed that once the woman's wound was healed, and no evidence extant concerning the existence of otherworldly life forms, her patient could be returned with no harm done.

He hadn't thought the consequences through while he carried the Earther back to the ship. Saving her life came first. That imperative outweighed all others.

Perhaps she'd rather be dead with her friends than on an alien vessel headed to worlds as yet unknown by her kind. Still, he could not have left her there dying. He couldn't have shot her to put her out of her misery. So Gemma's suggestion, as ship's med-tech, had seemed congruent with humanitarian aid. Especially when considering Goll's inhuman attack and her occupation as a fellow enforcer.

In effect, he'd already involved himself and his crew too much. But that was the situation and he was responsible as ship's commander.

He hung his head in weariness. Too tired to consider any thoughts of the future, he moved to his bed and sank onto it. Sleep came quickly.

• • •

"Commander, we have a problem in the med bay."

"On my way," Darius responded after Gemma's voice, via the intercom, jerked him from deep sleep. He quickly pulled on a robe and tied it closed as he raced through the passageways.

Once he was in the med bay, he saw Gemma holding down the struggling Earth woman. Barst and several medical staffers ran into the space a split second later.

"What's happened?" Darius asked, maneuvering himself to help contain the struggling Earther.

"She isn't breathing right. A bio-scan shows there's a problem with something in our environment but I can't detect what."

"She was decontaminated when we brought her aboard. All of us were," Darius quickly asserted. "Wouldn't that equipment have indicated a problem?"

Gemma shook her head as she gathered medical equipment on a crash cart. "You need to keep her calm. My job at the moment is to keep her breathing. She went unconscious then awoke again gasping. She's fighting to keep from suffocating. That's all I know for sure."

"I'll hold her," Darius ordered.

As Gemma moved away, Laurel tried to fight her way out of the incu-unit. He held her down though he could see the effects of horrible pain on her face. She acted as though there wasn't any air at all in her lungs or she was being crushed under incredible pressure.

As the others gathered equipment at Gemma's command, he held the patient down with one hand then used his other one to punch buttons that lowered the sides of the incu-unit. Several more moments of fighting took place.

In all his life he'd never seen a gasping person so determined to fight for every bit of air they could get. Clearly, she wasn't ready to give up.

"Almost ready," Gemma called out.

He turned his head to ascertain the staff's whereabouts. When he looked back at the woman he was pinning down, she looked straight at him. Without enough oxygen in her lungs, she couldn't speak. But there was fervent appeal in her pure blue gaze as she stared up at him.

As before, the communication chip embedded in her left temporal lobe made it possible for her to understand his words. He spoke softly, lifted her into his embrace, and cradled her in his arms as he uttered assurances.

"Quiet ... we won't let you die. You're safe. You're among friends and you'll be all right. I promise. I promise," he repeated over and over.

Among the bravest of all acts was her brief nod. With that slight movement of her head, she'd given her trust and was trying to calm down even as the last vestiges of air vacated her body.

In moments she'd be unconscious again. If the reason for her medical problem wasn't found quickly his promise of safety couldn't be kept.

"Hurry, Gemma! Hurry," he quietly ordered.

"Keep talking to her," Gemma replied. "I just need a little more time."

He glared at the med-tech, trying to convey urgency without actually saying anything else. A "little more time" might be all she had. He did his best to keep the fear off his face and out of his voice. "Hang on. Gemma is the best medic in six quadrants. That's why she's part of my crew. Just keep looking at me." The woman responded to his command, though she was beginning to turn blue. He held her closer as Gemma approached with a hypo-injection. What seemed like many minutes since he'd entered the med bay were probably only a few seconds. He was holding onto, and responsible for, a dying woman who'd trusted him to keep her safe.

"Why is all this paraphernalia going on your emergency tray?" Barst asked as he quickly decontaminated his hands with bio-spray and pulled on gloves.

"I'm going to sedate her so I can split open her chest," Gemma explained as she repeated Barst's actions.

"*What?*" Both men shouted in unison.

"Readings indicate the decontamination unit we brought her through might have wrongly interpreted something she needs to live as dangerous to us. I don't know what the element was and I don't have time to figure it out among the millions of permutations that might have taken place. Right now I have to deal with the results. She's not breathing so I'm gonna fix it!"

"How could such a thing happen?" Darius asked as he held their patient closer.

"By all my readings her physiology is almost exactly the same as *yours*, Commander. Like I already said ... there was something in her the decontamination unit didn't like."

Darius quickly lowered the Earth woman to the incu-unit platform again.

Gemma grabbed her tray, pushed Darius aside, and put an injection gun next to the Earther's neck, just below her left ear. When the med-tech pulled the trigger, the Earther's eyes closed.

Selfishly, he was grateful she'd gone unconscious. He sent a silent prayer to the heavens that all would be well. Everyone around him shared the sentiment evidenced in the urgency being displayed.

"Everyone get out of my way and hand me what I need when I say so. If you haven't scrubbed up, do it now or get out!" Gemma shouted.

"Have you ever done anything like this?" Barst asked.

"I've studied old holo files of such techniques," Gemma responded as she worked. "Usually, this kind of invasive stuff is left to specially designed computer equipment in major trauma facilities. But she's out of time and I'm all she's got."

"The incu-unit can't do what you require?" Barst asked again as he stepped backward.

Gemma didn't respond.

Darius gazed at Barst. The other man displayed a look of pure horror. He wasn't sure his countenance didn't bear the same expression.

He quickly turned to scrub up as the rest of the med bay staff did. It occurred to him that Gemma was risking her career and imprisonment for doing something so dangerous. Only the best surgeons were ever called upon to open a body. Technology was such that invasive surgery wasn't the norm. But Gemma had already pulled down the Earther's blankets, put a laser scalpel to the woman's chest, and was splitting it even as he stood there putting on a pair of sterile gloves and an emergency mask like everyone else in the space. As she cut, one of the other med staff officers slid a mask on Gemma's face, from beneath her chin. It was then affixed behind her head. A sterile gown was tied to her chest and around the back of her neck. Everyone in the med bay who had a reason to help was acting precisely as they should. He'd never been prouder of his crew.

But he still felt impotent. All he could do was watch as blood poured from the new incision in the Earther's open chest. Techs grabbed replacement units of all-blood from Gemma's tray, and began infusing them into Laurel via tubes attached to arm veins.

What if the all-blood didn't match an Earther's needs? Was there enough research to support the use of technologically advanced artificial blood replacement when speaking of a lower species such as an Earther? What if the gaping wound and open, beating heart—a heart that pulsed far too slowly now—was contaminated by atmospheric particulate in the med bay? What if Gemma slipped? What if … what if … what if …

"I can't believe I just closed one hole in her chest only to open 'er up again," Gemma angrily muttered as she worked. "That injection I gave her will keep her out as well as stave off pain and infection."

"But her oxygen intake—"

"Was also temporarily compensated for with the injection, Commander."

Gemma quickly called out for one piece of surgical equipment after another. Staff around the table acted with time-saving efficiency. He heard the frustration in their voices as they communicated with one another. Each of them was frightened they'd lose their patient. Caring wasn't limited to whether an injured person's race was less evolved.

Again, his chest swelled with pride. He turned to his second-in-command knowing he couldn't leave the Earther alone. Her safety was as much his responsibility as Gemma's.

"Barst … man the bridge," he ordered. "We're moving into uncharted space, someone needs to keep an eye on our scanners. I need to stay here."

"Yes, sir. I'll report on any unusual activity," Barst said, then hesitated before leaving the med bay. "I hope she'll be all right. Goll has done enough damage. She'd make an excellent witness at his trial. Diplomats would be hard pressed to ignore her account and use their oily machinations to get Gorm's son free."

"Indeed!" Darius nodded in agreement then put his attention back on the surgical procedure and the bloody, open mess that was now Laurel's chest. He sighed in relief noting how her chest rose and fell more evenly now. Clearly, she was getting oxygen though he wasn't sure what Gemma was doing with her lungs and heart to increase circulation. Such goings on weren't his strong suit. In the med bay, Gemma had total control. It was the only place on the ship where everyone, including him, yielded to her.

"Though I hit her with some heavy meds, she may still be able to hear what's going on so be careful what you say. Audible awareness isn't unheard of in these situations," Gemma softly advised as she kept cutting, snipping, and rearranging organs. "Commander … talk to her while I continue."

Darius's brows rose. He'd just been contemplating a question concerning exactly what Gemma was doing. Instead, he heeded her timely warning and moved closer to the injured woman.

The gore associated with opening Laurel's chest wasn't new to him. The site of it wasn't particularly shocking. He'd seen many casualties while enforcing laws in his assigned quadrant. But something about watching this backward little Earther lying there in the middle of her own blood and incised body tissue was so pathetic. He tried to come up with commentary that sounded intelligent. Something she'd grab onto assuming she *could* hear what was being said. He put one gloved hand on top of her head, noting the thick mass of hair as he conjured words of comfort.

"Don't be afraid. Gemma will have you right in no time," he whispered as he lowered his head to repeat the words through the barrier of the mask he now wore.

As the operation proceeded he actually saw the Earther's entire body tense. Later, she might not be able to remember what he'd said but right now, he was certain she really did hear every syllable spoken, just as Gemma had warned. He got the distinct impression she'd have reached for a hand to hold had she been able to move.

"Just a few more moments," Gemma relayed as she glanced between her surgical handiwork and holographic status updates generated by the incu-unit. "Okay. That's got it. I'll laser-suture the incision. The unit should remove even the smallest trace of the scar."

He recognized the sparkle in his med-tech's bright gaze, and heard the exaltation in her voice. Apparently, she was satisfied with her skills in saving her patient's life.

"She should start breathing deeper soon, sir. Her heart rate is already going back to its original speed. Of course, I don't know what normal is for her. I'm not that up on Earther vital signs but since her biology is almost identical to Lusterian specs, I think it's safe to say she'll be just fine." Gemma pulled off her mask as the incu-unit walls rose around her patient.

Other staff in the med bay sighed with relief and congratulated their head surgeon on a wonderful job. Darius simply stood there trying to hide such utter relief as to be nonsensical given his short acquaintance with the injured Earth woman. She'd fought so hard to live. As on the planet's surface, she'd displayed one more instance of utter courage.

He glanced at the patient and considered the creamy skin of her full breasts and perfect proportions of her body, as it'd been fully exposed when Gemma pulled the blankets back to make her initial incisions.

When one of his other crewmen caught him essentially gawking, he cleared his throat and turned guiltily away. That medical assistant snorted in amusement while pulling clean, thicker coverings over the injured woman's body.

"I … I was just thinking her physiology and mine might be similar for a reason," he defended. "Lusterian researchers speak of ancestors visiting many worlds in ancient times, before a ban was ever initiated regarding planets that were too backward to be exposed to higher technology. Earth might have been one of those planets. It seems logical to assume some of my home world's travelers might have intermingled with various populations, thereby producing entities whose physiology is similar. Even compatible."

"That's quite true," Gemma maintained as she took off her gloves and bloody surgical apron before handing them to a nearby attendant for sterilization. "Unfortunately … our decontamination unit didn't see the similarities, only the differences, Commander. The decon-unit actually damaged alveoli in her lungs. That's what I was repairing."

Gemma moved away from the incubation unit, and the presence of staff still cleaning and caring for Laurel. She crooked one finger and Darius bent to hear what she'd say.

"Sir … I had to add a third lobe to her left lung, move some veins and arteries around and reconstruct them. Primarily, I moved her heart to the back and center of her chest to accommodate the larger lung system." She briefly glanced back and moved further away from Laurel's resting space while lowering her voice. "The thing is … I can't undo what I've done. Not without killing her. To put her back the way she was would cause her to strangle in our atmosphere, just like you saw. She couldn't diffuse our air for more than a short time … a couple of hours at most." Gemma shrugged and shook her head in confusion. "I can run a thousand tests and never know exactly what the decontamination unit did. I really don't understand it since our atmosphere is so very close to Earth's. That being said … she'd be a medical miracle back on her home world. She could survive *there* with what I've done. In fact, her breathing there would be vastly improved. But once her chest was examined she'd never be left alone. I don't have to tell you that her current physical state would in no way resemble her former one. Any youngster with a basic knowledge of anatomy would know there was something very wrong with the placement of her chest organs!"

"But … you said she can survive this way … right?"

"Oh, yes, sir! She'll be fine. The prognosis is great. In fact, no one from an advanced civilization would question the procedure. But, like I've said, an *Earth* physician—"

He raised one hand to stop her. "This shouldn't have happened, Gemma! That decon-unit is supposed to protect us, not destroy the body tissue of other races!"

Gemma shrugged and shook her head. "Maybe someone higher up knows this is exactly why we shouldn't be engaging Earth citizens. But I stand by my decision to bring her aboard."

"That'll be my problem—"

"You won't have to answer for it alone, sir. Whatever's said or done in regards to her presence, I'll be with you. It was as much my call as yours."

He ran one hand through his hair. "I'm sorry to say her return to her home was always a moot point, despite this sudden turn of events."

"Sir?"

"I had orders to categorically stay away from Earth once Goll was caught and restrained. I can't countermand them for any reason, not without risking serious consequences for the entire crew. The law in this regard is standard League code."

Gemma snorted and sadly nodded. "I never really believed the admiral or any other official would give us permission to take her back, including the unusual circumstances. I just *hoped* I might make a case on her behalf." She shrugged. "Not to dwell on the obvious but … she's not going to like it. I wouldn't."

"I wonder if all Earthers would have been as damaged by our decontamination unit," Darius mused.

"I don't know, Commander. We may never know. We're on our way home and that's the way things are."

Gemma put one hand to the back of her neck and tilted her head left then right.

"You'd better get some rest. I'll stay with the woman," Darius offered as he walked to the incu-unit and stood to one side.

"You've barely had enough sleep yourself, Commander."

"Yes, but I've had *some*. When your patient comes out of this unit I fear you and your staff may need all the energy at your disposal. There'll be many questions to answer."

"Aye, sir. The instruments on the unit should alert you to any problems. Call if you need me."

"Good evening," Darius uttered as he watched Gemma walk out of the med bay. He took one last look at the patient then settled back in a nearby examining chair to get some rest. Thoughts of home filled his mind. But then his contemplation turned to Goll.

Unspeakable loathing filled him. He tried to tamp down feelings of vengeance but it was no use. But for their prisoner's sire, life would have been vastly different.

There was a point when harboring such vengeance would have been unthinkable. Something told him that once Goll was dispatched, the emptiness wouldn't heal.

For the minutes the execution lasted he'd have some satisfaction. After that, he wasn't sure of anything.

"I'll watch you die like the blood-sucking, soulless bastard you are!" he whispered. "Any race that would take a child's life deserves the worst punishment."

Bitterness filled him to the brim. It threatened to spill over and drive him to the prisoner section of the ship to do the deed now. It took everything he had to make himself stay right where he was. He mentally repeated his oath to watch the Earther.

No matter how he tried, sleep escaped. It'd been replaced by thoughts of the past, a past he couldn't undo.

His hands gripped the arms of his chair until his knuckles went white. For some reason, all his attention went back to the unit and the woman therein. At least one other on this ship would feel as he did. At least one more soul would have a reason to see Goll dead.

But to keep from making a victim of himself, destroying his family's historic reputation and all it stood for, he'd do his duty.

He dragged air into his lungs and reclined in the chair, trying to think about anything but the hole in his heart.

Also check out these books by Candace Sams:

The Peacekeeper's Soul

Fusion

In the mood for more Crimson Romance?
Check out *Savannah Sacrifice* by Danica Winters at
CrimsonRomance.com.